D0836863
the story of M . . .
A MEMOIR BY
Maria Isabel Pita

The Story of M
A Memoir

First Magic Carpet Inc. edition August 2003

Published in 2003

Manufactured in the United States of America
Published by Magic Carpet Books

Magic Carpet Books
PO Box 473
New Milford, CT 06776

Library of Congress Cataloging in Publication Date

The Story of M
A Memoir
by Maria Isabel Pita
ISBN 0-9726339-5-2

The Story of M
A Memoir

Maria Isabel Pita

Author's Note

In this book I wanted to tell the truth about being a beautiful, intelligent and intensely sensual woman, like so many other women out there who, like me, feel they don't fall into any politically correct category. I'm not a feminist, and yet I am fiercely independent. I'm not a silly sex object, and yet I am willingly, and happily, a masterful man's love slave. I am erotically submissive and yet also profoundly secure in my own being, and there's a world of women out there who know just what I mean. We have the Vote, and we've proved we can thrive on our own because we're as smart as any man, but that doesn't mean we have to give up the secret pleasures of our feminine soul, at the heart of which is a passionate belief in love. Obviously, we don't need to find our soul mate to survive, but it sure as hell is nice. *M* is the true story of my first shockingly kinky, and deeply instructive, year with the man of my dreams. We should never feel guilty about our innermost desires, or for living them should we mysteriously manage to make them come true, and I hope this book can serve as proof that they do.

Prologue

You have opened *M*, the true story of my training as a slave, the Prologue of which was originally published as the Epilogue of my erotic Gothic fairytale *To Her Master Born*. This is the beginning of my story, which I am writing even as I live it… the past is always present in a future forever shaped by whatever love dares desire…

I am writing these memoirs even though no words can truly express how much I love my Master. I must admit, I struggled with the term slave until I realized it has no more negative connotations than the word spirit, which is only a label placed on a force transcending the mind. Some say the spirit is not real and that a slave has no life of her own and both may be true, or not, but that is beside the point. For me to be a slave is to exist in a perpetual state of love, also another label for an invisible driving force. By this definition, a slave is not the lowliest creature on earth but rather an elevated being, for it all boils down to how much I love my Master that I am willing to do anything he says. The relationship between a submissive female and a dominant male is so ancient it is practically metaphysical in origin and nature. In the twenty-first century, when faith and marriage have degenerated into empty symbols, the terms Master and slave possess all the pure power of cosmic hieroglyphs branded into the human psyche with the same fire burning in the heart of the sun, sustaining it's beautiful 'slave' the earth. And the moon is just one of the many women and men my Master and I come into sensual contact with, their swinging orbit around us not in the least affecting our profound connection with each other even while hauntingly enhancing it.

Before I met my Master, I went by my baptismal name Maria Isabel Pita. I still fight depressing battles with her when I am alone, for MIP suffered much emotionally in the hands of men before she met her Master, who named her Missa. Missa is the beautiful phoenix that rose from the ashes of Maria Isabel Pita, who will never be burned again. Missa is everything that was beautiful about MIP like the pearl freed from its tension-filled shell. Missa is only six months old and as wise and timeless as an ancient priestess serving in the temple of her lord, who she never stopped believing in against all odds. I always knew my Master existed, whether it was in this life or another that we met. Fortunately, it was in this one, and he was the one who christened me Missa, launching me off the page of my fantasies into life and fulfillment. If we're lucky, or if Fate will have it, it will prove to be a long journey. I have no doubt it will be eventful, as it has been already.

He is so sweet and so tender. It never ceases to amaze me that my Master truly loves me. His firmness with me, both physically and emotionally, is the root of my happiness – how deeply he cares for me, as I literally care for him and worship him with my sexual submission. Almost every morning the first thing I do after I wake up is suck my Master's cock. Often my eyes are still closed as I open my mouth and slip his already semi-firm penis between my lips. I break my fast with the sweet milk of his pre-come. Often my mouth is dry, so I lick his shaft a few times to get my saliva flowing, and the way he moans instantly makes my pussy feel deep and warm. Half asleep, I am penetrated by all my dreams of love and happiness in the form of my Master's rigid penis.

When he told me, early on in the beginning of our relationship, going down on him every morning was going to be one of my slave duties, I laughed shyly and thought he was exaggerating. I soon discovered he was not when every morning without fail he gently urged my head down between his legs as we lay naked together in bed. Before I became a slave I always wore panties to sleep, now I rarely ever wear panties at all, and I have to ask permission to do so. I've grown to love the feel of my pussy and my ass beneath dresses, or the short skirts my Master likes me to wear, exposed to the air and the caress of strange surfaces everywhere. Since I began shaving, I am deliciously conscious of my labial lips rubbing against each other as I walk, whether it's in the slick penetrating heat of Miami in the summer, or through the cool caress of an air-conditioned space. There is no longer a barrier woven from conventional thoughts between the world and my sex.

My pussy is never so soft as after my Master fucks it hard. I touch my pubes in wonder they can be so tender and yet so resilient. It's strange, but the more violently my vagina is used the more it can seem to take, and the more it wants to endure. Last Saturday night, after hours in Plato's, my cunt was smoldering like the shrine of a burnt out temple, white towels and black lockers vestiges of a more relaxed pagan past and torch-lit catacombs. Yet the next morning on the sea of my Master's waterbed, the unquenchable vessel of my cleft was being rocked towards another cresting, crashing climax for him, and loving it. My clitoris glowed like the full moon at dawn, the intense satisfaction I felt listening to my Master come like the rising sun.

It's hard for me to reach orgasm. My clitoris can be described as eccentric. Like me, it is stubborn and intense. My Master says as my training progresses I will come more easily, and I believe him. Missa is gradually becoming the sensual and relaxed woman MIP always dreamed of embodying. My true nature is blooming beneath my Master's semen. The more I absorb of his being, in every sense, the more desirably erotic I feel and become.

I cannot possibly capture how beautiful my Master is to me with words such as handsome or attractive, which do not even begin to describe how devastatingly sexy I find him. I can set down a skeleton of details and say he has broad shoulders tapering down to narrow hips and long, strong legs. He is tall, six feet two inches, lean but tender, and his soft brown hair falls almost to his waist. His eyes are an indescribable color somewhere between slate-gray and green, and he has the most beautiful penis I have ever felt and seen. But now I've said too much and nowhere near enough. I will only add he has the most wonderful smile, soft and immutable, as though he is seeing all sorts of fascinating things and possibilities, all within his reach and requiring only a concentrated imagination to grasp and flesh out into reality. His smile, which I feel blessed to look at every day, makes me think of an ancient Etruscan wall painting, so perhaps it's not a coincidence his father's side of the family hails from Etruria, in Italy.

I told my Master last night that sometimes it hurts how much I love him; I don't feel there's enough I can do to show him how much I love him. He says I'm doing a good job, but I know I've only just begun. The only way to truly give myself and everything to him is to put my body at his complete disposal, to do whatever he tells me to and enjoy it without any emotional qualms or effort simply because it is giving him pleasure.

As I write, I am sitting beside the lavender roses he bought me last night, along with chocolate ice cream and a bottle of red wine – a hedonistic holy trinity. And I must confess, my greatest desire is to obey my Master's commands without any reservations getting in the way; without any thoughts of what I think I want, or don't want, damming the inspiring flow of his control. When I think about my Master I get so turned on that just picturing kissing him and fucking him is not enough, and sometimes it is not all he wants... so I imagine being bound and restrained from resisting as a stranger's penis penetrates me to intensify the pleasure he takes in possessing me, and I become so excited I wonder why in reality I hesitate to let other men enter me. If pleasing him is what I long to do, truly respecting his judgment in everything should enable me to relax in the most profound sense and enable me to take pleasure in fulfilling all his desires whatever form they take.

I am a beautiful woman, and yet how much I enjoyed my own physical attractiveness was eclipsed by perfect superficial images until I met my Master, now I am fully conscious of how powerfully sexy I am. My Master has given me possession of my body as society never did and no other man ever has. I always thought my breasts were not big enough, now I see how lovely they are, with such excitingly big and puffy aureoles, and I love the intensely erotic awareness of my pierced nipples. These are my slave rings and my most treasured possessions because they remind me constantly of the fact that I belong to my Master. My 'great legs' and 'fucking beautiful ass', my long black hair and full lips, my honey-brown 'Egyptian goddess' eyes and the soul behind them, all belong to him now...

1 Meeting My Master

Life has made me a firm believer in first impressions because I too often ignored them where attractive men were concerned. Looking back, that first feeling was always right, like a mysterious photographic flash that sees past the physical frame to the force inhabiting it. It is invariably accompanied by a sinking feeling in the pit of my stomach, in my womb, where another conceivable future is not meant to be and I know it deep down inside me. Then I met my Master and not a single blood cell in my body resisted; every part of me knew he was the one I had been pining away for. I was drawn to him from the second I laid eyes on his face, and when we met I had to fight an almost irresistible desire to fall into his arms. I had never experienced anything like it before. Instead of an instinctive flash pushing me back, I was magnetically drawn towards a complete stranger as though I had known him forever. And my Master felt the same way. He told me later that after he walked through the gate he had to resist a profound impulse to pull me into his arms as though we had always been together, which may explain the rather gruff way he thrust a dozen violet roses into my hands. The instant I saw him all my instincts transformed from cutting thorns into a budding sense of wonder that he truly existed and had somehow finally found me.

My Master is sometimes called a Keeper in his profession, and it was a rare form of palm tree that introduced us. I was walking Merlin, my beloved six-year-old Shiatsu, when I first saw the man who in the speed of light – the instant eyes take to meet – became the keeper of my heart. During that first meeting in the grass I gave him my virtual address and he sent me an e-mail later:

Maria,

Generally when I meet someone, there is great hopefulness that is slowly or more often quickly dashed. The mythology of the veil is understandable for a few seconds. With you it has been different so far. I am even more intrigued as the veil is slightly raised... taking it slow for a while would be fine with me. I think that you are worth it. I am also a survivor of some spectacular failures of relationships and take some time to jump into something serious. Dalliances are easy and plentiful, especially in Miami, and they keep things from getting desolate, but souls for joining are the rarest and most magnificent gift there is and get my complete respect and careful treatment. You are the only person I've encountered in a long time that shows some signs of being in the latter category. I want to know more about you however it comes, although I don't think a shared coffee would present any danger I am not ready to handle.

To which I replied:

You are so eloquent and such a gentleman, and you have a good sense of humor, too, don't you? A cup of coffee or a glass of wine, either one would be lovely, although I must admit, I would prefer the latter...

So he came over that first night with a dozen roses of my favorite color.

Amethyst is my birthstone and coincidence really is choreography because we met on my birthday, February 9th. My Master is a gift from the universe I strive to be worthy of as he never stops opening me up and showing me how much more there is to be excited about inside me. And what I have found is that everything comes wrapped up in fear and taped with emotional habits it is sometimes tough to break and discard. In the six months since I met my Master, I have experienced a tumultuous mess of feelings, but beneath all the newspapers used to package it and untainted by any cynical worldviews is the jewel of our love, which is real and makes anything feel possible.

We did not take it slow. We avoided penetration on our first date as a matter of principle, but we indulged ourselves in just about everything else; we couldn't help it. Nevertheless, a few of my most primitive ancient genes resisted going all the way to make sure he came back for the rest. My soul knew beyond a shadow of a doubt I would see him again, but my emotions often behave like vulnerable abused children who simply do not listen to my adult wisdom. Before I met my Master, I was more of a slave to unconscious doubts and fears than I realized, now more and more I enjoy the mysterious power of being a slave only to my deepening love for him.

On the first night with the man who would become my Master, I was a slave primarily to fear. I was afraid if we slept together right away the superficial merging of our flesh would short-circuit the profound long-term relationship I desired. I was afraid if I carelessly let him burn through traditional rules of courtship that his respect for me would go up in smoke, so I concentrated on not letting him plug his penis into my pussy's dangerously hot wet slot as though our future together was mysteriously in danger of being electrocuted for the crime of lust. Needless to say, I didn't enjoy myself as much as I could have because I was so busy worrying about breaking the rule I decided our future together hinged upon. The rule was we would not fuck on our first night together no matter what. My Master listened to me intently as I tried to explain to him how I felt and very patiently consented to abide by my superstition.

'I understand how you can feel that way,' he said in the deep and quiet, infinitely sexy voice that flows through my bones like magical marrow, 'and it's not a problem. You could be right. Maybe it is better if we wait... although I really don't think it would make a difference... but I respect that's how you feel about it.'

We were sitting together on my loveseat in the tiny living room of what I called my doll's house. I was fully clothed when I sat down, yet before I knew it, I was perched naked on his lap. I don't remember taking off my clothes, so he must have done it for me. All I remember is that, suddenly, he was cradling me naked in his arms while he remained fully dressed in black slacks and a long-sleeved white button-down shirt. I was somewhat shy about my body back then. I knew as a whole I was beautiful, but at the time I was still rather insecure about the facts that my cup-size is only 34B and I don't have a washboard belly. My sensual self-esteem was a tense bud, which has since bloomed to stunning proportions in his hands, but that night I was shyly insecure feeling his experienced eyes on me, and the beauty of his bone structure only intensified my own fleshly insecurities. I had seen such beautiful male faces before in Renaissance paintings but never on a living man of the twenty-first century, especially a man I had the miraculous pleasure of meeting and was getting to know fast, too fast, I felt, because there was still the superstitious rule I was determined to obey no matter how hard it got.

I don't remember how his clothes came off, either, and whether or not I helped, I was so lost in the purely wonderful sight and feel of him. His long brown hair was tied back, but it kept falling forward and caressing my naked skin with its soft fur as we avidly explored each other with our lips and tongues, hands and eyes. I do remember seeing his penis for the first time. I couldn't believe it. It seemed too much good fortune to swallow all at once that this intelligent, sensitive, strikingly handsome and understanding man with the face of a Davinci angel was also hung like a demon. He stood over me where I sat sprawled on the cloud-soft loveseat feeling as though I had just been flung there by my beautifully rough guardian angel gazing at his erection in disbelief as it stared back at me blindly confident. His light golden-brown skin combined with his divinely long hair, broad shoulders and narrow hips made me think of Lucifer sensually scorched by the flames of hell. I have since found out my Master has on occasion been called 'the devil incarnate', but he was also once mistaken for Jesus Christ in Africa. As I recall him towering over me, holding in his hand what to me was the perfect cock, I imagine I see large white wings rising behind him where there was really only a black television screen. I knew then it wasn't just a question of soul mates; my body had also been waiting and longing for his. Finally, real fulfillment was within my grasp, and very soon it was also in my mouth. I had had no intention of sucking him down on the first date, but when his head kissed my lips they bloomed open around him inevitably, willingly. Before I knew it, his magnificent dick was sliding in and out of my mouth resting contentedly on my tongue while I was torn between excitement and despair because I didn't see how I could possibly stop him from fucking me now. In the end, it was he who somehow resisted breaking my artificial rule. It seems strange, but I really can't be sure now if he masturbated and came all over my breasts or if I'm only fantasizing he did and he actually left without coming at all.

The next day felt endless. To say I couldn't wait to see him again is an understatement of biblical dimensions. It's like saying I can't wait to take my next breath, like saying I want my heart to keep beating. I waited for his phone call or for an e-mail from him like a snake-bite victim waits for an injection to assuage the pain caused by the venom of absence. How perfect I thought he was and the possibility he might not feel the same way about me were like fangs sinking to the very core of my being, and only his arms slipping around me every day and night could save me.

I live with my Master now, but at the time my physical address was south west twenty-third street on the border between Coral Gables and Miami. I am fortunate enough – or rather, I was stubborn and inspired enough never to give up trying to make my living writing – to work at home, and I was renting a little house just big enough for Merlin and me, with a tree-filled fenced-in yard and walking distance from just about everything. I loved my white tile floor and every other detail of the neat and lovely little home where I was relatively happy by myself until I met my Master, and then the place began to feel like what it was – a cramped, vitally empty shell I had been protecting myself with while I waited and searched for him. After knowing my Master less than forty-eight hours, I was already in the process of outgrowing and discarding my beloved doll's house. I could not distract myself from thoughts of him with simple domestic pleasures, and concentrating on work was nearly impossible. Then at last the bell sounded announcing the arrival of an electronic message.

Hey Beautiful,

Thanks for an excruciatingly lovely evening. I'm so relieved to have finally met you. I'll talk to you later.

Stinger

It was all I needed to hear, and more than enough to keep me blessedly happy until the phone rang a couple of hours later and we confirmed what time he would be coming over that evening.

If I have to pinpoint exactly when my Master began training me as his slave, I would say it was the moment he made me hold both our red wineglasses while we were sitting on my loveseat. It was the first time he put me in bondage, in an exquisitely subtle but highly effective fashion. I was wearing a white skirt, he was in a fresh button-down white shirt, and there was no table within my reach, which means I held perfectly still and submitted to his will. We had been having an intense conversation during which I sat gazing at his face in awestruck disbelief. I loved everything he said; it was exactly how I felt. It seems we were able to sense each other's thoughts from the beginning, because we kept anticipating questions and comments with amazing synchronicity, and when he gently took both glasses out of my hands, I knew it was time to let him inside me.

I spent a lot of money on my queen size bed, which is fully dressed with a white bed-skirt, a lush feather comforter protected by a shiny sage-green satin cover decorated with slightly lighter vertical lines, four matching sage pillows, two fluffy white ones and a diamond-shaped violet cushion thrown in for contrast. I love my bed. It is the perfect marriage of beauty and comfort as cum stains wipe right off the silky satin cover and a few firm caresses smooth out all the wrinkles. I'm talking about my bed because I can't really describe how I felt the first time I lay upon it with my Master, the first time he entered me, the first time his penis penetrated my pussy. I had been celibate for months before we met so I was tight and he was so thick and long it almost hurt when he thrust, but it also felt so good I wanted to cry. We were still fully clothed, our flesh merging only between our legs as he stared down at me where I lay beneath him gasping in mingled pain and ecstasy. The profound pleasure and the intense relief of at last being perfectly filled seems to have overflowed my brain's ability to hold those moments. All I clearly remember is the overwhelmingly welcome fullness in my pelvis and my Master's smile, which was as soft as his cock was hard. I remember his commenting on our perfect fit, and then illustrating how much he loved being able to push the envelope of my flesh with a violent plunge that made me cry out in blind panic at such absolute completion. There didn't seem to be a single microscopic piece of me he could not reach and touch, in every sense, and I feel that way more and more every day. All I wanted was to press him against me and keep him inside me forever. I was afraid of how empty I would feel when he pulled out and left me alone in my bed again.

'Turn around,' he said in the kind but inarguable way I was becoming wonderfully familiar with.

I obeyed him, thinking he wanted me in the traditional doggie-style on my hands and knees, but he had something else in mind.

'Remember this,' he instructed me. 'It's called the sleen position.'

'Spleen?'

'Sleen,' he repeated, pressing down on my lower back.

It took me a moment to realize he wanted me with my breasts pressed against the bed, my arms over my head, and my ass thrust up into the air with my thighs spread and the tips of my high-heels touching.

'That's it,' he murmured, 'show me your beautiful ass.'

My buttocks tensed instinctively.

'Don't worry I'm not going to fuck you there, not yet.'

I relaxed as I felt him positioning his rigid penis at the traditional entrance. My labial lips welcomed the full, unyielding intrusion of his head, parting around it willingly even as I clutched my silk comforter in trepidation. Tonight was the first time I had experienced penetration in months. My pussy was tight, and in the sleen position there was no way I could defend myself. At this angle he could ram himself all the way to the core of my flesh, which is just what he did.

'Oh my God!' I cried. 'Oh God!'

'Does it hurt?' he asked, his hand pressing even more firmly into the base of my spine to keep my back arched.

'A little,' I whispered.

'Do you want me to stop?'

'No...'

He kept driving into me, blinding me with stabbing, rending sensations that can't be considered pleasurable in a traditional sense, and yet I loved how hard he used me. My first time in the sleen position was a severe trial for my tense vaginal muscles, but his relentlessly therapeutic thrusts managed to relax my pussy enough for me to loosen my grip on the comforter and accept them, along with the promise of intense ecstasy they were stirring up inside me.

'Are you on the pill?' he asked me urgently.

'No, but you can still come in me!' I assured him breathlessly.

'Are you sure it's safe?'

'Yes!' I gasped. 'Oh God, yes, please...'

Even though he enjoys taking his time, when I beg him to come is the one time my Master doesn't mind obeying me.

Afterwards, he held me tenderly in his arms and asked me if I would consider going on the pill.

'We'll talk about that later,' I hedged, always having hated routine gynecological exams.

'No, let's talk about it now,' he insisted.

'Okay,' I sighed, so happy I could barely speak as I clung to him. Condoms were all right for a temporary affair, but the pill implied the desire for a long-term relationship.

'I'm almost certain I want a vasectomy,' he informed me, 'but until then, it would be nice if you could go on the pill.'

'I said I would.' I snuggled up against his warm, hard chest feeling I had finally come home after wandering lost and alone for centuries.

It was Friday night and my lover was taking me out to dinner, but first he wanted to tie me up and take some pictures.

I sat on my bed and fingered the smooth purple rope he brought with him while watching him set up the tripod and digital camera. I still couldn't believe how promising he was in every respect and how happy I was with him. I did not feel I would have to do any acting to hold on to him; I could just be completely myself. During the day, part of me still feared I might never see him again for some terrible reason – a car accident, or because he suddenly and inexplicably changed his mind about me – but it was not a real worry. I was not imagining or hoping we were always meant to be together, I truly felt we were, and my soul's conviction was stronger than all the mental and emotional doubts stoked by previous relationships. That afternoon, I had made an entry in the black ringed notebook of my journal for the first time since we met:

I have not written a word about Stinger, I almost don't dare.

Today a small black butterfly flew into the house and passed me heading straight for my journal, where it alighted and disappeared. I looked more closely. It had come to rest neatly on the top white border like a mysteriously enchanted adornment that matched it perfectly.

It felt like a reminder not to ever forget my faith in the magic of existence. I lose sight of this when I begin to worry about the nature of a man's intentions after we sleep together. It felt like a reminder that Stinger is a magical event in my life…

When he finished setting up his equipment, my Master told me to take off my clothes, leaving on only my red high-heels, and to kneel on the bed in the sleen position.

'But I'm already dressed for dinner,' I protested half-heartedly.

'Strip,' he commanded, and when I assumed the appropriate position on the bed, he began tying me up. He had mentioned during one of our in-depth conversations that if I really wanted it, he was more than willing to be my Master. I knew there was something kinky about my sexual tastes, but I had never fully explored this bent in my psyche. Even then, as he pulled my arms behind me and began tying my wrists together at the base of my spine, I still didn't quite grasp the fact that he was serious about becoming my Master. Before, with other men, ropes and blindfolds were all just part of a game that ended with the sex. On occasion, I had allowed myself to be dominated physically because it excited me. No man had ever come close to truly mastering me. But as the purple rope tightened severely around my limbs, I began suspecting this was about to change, at which point I went into a contented trance it is hard to remember, much less describe. He did a thorough job of binding me, and even though the muscles in my inner thighs ached they were spread so wide, and my cheek was pressed in a suffocating manner against the bed, I had never felt so profoundly relaxed.

He took some pictures of me dressed only in purple rope and red high-heels on my sage-green bed with my ass thrust high in the air and my eyes closed helplessly, then I heard the exciting whisper of clothes caressing flesh as he stripped. I felt him position himself behind me, and I moaned in anticipation when he gripped my hips, but I can't remember now if he entered me slowly, letting my pussy savor the full length and girth of his hard-on, or if he took advantage of my utterly vulnerable position and drove himself home. All I remember is I ceased to be aware of any discomfort listening to the quiet sounds of pleasure he made as I seemed to feel him plunging deeper and deeper inside me. My slightly anxious resistance quickly dissolved around him and I relaxed completely, opening myself up to his driving force. He fucked me so hard the ordeal transformed into a transcendent experience for me. It was as though my flesh was raw matter needing to be shaped and dominated by his energy, needing to be told what to do and what forms to assume. Instead of hurting, his head knocking against my cervix let in a host of divine sensations as I discovered my pussy was much more resilient than I believed, and that its mysterious dimensions were determined not so much by physical limits but by how deeply I felt for the man inside me.

2 Collared

One night sitting at the bar in the Bushwacker Lounge during our first week together, my Master said to me, 'I think I'm going to call you Missa.'

I took a sip of my scotch on the rocks and savored the vowels and consonants for a moment. 'I don't know, it sounds too much like a slave's name…'

He smiled. 'I want to collar you soon, if you think you're ready, Missa.'

'Oh yes!'

'Then I'll pick you up tomorrow after work and we'll go buy your collar.'

'Okay.' In my kinky soul, this was the equivalent of him slipping off the barstool, holding up a diamond ring and asking me to marry him. Actually, it was much better; the promise of a much more intense bond in which I would literally put my life and all my feelings in his hands.

'You'll need a safe word,' he told me. 'If you say that word, I'll stop whatever's happening right away. And you can use it whenever you feel anything is too much for you, not just physically but emotionally, too. Do you understand?'

'Yes.'

'Once I collar you, Missa, the correct response will be "yes, Master".'

I could not quite look him in the eye as I repeated softly, 'Yes, Master.'

'Mm, I like the sound of that.'

Finding the right collar was not as easy as we thought it would be. Petsmart was very disappointing. There was a plethora of colorful cloth collars that were all out of the question, and the leather ones were either too big or not exactly what my Master was looking for. So even though it was the heart of rush hour on US-1, we decided to drive to a sex shop in Coconut Grove, but that proved to be even more of a letdown than Petsmart. The bondage section was a pathetic pair of black cloth restraints and a blindfold, the rest of the store was filled with multi-colored dildos of all shapes and sizes. There was even a plastic fist complete with half an arm for those women with vaginas the size of small caves just about anything can swim in and out of. On display in the window was a life-size blow-up doll with a candy-red plastic 0 for a mouth it made me shudder to think any man could desire to buy much less use. Fortunately, my Master's jeep fit snugly between a big black SUV and the curb he drove over to avoid searching for a parking spot. It was technically illegal, but we were on our way before the authorities could catch us since the sex shop proved a complete waste of time.

'We don't have to keep looking anymore today if you don't want to,' I said, feeling guilty about the terrible traffic and the heat and how long the theoretically simple search for a slave collar was taking.

'I want to keep looking.' He glanced at me from where he sat with both arms draped over the wheel. 'If you don't mind.'

'Of course I don't mind!' I laughed in joyful disbelief, a double-edged emotion this beautiful man was constantly inspiring in me. 'I want you to collar me, Master... I want it more than anything.'

His smile deepening, he reached over and rested his hand on my knee. Then, keeping his eyes on the road, he moved it up to my thigh and squeezed my pale, tender flesh. 'Mm!' He glanced at me again. 'I have to get you to Haulover soon.'

'Haulover?'

He put both hands on the wheel again. 'You've never been there?'

'No. What is it?'

'It's a nude beach, the only nude beach around here.'

'Oh.' I had never felt the desire to go to a nude beach. I grew up on National Geographic specials, and when I pictured a stretch of sand crowded with tanned naked people part of me felt there was something animalistic about it, as though their lack of modesty and the way they willingly discarded the civilized titillation of clothing made them too much like seals to be considered sexually desirable.

'I'm not asking you if you want to go, Missa.' Stinger's firm voice penetrated my dubious reverie. 'I'm taking you to Haulover, and you're going to enjoy it. In fact, I'd like for us to start going every weekend if we can.'

'Okay.' Every time he said something that reinforced our future together it left me feeling not weak in my knees, which are quite strong from jogging regularly, but weak in my very soul. The relief and happiness that filled me as I looked at him and thought about seeing him every day, about letting his will and desires shape my life and in so doing fulfill my own mysterious needs, was indescribable.

Naturally, we ended up in South Beach. As my Master pointed out, we should have gone there in the first place. Miami's infamous strip was the only place to shop for a slave collar. Yet we found just what we were looking for not in a kinky sex shop but in a ritzy pet store. It was delightfully obvious many of the lovely collars on display in glass cases were not meant for cats or dogs, although, of course, there was no way to prove they weren't. It was rather like being in a head-shop and asking for a pipe to smoke tobacco in.

'Her neck is roughly the same size as our dog's,' my Master lied to the sales girl as he wrapped a black leather collar set with costume rubies around my neck. But it was still not exactly what he was looking for, and we enjoyed wandering around searching for just the right one. We found it in the shape of a black leather collar approximately one inch thick decorated with stylishly curved silver hearts. I knew it was my collar the moment I laid eyes on it, and my Master agreed.

'I'll just have to cut some off at the end and put another hole in it,' he observed, 'otherwise, it's perfect.'

We left the pet store with a small bag, but it was a big moment in our relationship. We had officially embarked together on the road marked Bondage & Domination traveled by people who call each other Masters & slaves. We had entered a metaphorical Mansion full of hauntingly exciting emotional passages opening up onto profound chambers of the heart, leaving the traditional marriage bed and boringly safe missionary position far behind.

We went to one of my Master's favorite bars, Mac's Club Deuce, a seedy dive boasting an ancient jukebox, a pool table and a U-shaped bar. The drinks are strong and cheap, the atmosphere is appropriately dark, and black-and-white photographs of old film stars line one wall behind the bar. My favorite is a classic shot of Humphrey Bogart as a detective wearing a raincoat and hat. He is leaning casually against the darkness, and smiling inscrutably at his early death of lung cancer while countless numbers of people keep smoking and drinking before him. His life passed in the blink of an eye, or at least it seems that way to me, and I wondered why he had taken the risk of smoking knowing it could kill him. It was a bit disturbing to think my life was passing just as fast, and that I was taking similar risks with my health all the time. On the other hand, I felt my life was just beginning now I had finally met my Master.

He ordered a scotch on the rocks for me and a Sapphire-and-tonic for himself, then he pulled the collar out of the bag, ripped the tag off, and slipped it around my neck right there in front of everyone. No one seemed to notice. 'That's the beauty of South Beach,' he remarked, 'you can walk around wearing a dog collar and no one even looks at you twice.'

The jukebox was playing, and a woman of some indeterminate old age (who could have been a man but didn't seem to be) was dancing by herself and singing along. She was totally lacking in talent, but she was drunk enough not to realize it. I could tell she believed herself to be moving sensually and gracefully to the music, and her heartfelt rendering of the lyrics was intense enough to drown out the fact, at least in her own ears, that she was painfully tone deaf. I watched her with pity and distaste mildly warring inside me while my Master talked to the man sitting beside him. I would never have dared walk into that bar by myself, but with my Master I felt so perfectly safe and happy that I could feel compassion rather than fear.

'I'm going to make her something,' the stranger talking to my Master declared, looking over at me. 'What would you like, a lizard or a grasshopper?' he asked.

I had no idea what he was talking about, but I said, 'A grasshopper' remembering the live Door's concert in which Jim Morrison hops around on stage chasing after a grasshopper. I judged from his appearance the stranger was homeless as he leaned over the bar and began working swiftly and skillfully with his hands.

'What's he doing?' I whispered.

'Making you a grasshopper.' My Master smiled cryptically.

'Out of a palm leaf?' I asked dubiously.

'Yes, he's very good at it. He sells them for money. He's been living on the corner outside for a few years now, but he used to live in the apartment just above it with his girlfriend. Then she died of breast cancer and he couldn't deal with it, and now he's on the streets.'

Dying of breast cancer was my pet fear, and I thoroughly respected this seedy-looking man for his grief-stricken reaction to his girlfriend's death even as I felt sorry for her and frightened for myself. Then suddenly he handed me the finished grasshopper and I was amazed by how lifelike it was. 'It's lovely,' I exclaimed. 'Thank you, thank you very much.'

'How much do I owe you?' my Master inquired.

'Nothing, its for her.'

My Master signaled to the bartender, indicating he would be paying for the 'artist's' beer.

'I'm going to keep this forever,' I declared fervently, holding the delicate grasshopper fashioned from a palm leaf reverently in my hands. 'It's a little work of art, true folk art.'

'It is,' my Master agreed.

'And it will always remind me of our first days together, Stinger.'

'And of the night I collared you.'

'Yes...'

'When you finish your drink, let's do some more shopping.'

My hand rose uncertainly to my throat. 'Should I wear my collar?'

He regarded me intently for a moment before replying, 'Of course.' He caressed my hair back over my shoulders. 'I'm really liking the look of you in that collar.'

'I was meant to wear one,' I said quietly.

'You were meant to wear my collar.'

'Yes,' I agreed fervently.

'Look me in the eye, Missa, and repeat I'll do anything you say, Master.'

'I'll do anything you say, Master.'

'You are my slave.'

If it's true sex is the way adults play, then Washington Avenue is lined with stores catering to the imaginative child in us all. Washington Ave is the concrete line between sexual fantasy and reality, and at some points dreams of beauty are amazingly cheap, but inexpensive treasures can also be found in the mountains of bad taste. For less than twenty dollars, my Master bought me the faux diamond bracelet I had coveted since childhood, and a diamond choker to match. Then I simply had to have the long black gloves Cyd Charisse was wearing with her diamonds in the photograph that branded itself into my little girl's psyche as the hieroglyph of ultimate seductiveness. I couldn't understand why it had taken me so long to end up owning simple items that made me feel so sexy, which made me disturbingly aware of all the subconscious barricades we live with every day. In my brain, a voice had been saying things like, Women with good taste don't buy two-inch-thick faux diamond bracelets and What earthly good are long black gloves in Miami any way? etc. etc. When I was very young, I was looking through a clothing catalogue with my grandmother. I pointed out a short red dress I thought was really pretty and she told me I had bad taste. For the life of me, I couldn't understand why she said that since she seemed to find other red objects acceptable, and I realize now this is one of the bricks that went into building an artificial wall between my mind and my real sensual self-esteem. The minute I met my Master, the expressive warmth in his eyes when he looked at me began dissolving the moral mortar holding countless psychological bricks in place, and one by one he began knocking my artificial defenses down with his kind but firm commands.

We ended up in a store that sold the most incredible shoes I had ever seen.

'What do you think?' my Master asked me, holding up one half of a shiny black vinyl pair. 'Could you walk in these?'

'I don't think so!' I laughed.

'Why don't you try.' It was not a question.

'Do you really want me to?' I eyed the six-inch heels with disbelieving respect. 'I mean, do you really like them?'

'Oh yes, I like them.' His smile deepened dangerously. 'And if you feel comfortable with them, I'll buy them for you.'

'Oh no, you don't have to...' I felt guilty about all the money he was spending on me. We went out every night to bars and restaurants and I never contributed a penny, being in between paychecks and flat broke.

'I want to,' he assured me. 'What size do you wear?'

'Seven-and-a-half.'

My Master turned to the salesperson hovering just behind him. 'Do you have these in her size?' he asked a young man with unruly black hair and smoldering dark eyes who, surprisingly enough, struck me as being straight.

'I'll check,' he replied, and returned from the back room almost at once holding a large box. 'All I've got is a size seven.'

I shook my head, torn between relief and disappointment.

'Try them on, Missa,' Stinger insisted.

'But-'

'Missa...'

I already recognized that particular tone in his voice, and the profound thrill it gave me made me hasten to obey him.

The astronomically high heels fit perfectly. I even found I could walk in them, albeit slowly and carefully, and with two pairs of admiring male eyes supporting my efforts. A mirror told me my shapely legs looked even more stunningly sexy now. I ended up walking out of the store in the close-toed, single-strapped black vinyl shoes with six-inch heels, feeling more as though I was floating as I braced myself on my Master's arm, supremely perched on the cloud of our love for each other. It was like learning to walk again. My new sensually unrestrained sense of self took its first steps that day on a sidewalk in Sobe.

I felt my grandmother turn in her grave as I tripped at the curb.

Stinger caught me safely in his arms. 'Are you okay?' he asked, his lips smiling even as his eyes expressed concern.

'Yes... the street sloped there a little...' I wasn't about to let a slight mishap interfere with how intensely erotic the impossibly high heels made me feel. 'I just can't handle uneven ground in these yet,' I apologized for my clumsiness.

'I understand. You're doing very well, Missa. I'm very proud of you.'

I clung happily to his arm as we kept walking.

'Do you know how much the way you look in those shoes makes me want to fuck you, Missa?'

'Mm...' I smiled, enjoying the looks I got from the rare straight males we passed.

'You'd just better hope there isn't a porno shop between here and the jeep.'

'Why?' I inquired innocently.

'Because if there is, I'm going to fuck you in it.'

There was an adult video store a block away, and true to his word, my Master led me carefully over the seedy threshold. I felt the eyes of the man behind the register following me all the way through the harshly lit room – blooming with hundreds of unnaturally bright and colorful cardboard boxes – to a row of dark private booths in the back. My Master pulled a curtain aside and I stepped into the cramped space. He followed me in, and yanked the black curtain closed again. After inspecting it for cum stains, he set our bags down on the plastic seat. Several small viewing screens were flashing advertisements for X-rated films catering to a variety of appetites.

'At least it looks relatively clean in here,' my Master remarked as he turned me around to face one of the black walls. I leaned against it, bracing myself with my hands as he lifted my dress up around my hips. 'From now on, Missa,' he quickly slipped my black cotton bikini panties down to my knees, 'I want you always to be ready for me.'

'I am, Master...' My pussy was always ready for him; just listening to his voice made me feel warm and wet.

'From now on, Missa,' he unzipped his jeans, 'you are not allowed to wear a bra or panties without my permission. Is that clear?'

'Yes,' I murmured, and then gasped in shock and pain when he suddenly smacked my ass with his amazingly hard hand.

'What did I tell you the correct response would be?' he asked me softly, gently caressing my smoldering cheek.

'Yes, Master...' It was impossible to think straight in the charged seconds before his penetration. My mind offered a brief, anxious resistance to the thought of always being completely naked beneath my clothing just as my labia clung to his head for a tense instant. Then the indelible statement of his erection surged into my pussy and I knew whatever he desired would always make perfect sense to me, even if it made me uncomfortable at first and I had to force myself to relax around the concept. He shoved his deliciously stiffening penis up inside me from behind, and I moaned from the intensely satisfying pleasure I experienced on all levels being able to hold him and embrace him with my deepest self anywhere.

'Quiet,' he whispered, his breath hot against my cheek. 'Step back a little and spread your legs more… that's it, Missa, good girl…'

Arching my back, I braced myself against the black wall relishing the contrasting textures of his slightly rough cool blue-jeans and his smooth warm dick. As he gripped my hips to brace himself, the metal teeth of his zipper nipped my vulva, and the subtly sharp sensation heightened the rapidly escalating pleasure of feeling his hard cock pumping in and out of me faster and faster, relentlessly expanding my tightly clinging slot around its driving energy. The six-inch heels placed my pussy at just the right height and angle for his increasingly urgent thrusts, and I almost cried out in excruciating ecstasy as he stabbed his pulsing erection to the hilt inside me and suffused my body with his liquid heat, groaning breathlessly into my hair.

3 Ready All Ways

I could hardly bear the few hours my Master and I spent apart every day. Only years of discipline enabled me to concentrate on work even though I never stopped thinking about him. My Master is a scientist and a busy man, but he always finds time to send me e-mails, virtual touches that help soothe how much I miss him. Yet my soul doesn't stop aching until he comes home and I greet him wearing only one of my collars and high-heels. Stockings and a garter belt are optional additions to my slave's uniform. This is now that we live together. When we first began seeing each other, I couldn't seem to take a deep breath until I saw his jeep pull up in my driveway every evening. Merlin ran out first to lick his feet, and I met him halfway down the walkway. I slipped into the magical cradle of his arms and rested my head against his chest, infinitely relieved I hadn't just imagined him, that he was truly real and there with me.

'I don't want to be apart from you,' he confessed, as always expressing my own feelings perfectly as he held me close. 'I love being with you, Missa. I feel so completely comfortable with you. I don't even think about it now, but I've been searching for so long.'

No matter how hard I hugged him or how passionately I kissed him or how fervently I caressed his soft hair and warm skin, I couldn't seem to get close enough to him or to adequately express how he made me feel, so I just kept trying and trying, and I still am and always will be.

He pushed me away gently and held me at arm's length to gaze down at my face. 'I love you when your eyes are brown, Missa,' his earnest expression sharpened his beautiful masculine features in a way that cut mysteriously between my heartbeats, 'but when they turn golden, like they are now, it's a metaphysical thing.'

'Oh Master,' I sighed, clinging to him, 'I feel the same way!'

'I couldn't stop thinking about you all day,' he confessed.

'I couldn't either, Master. I think about you every second!'

'I'm so happy with you. Do you know how happy you make me, Missa?'

'As happy as you make me, Master.'

He pulled me to him with one arm and reached behind me with the other. 'You drive me wild!' He squeezed my ass. 'Mm... good girl.' He was referring to the fact that I wasn't wearing any panties. My pussy was completely exposed beneath my short skirt, and the feel of his hard fingers stroking my moist labial lips was reward enough for obeying him. 'I can't tell you what a relief it is to meet a woman I can respect intellectually and who I'm also so strangely drawn to.'

'Strangely?'

'In that it doesn't happen often... ever. I'm so glad you are who you are, Missa.'

'I'm your devoted slave.'

'Yes, but your training has only just begun, dear.'

Before I met my Master, I stayed home with Merlin a lot. I've never been the club or bar type, and I'm still not, although I regularly enjoy them much more than I ever thought I would. I've learned to question just how much is actually personal taste vs. fear masquerading as individual preference. The truth is, I am much more open to things than I believed. As my Master pointed out the other night when we were cuddling on the loveseat, 'You're in a stable environment now, Missa, the only instability is the one we create for excitement.' He's right. I have never felt more at peace on all levels of my being than I do now after breaking countless conventional rules of stability in life and security in love.

Suddenly, Miami bloomed around me wild and lush with the cultural rampant invasive exotics of nightclubs and bars, branching neon lights in endearingly naïve primary colors. I could sense irresistible drugs' undertows and drank in the intoxicating blend of people from every part of the globe. Leaning on the open window of my Master's jeep surrounded by the luminous honeycombs of skyscrapers, I felt like an explorer in my own home. I used to have a recurring dream that the house I lived in, which was always different, possessed many more rooms than I ever imagined. I would come upon a door I never knew about, and my heart would fill with wonder and joy when I realized there was much more to my home; many more rooms and views for me to discover and enjoy. I have not had this dream since I met my Master. What was a subconscious desire before is reality now.

My Master seemed determined to claim Miami as our own exclusive sensual playground by fucking me everywhere he couldn't. True to his command, I refrained from wearing a bra and panties beneath my clothes even though every time I dressed, I struggled with a mental urge to don the undergarment armor protecting me from the dangerously dirty world out there. At first I chose knee-length skirts and thick cotton tops to make up for my lack of a bra and panties, but gradually, emboldened by my Master's appreciation and the knowledge he would protect me, I began wearing short skirts and more clingy shirts. I felt very daring and sexy every time I glanced down at my breasts in a public place, and glimpsed my nipples carving themselves out of fine material suggestively veiling rather than concealing them. I have very long, pronounced nipples thrusting from puffy aureoles almost too big for the pert mounds they crown.

One evening in February, I walked into the Eden Roc hotel relishing the firm, warm grip of my Master's hand holding mine, the feel of my warm wet pussy lips caressing each other just above the hem of my white skirt, and the subtle titillation of my nipples roused to stiff peaks by the ocean breeze outside poking eagerly against my purple silk button-down shirt, which was open a daring way down. My Master always looks handsome and elegant, even when he is only wearing blue jeans, brown leather sandals and a long-sleeved button-down shirt, his soft brown hair pulled back. We perched on two comfortable black bar stools slightly facing each other, and he promptly slipped his hand up my skirt, which was hiked shamefully high up my thighs now that I was sitting down. His fingertips explored between my full moist labial lips for a delicious moment, and I wasn't sure if I was afraid someone might see or if I wanted someone to be watching, but either way it added an exciting charge to the natural pleasure of his touch.

We ordered dirty vodka martinis, which were as good as they were expensive, and then my Master led me across the luxurious lobby to the elevators. We rode the car all the way up to the penthouse. The elegant hallway was deserted, and the door to the stairwell was unlocked.

I preceded my Master into the bare concrete space feeling as sensually relaxed and happy as a genie floating out of the bottle from which our drinks came. 'Oh wow!' I exclaimed, leaning against a white honeycombed wall open to the cool night air and offering a bird's eyes view of the luminous traffic down on Collins Ave.

'It's nice,' my Master agreed, unzipping his jeans.

I glanced anxiously at the door leading out into the penthouse hallway.

'Bend over, Missa.'

'But...'

He gripped my arm and positioned me facing one of the blank concrete walls. 'Brace yourself,' he instructed.

Bent at the waist and perched on high-heeled sandals in a hard concrete nest beside a green metal door that could open at any second, my pussy felt excitingly soft and vulnerable. I was tense at the thought of being caught, but also turned on by my Master's virile daring, and I sensed this made my hole feel just right to him, tight but slick.

'Oh yes, Missa,' he whispered as he penetrated me.

Knowing how good my cunt felt to him gave me as much pleasure as the experience of his erection filling me. His cock was so thick and long and hard, I moaned and closed my eyes as my innermost self clung to him even while inexorably expanding around him. Only how much I wanted him enabled me to take him right away all the way, and when his head touched what felt like the core of my flesh, I braced myself against the wall as he began thrusting. I gasped and arched my back so my cushy ass absorbed some of the impact of his hips beating as relentlessly as a piston at the heart of everything, but he was fucking me so urgently and selfishly the wall was in the way. I ended up bracing myself on the floor with the tenacious roots of my fingers while his penis kept getting harder and more demanding between my soft thighs, my cervix like a castle door being rammed by an overwhelming force I longed to let in because it belonged to the man I loved. By the time he climaxed, I couldn't take much more, and it was with relief and pride I slowly straightened up afterwards as he zipped his jeans closed.

'Very good, Missa,' he said a bit breathlessly, and a smile touched his firm mouth as his deep stare sought to gage my feelings. 'Are you okay?' he seemed compelled to ask even though I knew he could see it in my eyes that I was.

I slipped my arms around him and purred against his chest.

After the Eden Roc, my Master took me in a variety of public places. There was the pitch-black laundry room just off the patio at Churchill's; the small park near his apartment beside the lake when we were walking home from our favorite bar Fox's one night; a parking lot near Fox's another night; a lifeguard's stand across the water from the Red Fish Grill; and just off the trail in Matheson Hammock where we heard a group of hikers approaching as he was fucking me from behind. I was leaning against a rough tree bark, my shorts around my thighs, my labial lips blooming around his shaft willingly, happily. The more he took me like this, impulsively and out in the open, the better it felt, and I was possessed by the overwhelming pleasure of feeling him starting to come inside me when we heard the sound of voices on the trail and glimpsed figures approaching. I loved the sensation of his cock pulsing deep between my thighs, which always culminated in his excruciatingly delicious ejaculation, so when he pulled out abruptly he also had to cover my mouth with his hand to stifle my cry of passionate disappointment at the loss of his orgasm. I yanked up my shorts and started back towards the path, walking behind him and pouting because some silly nature lovers were depriving me of the physical joy of my Master's semen drenching my pussy. It was like being baptized over and over again with the blessed sense of his desire for me, the trickle of his warm spunk down the insides of my thighs a wordlessly eloquent script expressive of how beautiful I am and how much he loves me.

Constantly being fucked was making me aware of my pussy as I never had been before. Now that it was being exercised regularly, two, three, occasionally four times a day, I realized it was a muscle that could be stimulatingly aggressive as well as passively yielding. One afternoon lying on my bed, I kept consciously clenching and relaxing my vaginal muscles, until I was satisfied I had full control of this deep, dark part of me I could never see, only feel. I was beginning to grasp I had a say in what went on down there, that this tightening and loosening I was sometimes aware of was not just an unconscious spasm. Just then, the bell of an incoming e-mail sounded at my workstation beside the bed, and when I read it, I found the continuing synchronicity between my Master and me truly amazing.

Attached to his message was a document outlining Kegel exercise routines designed to strengthen a woman's vaginal muscles and make her more aware of how subtly, but effectively, they can be used to heighten a man's pleasure as well as her own. I learned exercising the muscle directly linked to the clitoris and climaxing can make achieving heights of pleasure much easier. I've worked out regularly for years, yet I never thought to apply the same logic to my pussy as I do to the rest of my body. Eastern sexual traditions such as Tantric yoga and the Kama Sutra don't appeal to me because I never studied for tests in school and yet I always passed with flying colors. Perhaps I suffer from a touch of feline laziness, but all these advanced sexual positions struck me as complicated equations it would turn me off trying to figure out so they might theoretically add up to ecstasy. Kegel exercises, however, made perfect sense to me with their simplicity and potentially devastating effectiveness.

These exercises should be done up to three times a day, every day if possible. Tighten your vaginal muscles a little and count to five. Tighten a little more and count to five again. Contract your inner muscles as much as possible and count to five. Other exercises include contracting your muscles for three seconds, releasing, and repeating this process ten times, and squeezing and releasing your muscles as quickly as possible over and over again for a few minutes at a time.

I will admit, I don't do these exercises exactly as outlined, much less three times a day, but they seem to be working anyway. I can grip my Master's erection at will now as hard or as gently as I want to, and I can choose whether to hug his whole cock with my pussy or to only squeeze the head or the base, contracting and expanding my inner muscles like a wave rippling up and down his shaft. The way he moans and how hard he gets, and how much more I enjoy having him inside me, makes me glad I'm always making an effort to better understand my deepest feelings, in every sense.

I printed the Kegel exercises and pasted them in my journal, where I regularly jotted down things my Master and I said to each other that I never wanted to forget, as though I ever would.

Last night at the Bushwacker when he was playing pool with some of his graduate students who we happened to run into there, I was feeling a bit bored and petulant, and he said to me, 'I'm your Master, but if you told me to or wanted to, we would leave right now.'

I knew willingly becoming this man's slave was the best thing I could ever do for myself. This may seem like the ultimate paradox, but it isn't really, as I hope this book will help explain. My Master keeps proving he often understands my emotions better than I do, and I have learned that always telling him what I am thinking and feeling – as he regularly and firmly commands me to do – instantly resolves any conflict I am experiencing, helping me move on to a higher level of awareness and profound relaxation. Communicating with him with absolute honesty is gradually exorcising all my demons, large and small. My inner self must be naked and exposed to his appreciation and scrutiny at all times, just as my slave's uniform at home (unless my Master indicates otherwise) consists of a collar and high-heels and nothing more, except when I wish to punctuate my absolute submission to the wisdom of his will with stockings and a garter belt.

One evening my Master and I sat at my workstation searching the Internet for other couples like us. From the moment I met my Master, I knew all my fantasies had the power to come true and that life really was worth living. I knew almost without it having to be said that sensual exploration and adventure was going to be a part of my relationship with Stinger, and I was intensely excited about it without quite being able to grasp how our unconventional desires would take flesh. Obviously, I was aware you could meet single people online, but I was somewhat shocked to discover that couples also post their profiles on Swinger's sites searching for other couples to play with, or single girls.

'Well, we're definitely not looking for a single girl,' I remarked tersely.

'No,' my Master agreed, flashing me an enigmatic smile, 'right now we're looking for another couple to have some fun with.'

I stared hard at his beautiful profile for a moment as he continued perusing the site Swinger's Date Club, but I was really only seeing the fierce jealousy that overwhelmed me imagining sharing him with another woman. The sensation was as terrible and inescapable as a black hole suddenly forming in the very center of my being directly over my heart and sucking all my thoughts and emotions into a crushing void. I could see no other side to this feeling; I didn't see how I could possibly ever survive much less get over it. I knew of only one universe, where sexually sharing the man I loved with another woman was out of the question. She would have to possess a husband almost as sexually exciting as my Master (because no man could ever be more desirable to me than Stinger) making it an even swap, at least physically. I had much to learn and a long way to go as a slave, but my training was only just beginning, so when my Master pulled up a couple's profile, I focused exclusively on the photo of the man, if there was one. Often there were dozens of pictures of the female in the relationship but none of the male, except perhaps a few overly lit close-ups of his genitalia, which for me were a total turn-off.

'Why are we doing this?' I asked abruptly, propelled by sheer disgust into the abyss jealousy opened up inside me. 'I mean, what does it say about us, Stinger, that we've been together less than a month and we're already looking outside ourselves for excitement?'

'It says we're having the relationship we always dreamed of,' my Master replied in the calm, even voice he reserved for those times he sensed me panicking, and hence rebelling against what he knew perfectly well I desired as much as he did. 'It means what we have is so special that we're already at a point most couples never reach at all, and if they do, it's not for a months or even years. It means we're not wasting any time. We're choosing to be explorers and to make life as exciting as it can be now that we were lucky enough to have found each other.'

'I don't believe in luck,' I snapped, still suddenly profoundly tense about breaking our miraculous orbit around each other. 'I believe in choreography.'

'Missa, what's wrong?' His soft smile vanished and the look in his eyes grew painfully sober. 'You wanted to do this as much as I did, and now you're freaking out for some reason.'

I looked at the computer screen, at the photograph of a beautiful exotic dancer sitting next to her husband, who was so ugly he almost looked like a cartoon parody of a man. 'Most of these women are all pretty,' I declared cattily, 'and yet they're all married to dogs! I mean, what if you saw a girl you really wanted, that you were irresistibly attracted to, and her husband was-'

'Missa, look at me,' my Master commanded quietly.

I obeyed him sulkily.

'This is all about us, remember? You're the only woman I'm irresistibly drawn to.'

'And I feel the same way about you, Stinger!' I whispered desperately. 'You're the only man I really want.'

'And if that wasn't the case, then we'd have no business being together. It's true that, for some reason, especially here in Miami, there are lots of couples like that, where the woman's gorgeous and the man is old or fat-'

'Or plain hideous.'

'We've only just started looking.' He ignored my interruption. 'But if you feel this isn't something you're ready for yet, we can wait, I just thought-'

'We don't have to wait,' I murmured. The idea of Swinging was like a sword hanging over my head. Waiting would only prolong the torture of discovering if I could learn to handle it, or if it would end up cutting me to pieces inside.

'Are you sure, Missa?' my Master asked me quietly.

'Yes, I'm sure.' I couldn't take my eyes off Beauty and the Beast. 'It's just that this is... I don't know,' I shrugged. 'I mean, we just met, and yet I'm thinking about fucking other men? You say it's all about us and enhancing our intimacy,' I looked into his eyes, 'and I believe you, but it's just all so new to me...'

'I know,' he said gently, kissing me on the lips, 'you just have to trust me. You'll find out there's nothing to be afraid of and no need for jealousy because it really is all about us. You're the most important thing to me, Missa, and you know that. Never forget it.'

'I won't,' I whispered fervently, resting my cheek against his chest.

'I want us to be bad together,' he said quietly, stroking my hair, 'very bad.'

4 Learning To Obey

I'm writing this sitting on the balcony of a hotel in Indiatuba, Brazil. I'm here with my Master at a conference crowded with brilliant minds mingling and merging to determine all our virtual futures for years. It's a strange place to write about my first experience at a Swing club, where only bodies go to mingle and merge. On the other hand, it seems strangely appropriate; the perfect expression of how rich and varied life is with my Master.

How to describe my first sight of Miami Velvet? It is tucked away near an expressway in a dark lot subtly lit by a lovely lavender neon light that can only be seen if you're looking for it. There is something perversely enchanted about the realm of Swinging if you're truly in love. Obviously, there are utterly disenchanting reasons for belonging to a club like Velvet, but they do not concern me. I know how my Master and I feel about Swinging, and that's all that matters. The emotional waves were rough at first, there's no denying that; I came close to drowning in conflicting emotions more than once. But it was more than worth the effort to reach the smooth open sea of a beautifully strong relationship able to explore the depths of sensuality without sinking to infidelity. Love is only cheated by lies, not by sexual contact with other people. If a relationship is truly sound, it can pull in and out of as many inviting harbors as it pleases and only be enriched by the experience. The bed sheet a man and a woman share has to be a sail alive with desire, which is what keeps the blood flowing even if it means going against the normal current. The mast of a marriage of souls can never be broken by the fickle winds of lust because its force is used to reach and revel in almost paradisiacal plateaus of intimacy...

That first night I was daringly dressed in a sleeveless low-cut black dress that clung gently to my curves and glimmered like the star-filled sky before light pollution. It flared gently out from my hips and barely reached the tops of my thighs. My Master had consented to my wearing a black lace thong panty beneath it, but I still felt wickedly sexy perched on six-inch heels with barely anything between my most private parts and the world. My Master looked stunningly handsome in black shoes and slacks and a long-sleeved button-down shirt, his hair flowing freely down his back between his breathtakingly broad shoulders.

Admission was not cheap, but we could bring our own liquor, and my bottle of scotch along with my Master's bottle of gin received circular orange labels printed with our membership number in black ink. Carrying my vice openly in my hand, I walked into a Swing club. It was still early; there were only a handful of people in the main room surrounding the empty circular dance floor as we sat down at the bar. I wriggled self consciously on the hard stool facing my Master, who immediately reached down and fingered my pussy through my panties, his smile telling me how much he loved having easy access to my intimate warmth in public. He was always telling me how beautiful I was and how much he loved me and tonight was no exception. We sat as close as possible while we sipped our drinks, and I immediately appreciated a venue that essentially allowed us to behave as we would in private with the added stimulation of being watched. Both emotionally and physically, I clung to my Master's passionate assurance that Swinging was all about us; I couldn't stop touching him and caressing him and kissing him. I was more turned on by his physical presence than I ever had been, which is saying a lot, but fear and excitement were sharpening all my feelings and sensations. I knew Swinging was a double-edged sword, and I still wasn't convinced I could handle it. There were only two or three other couples seated at the bar, and it at once reassured me and made me feel profoundly queasy that none of them were anywhere near as attractive as my Master and me. I still had not truly grasped the meaning of the statement 'It's all about us' or rather, part of me did not believe it. A cynical conventional part of me was convinced Swinging was a way to let my Master satisfy his male need for variety without him cheating on me, which he wouldn't be doing if he had my permission and I was there to watch him fucking another woman while he observed me being taken by another man. This lack of faith in my Master's depth and integrity is the only thing that has truly caused me pain since we met.

'Let's take a look around,' he suggested, and drinks in hand, he proceeded to give me a tour of the club.

I liked the first level, which boasted a spacious shadowy area separated from the bar and dance floor on one side by a glass wall. It was cozy with cushy black divans and black chairs and afforded a good view into two 'private' rooms, each furnished only with a large wall-to-wall bed and floor-to-ceiling mirrors. One way led out into the main area of the club, another opened onto the multi-leveled Jacuzzi room, and a third door took us out into a narrow corridor lined with truly private rooms. I liked the doors, especially the fact that they locked, and the intimate space surrounded by mirrors. I also loved the mattress, which was just the right height for my Master to fuck me while standing up as I lay on my back. He shoved me back across the bed, unzipped his slacks, pulled my panty aside and swiftly penetrated me as I raised my legs up around him. He took a few moments out of the tour to stroke his hard-on with my pussy, dipping his rigid cock into my welcoming wetness for a few delicious seconds. I was disappointed when he pulled out of me so soon and yet not surprised, since we had come to play in public. This was another thing I still didn't really believe – that just being there with me turned my Master on whether someone was watching us or not. Another reason for his brevity, as he explained, was his desire to show me the second level of the club before the 'robes only' rule was enforced.

My stomach clenched. 'What do you mean, robes only? You mean I can't wear my clothes up there later?'

'No, just a robe.'

'I can't even wear my panties?' I was outraged at the prospect of my individuality being stripped from me, and replaced with a generic white robe I imagined would feel like a shroud adorning the terrifying death of my sexual privacy. 'And what about my shoes?' I added in despair.

'I think you can probably keep your shoes if you want to.' He smiled. 'I hope you can.'

At the moment, no one was guarding the curtain over the narrow stairway leading upstairs. I ascended carefully, placing my treacherous shoes sideways on each step as my Master walked behind me to break my fall should it prove necessary. It did not, and yet I felt myself falling inside as my heart grew heavier and heavier beneath a weight of dread. I was not only afraid of what my Master might expect me, command me, to do there, but also of how his desire for us to come to such a place might affect my respect for him. With each step I took, I became increasingly worried that our souls were not really as magically in tune as I had believed. Fortunately, deep down in the core of my being, I knew this was a foolish fear, and it was the indelible knowledge that we were indeed meant to be together that got me up the stairs, past the small open area half-filled with a comfortable looking couch, and into the heart of the club.

Apparently, there were still hours of foreplay left to go downstairs in the form of drinking and dancing and whatever, because for the moment we had the whole second floor to ourselves. My Master led me into a 'hallway' the likes of which I had never seen before. One side was a wall with waist-high alcoves, apparently made for holding drinks, facing a row of elevated wall-to-wall beds framed by mirrors, which also covered the ceiling. It was clearly a space designed for people to stand and watch other people fucking as they watched themselves. And this carpeted corridor ended in a spacious room entirely filled with low mattresses allowing for no walking space between them. The sheets were black-and-red and artificial torches reflected in the mirrored ceiling gave the shadowy, slightly sinister atmosphere a disturbing cheapness.

It is impossible to describe what I felt in those moments as I gazed at this blatant 'fuck room'. I did not want to be there, that's all I knew for sure. In fact, I couldn't believe I was there, that the man I loved had brought me to such a tasteless den of iniquity. I wrenched my hand out of his feeling my soul mysteriously arch inside my flesh like cat's back as I was threatened by waves of undulating human flesh this man had the gall to think he could plunge me into so casually. Only how much I knew I loved him – not to mention my six-inch heels and the fact that he had driven us here in his jeep – kept me from bolting down the stairs and out of the building.

'Stinger, I'm not into orgies!' I gasped, my heart beating fast and furiously. 'I told you how I felt about that. It's like being a worm in a box! I'm not going in there and letting just anybody fuck me! I'm not just another body, I-'

'Missa, relax.'

I don't remember exactly what he said to me. I think he assured me he was not into orgies either, and that he was not expecting anything from me I didn't want too, even though as his slave it was my duty to obey him without question whether the prospect pleased me or not. This was a terrifying paradox to me at the time, because even though I was madly in love with him, I was still learning to trust him. I do remember, however, how firmly and inexorably he put a lid on my hysteria. Grasping my hand securely in his again, he showed me the rest of the second floor, and I followed gingerly behind him feeling as though I was being given a tour of hell by a beautifully relentless angel. His divinely long hair flowing down his back, he kept glancing back at me with a stern, determined expression that at the same time was full of love and concern.

There wasn't much more to see, just a narrow corridor lined on one side with rooms that were intimate in comparison with the main play areas, but still large enough to accommodate a generous group of people. The room at the very end of the hall was the most interesting of all. The smallest and darkest space, it contained not just the requisite bed, but also a black iron cross and a black leather combination sawhorse/scaffold. I was very happy when my Master closed the door so we could be alone in there. I was more than willing to kneel on the contraption and drape myself forward across it so he could carefully manipulate my hands and head into the appropriate grooves before bringing the top half of the wooden frame down, thus securely locking me in place. I was now perfectly vulnerable to being spanked or fucked from behind, and I found it quite a comfortable position. A tendril of excitement sprouted inside me at the thought of the door opening and people watching me like this without my being able to look up at them or protect myself, but this bud of erotic enjoyment was immediately killed by the frost of fear. I had no desire to be touched, much less prodded, by anyone except my beautiful Master, yet as he freed me from my bondage and opened the door again so we could go back downstairs, I knew it was going to be a very long night, during which I had to accept the fact that sensual contact with other people was why we were here even if we only ended up playing with each other. My Master repeatedly assured me he would consider it a totally fulfilling evening if all we did was watch and be watched. He kept telling me how beautiful I was and how proud he was to be there with me, and his attitude was such a relief that, paradoxically, as the evening progressed, I began feeling the night would be a failure if we didn't find another couple to play with. I began feeling guilty about letting my doubts and fears limit us to just being with each other, which I didn't believe was really enough to satisfy him. I was sure variety was what he was after no matter what he said to make me feel more comfortable with being there. I was an emotional mess that first night at Velvet, and I find it painful to write about the unnecessary torment it caused me to so seriously underestimate my Master and not fully trust in the truth of everything he said. It took me some time to understand that when he told me 'It's all about us' that was exactly what he meant. It was a statement full of deeply exciting implications and possibilities, not a pat excuse he gave me just so I would agree to let him fuck other women.

I spent most of the rest of the night at Miami Velvet with my head down, in my Master's lap. My hand clung to his as we walked slowly around the club, and my mouth clung to his dick when we came to rest on one of the black divans. I let the curtain of my hair fall around my face, but my Master caressed it away so the couples standing and lounging around us could watch me going down on him. He wanted them to see my beautiful features riding his erection. He wanted them to see my full red lips gliding up and down his slick shaft. I closed my eyes at first, as though the fact that I couldn't see them meant it didn't matter there were other people around, but then I opened them again and kept them open as shadowy forms rose in the corners of my eyes and my Master's cock rose in my hand and in my mouth. I was tense, and yet I could not help succumbing to the strangely dark thrill of sucking him in public. A porno film was playing on a television in the corner, the scene harshly lit and much more graphic than my subtle head-bobbing in the shadows, and yet what we were doing was real and therefore much more exciting. When I glanced up at my Master's face, I saw he was looking around him, smiling, which initially upset me because I wanted him to be looking at me. I quickly got over it, since the important thing was that he was feeling me, and even though I was studiously ignoring them, I wanted everyone there to see how big and hard he was for me. In my opinion, he was the most beautiful man in the club, and I felt as though I was stabbing every woman there with the enviable knowledge that he was all mine every time his head touched the back of my throat; every time I took his entire hard-on into my mouth; every time his pleasure and desire were surrounded by me. I suppose it was also a turn-on that other men could observe my skill and devotion, and I was sure we were the center of attention. But after a while – when my Master finally told me to stop and pulled me up into his arms beside him on the divan – I realized with a shock of annoyed disappointment that we were only part of the shadowy show.

'See what you did?' he whispered.

'What?' I asked sulkily.

'You inspired them.' He glanced around us at two other couples engaging in oral sex.

I looked away indifferently. Neither of the men was what I considered attractive, which made watching them being serviced less than appealing for me.

'What are you feeling, Missa?'

I shrugged. 'Nothing.' In a sense it was true; all the emotions clashing inside me were canceling each other out and I was mysteriously numb.

'Do you know how proud I am to be here with you, Missa?'

I tried to burrow into his chest. 'So am I.' I didn't mind showing off for other people, it was the thought of letting them into our sensual orbit that burned me up inside. Part of me was angry at my Master for not being content to be alone with me. Everyone else was a mere undesirable mortal, so I was defensively surrounding myself with a moat of negative thoughts, zealously protecting the sacred shrine of my pussy. I was finding it very difficult to accept that my noble and beautiful knight, who had rescued me from a life of frustration and loneliness, was willing to share my body with other lesser men. As the evening dragged on, the dreaded moment when I would have to strip off my clothes and don the anonymous white robe drew closer and closer, and there was no avoiding it because I wanted to obey and please my Master more than anything in the world. All I could do was hope that there really was love after group sex, which I regarded with the same horror of having all my values shot down and my body tossed into a mass grave.

The music was terrible, mainstream pop dance tunes that did nothing to inspire me in any sense. However, when my Master told me to get up and dance for him, I did so willingly. I find moving my body to music almost more sensual than any sexual act. I know I'm good at it, and I felt intensely beautiful as I undulated my hips for him, caressing myself while feeling other men's and women's eyes on me. My extreme high-heels arched my back and thrust out my ass so my center of gravity was aligned to the ageless power a woman has over a man as she dances for his pleasure.

When the song ended, I sank gracefully off my pedestals onto the divan again, but my Master decided it was time to take another leisurely stroll around the club. He told me to point out to him any couples I thought attractive. I nodded, but I did not see anyone who even slightly interested me sexually, and because I'm not bisexual, I mean I did not see any men who appealed to me. I didn't want my Master to desire other women, and I didn't want other men inside me, yet I also knew I wasn't content with just staying home alone all the time either. I hungered for the thrill of the hunt, but I was terrified of the kill – of actually watching Stinger's penis stabbing another woman's pussy. And the thought of an anonymous latex-clad cock plunging in and out of me while another girl enjoyed the much greater honor and pleasure of my Master's beautiful erection was intolerably exciting; I couldn't stand it. Nevertheless, when my Master asked me if I wanted to leave, I said no, and not just because I didn't want to let him down.

We danced, we had more drinks at the bar, we walked around, and around the first floor again, and oh yes, I forgot to mention we even had dinner. The food, included in the price of admission, was not very good, but I didn't have much of an appetite anyway. Then finally the moment I had been dreading arrived. We made our way to a locker room that might have belonged to an ordinary gym, except it was smaller and carpeted and full of both naked men and women who did not look away tactfully. Everyone was smiling and seemed perfectly relaxed and happy, a fact that made me even more profoundly wretched and anxious. There was no one there I considered even remotely attractive. I was not yet familiar with the concept of 'body acceptance' (I still don't fully accept it) and it was with the reluctance of a condemned witch being led to the stake that I pulled off my starry black dress and quickly replaced it with a rough white robe. I stubbornly kept on my black thong panties and high-heels, however, as well as all my jewelry.

There was a big black man guarding the gaudy silver curtain in front of the stairs who thankfully did not ask to see if I was wearing anything beneath my robe and let me pass with my shoes on. Almost all the rooms upstairs were alive with people fucking, in groups of two or three or four or more, I really wasn't counting. They were also full of respectfully quiet voyeurs, and my Master and I joined one white-robed rank of spectators looking in on a moaning trinity. The sight did absolutely nothing for me.

'Does this really turn you on?' I whispered incredulously.

'Yes.' My Master smiled at me as he led me towards another playroom.

'Why?' I insisted. 'Why does it turn you on? Did you come to these clubs before you met me?'

'Only a few times, and there was always something missing...' He squeezed my hand. 'You.'

The other two smaller rooms did not offer up any more interesting scenes, so my Master led me to the mirrored hallway where several exhibitionist couples had taken up positions on the elevated beds. I felt as though I had entered the bowels of some perverse underground temple I had never really been aware of, but which for years had existed beneath the normal streets of the city in which I lived, unbeknownst to me or anyone else not inclined to publicly worship sex. I deliberately let my

Master's broad shoulders block most of my view of the large, demonically lit back room seething with gasping, writhing flesh.

'I'm not going in there!' I whispered in terror.

'I'm not asking you to yet,' my Master replied firmly. 'Just look, it's not what you think. There's nothing to be afraid of, Missa.'

Forced to obey him, I gradually realized it wasn't just one big orgy in there, but I didn't care; everyone was still too close to each other for comfort, meaning for safety. I didn't see what was to prevent some man from just plunging into me from behind when I wasn't looking. Certainly I knew my Master would protect me, but he would be otherwise engaged and perhaps not see the threat coming. Plunged into a whole new realm, I didn't understand it was governed by intangible laws, just like the 'normal' world; rules had not been shed with our clothes.

When I saw the mattress to the far right in the mirrored corridor become available, I prepared myself for my Master's command.

'Take off your robe, Missa, and lie back... no, not like that, this way...' He meant facing the spectators. 'I want to go down on you.'

As if in a dream, I shed the rough heavy robe and let my Master pull down my panties as I lay back on the dark sheet. Only my own reflection lay to my left, and I watched my Master's head sink between my thighs feeling nothing, really. I caressed the silky-soft hair against his unyieldingly hard skull wishing he would cover me up with his body and fuck me rather than leaving me exposed like this, so I could see everyone's eyes except his, everyone's face except the only one that mattered to me.

'Please fuck me,' I begged quietly, and clung to him gratefully when he stopped eating me and spread himself on top of me. The mattress to our right was now occupied by a young white man and a petite black girl with heavy pendulous breasts. I don't exaggerate when I say that her face was ugly as sin, but she was passionately devoted to her partner, whom I perceived as her white master. I didn't care how politically incorrect the thought was, it turned me on in tandem with my Master's big hard cock penetrating me and mysteriously protecting me even as he fucked me openly in front of countless strangers.

'I want you to come, Missa,' he urged, supporting his weight with his arms so I could slip my hand between us and caress my clit while watching him pump in and out of me.

I was so far from an orgasm I believed coming now on command would require a sensual quantum leap... and yet, as my gaze kept darting over to the light-and-dark couple energetically fucking beside us, I felt a climax stirring to life in my pelvis like an awakening snake flicking its tongue teasingly, with a divinely forking heat, against the cold stone of my clitoris, which was miraculously coming to life beneath my digging fingertips as my Master looked down at me, the expression in his eyes fertilizing my pleasure with its intense encouragement... I was torn between my Master's eyes and the vision of contrasting white and black flesh merging at the borders of our personal space. The troll-faced black girl had finally stopped sucking her handsome white Master's dick and was crouched beneath him in a semblance of the sleen position as he fucked her furiously from behind even while staring at me the whole time. All our combined pleasures was like a disembodied smoke rising from the fire being stoked by two hot cocks stoking two warm wet pussies. I felt myself intangibly caressing this total stranger more and more openly even as all I did was meet his clear, direct stare. When he suddenly reached out and grasped one of my ankles, getting a firm grip on it to help hold my leg open around my Master's thrusting hips, I started coming. It aroused me beyond reason to be held by one man while another man fucked me. All it took was this slight taste of what until that moment I had considered an inaccessible pleasure to make me climax. My Master was pleased with me, and I was weak in the knees and in my whole being afterwards. I had taken my first sip of an intoxicating excitement – my first small tentative, insignificant sip – and it had blown me away with the delicious knowledge that all my fantasies could, and were actually going to, come true if I had the courage to let them. And all I had to do in order to live my wildest dreams was obey my Master without fear or hesitation.

Stinger is the most considerate of men as well as a scientist, and he did not push me too far that first night at Velvet. After our orgasms, we went downstairs to the Jacuzzi. The hot foaming water was alive with couples, some just relaxing together, others intimately engaged. The massaging currents felt good against my skin. I was tired. It had been a long night and it was very late. My Master had promised we would be leaving soon, but first he wanted to fuck me some more. He sat on the edge of the tub while I bent over and sucked his cock, only half immersed in the water. I didn't quite want to admit to myself what a thrill it gave me to offer my naked ass and pussy up like that. And yet, vulnerable as my orifices were in that inviting position, I also felt them surrounded by the force-field of my Master's ownership, which was clear for all to see. It only took me a few seconds to make him rock-hard again, at which point he slipped down into the Jacuzzi with me and turned me around, indicating he wanted me to bend over in that direction. I obeyed, pushing back against him because I was dangerously close to plunging my face into a woman's cleavage. She, too, was being penetrated from behind by her partner, and as my Master rammed into me, his penis almost painfully rigid, I became increasingly aware of the fact that he wanted me touch her somehow. She was smiling impassively, not quite meeting my eyes even as I couldn't seem to take mine off her generous breasts. I stubbornly refused to admit it, but I really wanted to touch her tits. I was aching to handle those full soft mounds of white flesh crowned with big pink nipples, but I was also afraid of violating her personal space. Later, my Master assured me that under the circumstances she certainly wouldn't have minded, but I was a virgin to Swinging. Afraid of where it might lead, not yet understanding that I didn't have to become bisexual to enjoy sensual contact with my own sex, I anxiously resisted this novel longing to touch and caress another woman.

5 Possessed By Sharing

I must admit I reacted like an addict to my first taste of Velvet. Part of me dreaded it, yet I couldn't wait to go back. And the truth is I still feel that way. Part of me thinks Swing clubs are disgusting and hates most everything about them, and yet another part of me accepts they're the only place you can go to enjoy a sensual communion with others that mysteriously intensifies the pleasure of sex with the person you love.

I've somewhat lost track of the order of events at this point in time. I've not experienced a dull moment since I met Stinger, and I doubt I ever will, for he is a man who truly knows how to live life, which makes being his slave an ever-deepening pleasure. I am able to weave events together again now in chronological order thanks to the fact that I had begun a section in my journal entitled Missa's List of Firsts. I attach this list at the end of my story as a testimony to how fast and how far my sensual horizons began broadening the instant I met Stinger. My Master's will sometimes feels very much like a direct shaft of lucid force penetrating to the very depths of my being and the seeds of desires latent within me, which keep blooming into realizations that change my life for the better with the beautiful sense they make. It's also true that my second trip to Velvet is a bit of a colorful blur now, punctuated by vivid highlights, moments I'll never forget. Amongst the important things I learned that night was never to drink half a bottle of red wine before imbibing several scotches, although I felt so good that what I suffered in the morning was worth it, and I seriously needed to lubricate my inhibitions. Fortunately, when I get drunk all that happens is I feel less restrained; I don't lose motor or mental control. I mixed two heady liquors that night as well as two heads, as in cocks. For the first time in my life, after fantasizing about it as often as there are stars in the galaxy, I had sex with two men at once. In order to protect the guilty, I will call this guy Ray, but he came later...

First my Master and I had a little superficial fun on the dance floor, where what I mainly enjoyed was pleasing him by fondling a woman as she laughingly reciprocated, another entry for Missa's List of Firsts, which seemed to be growing at the speed of light. She was a petite blonde and she wasn't young, more like well-preserved, and her equally small husband was pathetically ugly. He was pushing his wife, or his partner, or whatever she was, up against me as we all faced each other in the middle of the crowded dance floor. I was leaning back against my Master, who was caressing me with growing fervor as he watched my hands cupping and fondling another woman's naked breasts for the first time. It wasn't exciting me at all, but caressing flesh to music is always relatively enjoyable – whether or not you particularly like the music or the flesh in question – but I could feel how much I was turning my Master on and that was all that mattered.

As if in a dream, the next thing I knew we were in the 'voyeur's hallway' with the blonde we had been playing with on the dance floor and her elfish spouse. My Master had made it clear to him that a full swap was out of the question, but apparently he was content to just watch his wife have fun. Meanwhile, a handsome man with black hair and a black goatee named Ray was standing as close to me as possible, and although I would normally have considered the gold chain around his neck cheap, in those highly intoxicated moments, framed by the folds of his white robe, it just made him look even more masculine. I realize now what his main charm was – the fact that I could indulge my superficial physical attraction to him without worrying about any other dimension to our relationship. I had already met the man of my dreams, the man I connected to on all levels of my being, the man I wanted to spend the rest of my life with, and he was standing approvingly beside me as Ray kissed me. Too late, I glanced at my Master to make sure I had his permission to kiss him back. He smiled and gave me a slight, almost invisible nod even as he leaned down to kiss the blonde. He is so tall and well-built and she was so slight, I think I was turned on merely by the logistics.

Soon we were all in the middle of the big play room. My senses swimming in red wine, I surrendered to the flow of events as to a current directed by my Master's words and expressions. I felt perfectly beautiful and natural following the lead of his desires. I also felt like the center of attention lying on my back as the blonde arched her slight body over mine and presented her pussy to my lips. I touched the tip of her clean-shaven little slit tentatively with my tongue, not so much seeking her clit as avoiding the juicier opening of her vulva. I was surprised and relieved by how clean and smooth and relatively dry her sex was, but apparently my Master did not want me beneath her, because a moment later I found myself sitting up facing Ray's cock. He was kneeling at the edge of our group, his body proud and straight as a statue's, his impressive erection clearly waiting for some oral devotion I had no intention of giving. I looked up into my Master's eyes again, and reached for the condom he handed me. I offered it to Ray, who promptly slipped it on as I watched my Master attempting to sheath his own flesh-weapon. Then I lost sight of everything when Ray pushed me back across the mattress and thrust into me as I lay soft and yielding as sand beneath his driving rhythm, oblivious to everything except the experience of a complete stranger ramming his rigid penis into my clinging pussy.

'Missa...'

My Master's deep, quiet voice reached me over the storm of Ray breathing in my ear with an almost divinely effortless authority my soul heeded instantly. The fact that my flesh was relishing Ray's energetic penetrations was irrelevant. I don't know how I got him off me, but almost the second after my Master said my name, I was on my hands and knees before him gazing worshipfully up at his face.

'I want you to suck me, Missa.'

I didn't understand why he wasn't busy fucking the little blonde, who I had glimpsed eagerly awaiting his cock doggie-style while he struggled with a condom. I didn't know what had happened, but I was overjoyed by the turn of events. He was only partially erect and it thrilled me to think she hadn't turned him on like I did. I also dared to hope watching me with another man had made him jealous enough to affect his performance. It was with a blessed sense of triumph that I took my Master's beloved cock into my mouth, even as Ray gripped my hips from behind and thrust his erection into my grateful pussy again. I was finally living my favorite fantasy, and for a while I was aware only of how good the reality felt. But then I had to turn my face away from my Master, gasping as Ray banged me faster and harder, coming aggressively into the plastic pouch at the tip of his spurting cock buried deep inside me. He had stroked himself to an orgasm with my sex yet had never really felt it. Only my Master's erection is meant to experience the warmly loving caress of my innermost depths where other men are only superficial divers.

As though a cresting wave of sexual energy had just literally broken over the hedonistic beach of bed sheets, I knew this particular erotic scenario was washed up as Ray pulled out of me, discarding the latex tunnel heavy with his semen, and teasingly coated with my juices which had not for a single second merged with his despite how hard he fucked me. I rolled over onto my back feeling wonderfully surfeited, given permission to relax for a moment by my Master's smile. As I lay there, Ray began licking one of my nipples, his tongue tasting the more delicate aspects of the lush feast he had just enjoyed deep between my thighs, which were spread shamelessly wide. And apparently the sight of my freshly fucked pussy proved an irresistible temptation to a muscular black man kneeling on another mattress, because he suddenly leaned over and gave my slick hot vulva a quick, hungry lick. I did nothing to stop him; I felt no reason to do so. For a delicious instant I had a handsome Latin man suckling my tit while a virile black man licked my slit. Then came my Master's softly resonant command again in the form of my name 'Missa' snapping me out of my sensual reverie as he helped me up, and hand-in-hand we walked out of the room whose shadowy atmosphere was sinfully rich with the heady perfume of countless orgasms.

The following Saturday night, we were back at Velvet again. This time, however, I remained relatively sober sensing my Master had an important lesson for me to learn. Last weekend he had proved he could get over the hurdle of watching me being physically possessed by another man. The fact that he had had to make some effort to do so afforded me a comforting degree of satisfaction, but also made me even more nervous wondering how I would react when forced to watch him fucking another woman. Actually, I wasn't really sure what he wanted out of the evening. He hadn't told me he had decided it was all about my watching him tonight. I believed our objective was to swing with another couple (which we had not actually succeeded in doing last week) and that if the opportunity presented itself, I should be willing and obedient.

I was beginning to find it frustrating how few truly desirable couples there were, and of this handful, they all turned out to be into 'soft swinging', meaning oral sex only and mainly amongst the girls. I have always considered oral sex to be a much more intimate act than penetration with a condom, which gives you all the clean hard pleasure without any of the messy risk. I was not into the idea of taking a total stranger's sexual juices into my mouth without protection, so my Master and I went shopping for flavored condoms I could theoretically use to make other men's penises more palatable to me, not to mention safe. I was astonished by the casual way many of the people at Velvet went down on each other, as though they had never heard of AIDS or any other sexually transmitted diseases. Ever since I met my Master, I learn things every day, and he has since broadened my education on a number of subjects, oral sex being one of them. According to the medical experts, it is not as easy to catch anything from oral sex as I had believed and feared. Our mouths seem to kill any viruses they come into contact with. Our saliva is full of germs and bacteria, a fact that doesn't make the thought of kissing someone very appealing. Fortunately, the experience is pleasurable enough it's easy to forget the invisible microbial war being waged as our tongues dance around each other...

My Master was fucking me from behind on one of the mattresses in the mirrored hallway. I was on my hands and knees looking at our reflections in the mirror before us, and I was literally flowing with admiration gazing at the intense cast of his features framed by his long hair, which he had flung behind his breathtakingly broad shoulders. I know that sounds like a romantic cliché, but to me it felt like anything but watching his magnificent physique thrust into my lucky cunt. Then suddenly a woman crawled up onto the mattress with us, very much like a cat rubbing up against my Master, who did not seem surprised by her appearance. He pulled out of me nonchalantly and I sat back, languidly watching as he fished a condom out of his robe, which he had spread across the sheet for me. He shoved it aside now as this smugly smiling woman with short black hair took my place before him. I watched as he grabbed her plump hips and penetrated her without further ceremony, swiftly wrapping her pussy around his erection. I watched as he began fucking her fast and hard from behind. She reacted to his violent strokes with an occasional soft moan as I tried to get in on the action by caressing his tight ass, but his hips were moving too furiously, so I gave up and sat back again to stare at my beautiful Master possessing another woman. Then I glanced at him in the mirror and realized she was seeing the same thing I had seen only moments ago. He looked just the same now fucking her as he had fucking me only a few heartbeats ago, exactly the same. The vision of his long hair and broad shoulders beneath the almost grim concentration of his features was as riveting now that his dick was buried inside another girl's body. And watching him, it seemed to me he was feeling the same thing he had felt with me, except of course that he was wearing a condom so she couldn't feel quite as good. I wondered if her pussy was as tight as mine, and it was as though my soul was bleeding out of me. I felt increasingly weak and indifferent to everything, vitally wounded by the realization that, physically, I was essentially the same as her or any other woman. A few minutes ago I had felt beautiful and special as my Master possessed me, but now it seemed there had been nothing truly special about it at all because here he was taking a girl who meant nothing to him in exactly the same way.

When she climbed onto the bed with us, she appeared to be alone, but apparently the slender man insinuating himself beside me now was her partner, and he was obviously willing to go for a 'full swap'. I thought this was what my Master wanted, and since all the life had gone out of me along with his attention and his erection, I succumbed to this soft-spoken man gently urging me back onto my hands and knees beside his companion, who had the great honor of being completely occupied by my Master's driving force at the moment. I glanced over my shoulder to watch the stranger wrestling with a condom, and was both surprised and infinitely relieved when my Master abruptly pulled out of the new hole he was enjoying, and stopped the man just as he was about to penetrate me. I was too dazed to understand what was happening, all I knew as my Master grabbed his robe and quickly put it on was that he was angry, and this was the most terrible thing of all. He barely allowed me enough time to get up and slip my own robe back on before he strode downstairs with me trailing behind him in despair.

Back down at the bar, my tearful intensity succeeded in diffusing his anger. He could see I was genuinely confused by his reaction upstairs, because I had believed our ultimate goal was to fuck to another couple together, and yet when it was about to happen, he suddenly stopped the action. He agreed this was one of our goals, but tonight was supposed to have been about me watching him just as last weekend he had watched me with another man. I assured him I had indeed been watching him, but all it had made me want to do was cry, and it was all I still wanted to do; I was having a hard time keeping up appearances so people wouldn't stare at us where we sat at the bar wearing the incriminating robes. My emotions were in full flood and my Master, blessedly his firmly understanding self again, calmly rode the passionate wave of my reaction to watching him fuck another woman while leading me by the hand into the Jacuzzi room.

We didn't get into the water; we stepped up onto a raised platform of cushy black foam mattresses. He spread our robes out in one corner, and our feelings and flesh became indistinguishable from each other as we lay back across them and began making passionate love. I didn't need to be told that what we were doing now was not fucking and bore no relation whatsoever to what I had been watching him do with a stranger only a few minutes ago. Our merging, undulating bodies on the black mats were the center of the universe and no one and nothing else existed. There was only his presence inside me, which I couldn't live without, and his face beneath me. He was saying things, but all I remember is the moment he finally spoke the words I had been longing to hear.

'I'm falling in love with you…'

I was crying as the pleasure of his unique personality in the form of his cock planted deep inside me merged with the pain of still seeing in my mind's eye his beloved manhood sliding in and out of another woman. 'Well, I'm already in love with you!' I sobbed, kissing him and riding him and clinging to him.

'It's true,' he said. 'Part of me keeps thinking it's too soon, but it's true… I love you, Missa.'

Only recently my Master explained to me that this was a necessary order for events to take in our relationship. He wanted to make sure my love for him was not conditional upon anything. I don't know exactly what he was thinking, but I understand what he means. He needed to make sure I truly did love him and desired to be his slave and that I wasn't just saying that in order to tie him down. He also wanted to see to it I didn't make the mistake of confusing our profound feelings for each other with sex. If he had told me he loved me before I watched him fucking another woman, I would have seen it as a betrayal of our bond and not as an exciting part of it. He was also wise to let me be the first to prove with Ray that having sex with other people in no way affected our love for each other.

I was so happy now it was though my soul was climaxing and not just my body. So when he turned me around and told me he was going to fuck my ass, I wanted him to more than anything. I don't think we had officially begun my anal training yet, but I was so open to him, so relieved and relaxed and aroused anticipating our future together – painfully challenging as it might occasionally prove to be – that when he thrust his hard-on through my sphincter's tight ring I felt truly and fully betrothed to him, my Master. Our passionately kinky engagement was witnessed by four black men, who my Master later told me watched him jealously, apparently amazed such a beautiful woman was not only letting her lover fuck her up the ass but loving it, too. He had to hold them back.

6 Inhibition Stripping

Mirrors provide a mysterious form of lubrication. I had always instinctively known this to be true, but I really came to appreciate it at Miami Velvet. I'll never forget Stinger's black-clad figure fucking me from behind reflected in front of me along with the sight of my face and quivering cleavage responding to his undivided attentions. Intense satisfaction cast my features even more beautifully, and my dark eyes were molten with the pure fulfillment experienced by women throughout the ages when a handsome, virile man deepens her metaphysical wound with his relentless energetic thrusts.

After a Saturday night at Velvet, we invariably slept in late on Sunday either at my place or his, but wherever we were, my little Merlin was always with us. At first he was jealous of sharing my affections with a man, but now we form a happy trinity free of children. My Master and I agree a child would essentially ruin our life since the ways we desire to play are not rated G. Therefore, I began taking the birth control pill only a few days after we met, as he had politely commanded me to do on our second date.

When we finally got out of bed after one o'clock, we left Merlin with a treat in his mouth and drove to the local Starbucks for ours. We sat sipping our non-fat lattes feeling wonderfully relaxed, and while my Master read the paper, I basked in his presence suffering hot flashes of excitement mingled with a shock of disbelief recalling the events of the previous night. Part of me cringed from the thought of Swinging, yet my imagination went wild over it, and the effect was feverish as these two conflicting reactions battled inside me. For months, I had Swinging on the brain, and if I made the mistake of thinking about it when I was feeling tired and vulnerable, I just wanted to curl up alone and safe beneath the pure white sheets of my bed. But this would mean the nightmare of returning to a world without Stinger, my beautiful Master, so I am forced to be strong and adopt a more healthily balanced perspective on the matter.

It was the first Sunday of what became our ongoing ritual while we still lived in Miami. From that day forward, we religiously made it a point to attend our open-air church – the nude beach at Haulover. Instead of putting on confining clothing and entering a man-made structure to worship, we stripped off all our garments to let the wind caress and the sun penetrate every inch of our flesh. All we needed was a big towel and each other. It's easy to forget your blood is always flowing as a result of your heart beating, just as waves endlessly break on the shore and flow back into the deep, which must be one of the reasons why lying on a beach is so soothing. Physical laws come together there like fingers massaging your skin down to the mystical muscle of your soul. Sometimes the wind is too cold or the sun is too hot or the tide is too low, but more often than not the elements were in perfect harmony for us at Haulover, and for a couple of hours every Sunday we worshipped our embodiment – the miracle of conscious love and desire made possible by the Divine's temple of flesh and blood.

The parking lot was nearly full, but the jeep effortlessly found a spot on the grass under a tree, and a concrete tunnel beneath the street led us across a wooden bridge to the only all-nude beach in Miami. The flesh-toned sand was decked out with towels and beach umbrellas, two volley-ball nets and evenly spaced lifeguard houses alternately painted shocking lime green, neon lavender and radioactive yellow, colors conceivable only in South Florida where blatant bad taste can almost pass for a perverse worship of the blinding sunlight. With my hand safely curled inside my Master's as always, I stepped boldly onto the sand with my black thong sandals, which I soon paused to slip off as we made our way towards the water. Naked bodies walked and reclined around us, but any possible par-adisiacal effect was ruined by baseball caps, sunglasses, plastic coolers and other technologically rooted accessories. A thin man, his limp penis dan-gling between his thighs, strolled past us, dramatically contrasting with a reclining woman's rolling folds of flesh. I glanced at her, incredulous she did not feel the need to hide her body from the world while she did her best to trim it down, like a sculptor whittling away excess clay to reveal the work of art buried within it. Here was a blatant example of the 'body acceptance' concept I had only briefly wrestled with before rejecting. I don't believe anything that is bad for the haunting muscle of my heart can be considered a good thing. Unless it is genetic, I consider obesity disre-spectful to one's self and I see no reason to be politically correct and pre-tend I approve of it just as I am not politically correct about a lot of other things, my own sexual tastes included.

I was scanning the beach for potential rivals and I spotted more than one annoyingly slender yet full-breasted physical nemesis. We walked past one lovely woman who lay on her back, her tanned skin covered with sunscreen giving her the glistening aura of a bronze idol fallen from the temple of ideal sexuality.

'Implants,' my Master commented.

I smiled triumphantly.

The beach was only comfortably full; it was relatively easy finding a spot with no one between us and the water and far enough away from other people to feel private. I imagined all eyes were on me as I pulled off my tight tank top and exposed my breasts. Caressed by the ocean breeze and kissed by the warm sunlight, my nipples instantly hardened in response to the subtle sensual assault. But it was nothing compared to the thrill I experienced pushing my shorts and panties down my legs to my ankles and stepping boldly out of them, exposing my naked ass to everyone behind me and the pink shell-like folds of my labia to the pounding sea before me and the people walking along its edge. I sat down on the towel beside my Master, who had commanded me to keep my pussy shaved for him at all times, but it was such an ordeal that I wasn't obeying him properly. I wanted to get better at keeping myself smooth down there because I loved the feel of my naked pubes and being able to caress my clit without any prickly hairs distracting me from the slick feel of my deepening pleasure.

Leaning back on my arms and spreading my legs slightly while bending one of my knees, I felt very daring exposing my unprotected sex to strangers' eyes, but the truth is, it also just felt really nice. Apart from the fact that almost everyone was naked – some women and even some men were modestly wearing bikini bottoms – Haulover was like any other beach and yet better in that there were no children running around screaming or boom-boxes blaring. Nothing disturbed the peace of skin communing with the elements, which was pleasantly intensified by the constant hum of intimate conversations rising over the sound of the surf. But while it was the sun sustaining my flesh, it was my Master's loving gaze my soul was blooming beneath and fully taking possession of my body through. Even when I couldn't see his eyes, only my own slightly distorted reflection in the silver panes of his sunglasses, the way he looked at me made me believe in my beauty. We took turns rubbing each other down with suntan lotion, and I was careful to wipe all the gritty sand off my hands before I concentrated on his groin area. I did him first, relishing the shaved smoothness of his tender ball-sack, the rosy porous skin of which I saw more clearly than ever in the sunlight, and his deliciously full limp shaft threatening to stiffen beneath my ministrations. Then it was his turn to do me, and I came to love the feel of his big strong hands rubbing the oil into my skin, a teasingly brief massage that made me crave a much longer one. It is amazing to me how many muscles I became aware of, like musical notes I'd never heard/felt before, when his fingertips pressed skillfully and lovingly into them.

As my Master put it, if we couldn't be naked he wouldn't care for the beach, and I agreed. We lay on our backs and on our stomachs with our chins resting on our hands, talking or merely smiling at each other and kissing occasionally, watching people strolling up and down the beach just as we did after a playful stint in the water. I felt so proud to be walking hand-in-hand with my handsome long-haired Master, as though I was exposing the full extent of my happiness at belonging to him by appearing naked beside him in public. I was also proud of myself for feeling so at ease my first time on a nude beach. The slight flaws I had always perceived in my body were gradually flowing away on the tide of my Master's pleasure, which was literally beating into me a sense of my own special sexiness. It was walking in Haulover gazing up at his profile outlined against the sky that his smile first made me think of an Etruscan painting. I absolutely love his smile, how soft yet immutable it is, as though he is seeing all sorts of fascinating things and possibilities, all within his reach and requiring only a concentrated imagination to grasp and flesh out into reality...

When it came time to put our clothes back on – instead of being shy I relished the fact that everyone around us seemed to be looking at us while we did so – it dawned on me how constricting the materials I willingly choose to wear everyday are. My skin sticky with remnants of sunscreen and invigorated by the constant caress of the wind, the penetration of sunlight and the primal baptism of seawater, it didn't feel quite right to be sliding panties up my legs, then tight shorts followed by an even tighter Tank Top. What I had thought of as a skimpy sexy outfit suddenly felt like a prison. My Master seemed to read my feelings as he said, 'We're going shopping for a Sarong now' and the following Sunday, when we once again decided we had spent enough time at our hedonistic church, my whole being seemed to sigh with delight as I lifted my arms so he could wrap the purple-and-white Sarong he had bought me around my body, deliciously sun and wind kissed everywhere. He tied the soft material tightly over my breasts, and it fell loosely over my curves even while clinging gently to them as I walked. The panties and constricting shorts belonged to MIP, the Sarong was Missa's. It felt so much better, so much more natural, and made me acutely aware of the sad fact that our culture is not so much concerned with sensuality as it is with sex on a rather adolescent level. Tight shorts and tops are not designed for a woman's pleasure; she wears them to attract men. Thankfully, my Master's tastes are more varied and refined, and how beautiful he thought I looked in the Sarong made it feel even more wonderful. Those moments after spending a couple of hours on the beach, walking back to the jeep with the sun beginning to set in the West and the sky growing softer and more luminously colorful, soon became our favorite time of the week. All the inevitable tensions created by modern life were temporarily soothed away by the sensual rhythm of the tide, which helped wash away some of the excessive thoughts cluttering my mind. I felt so peaceful and relaxed it was as though our whole life stretched out before us with the easy promise of a Sunday night at Fox's.

On that particular evening, when I was relishing breaking out of MIP's contemporary confines and discovering a more timeless sensual realm as Missa, I was possessed by an irresistible craving for raw oysters accompanied by a very dry gin martini. Once we were underway in his jeep, I expressed this desire to my Master, who declared it was just what he wanted as well. So we embarked on the adventure of trying to find the best place to fulfill our desire, which became more and more intense with every unsatisfactory bar and restaurant we passed. Finally, Stinger had an epiphany and we ended up on Lincoln Road in South Beach at an outdoor table. At last we had large martini glasses in hand and a plate of equally big oysters on the half shell laid out on a bed of ice before us. The setting sun was shining in my Master's eyes in a way infinitely more eloquent than words as we gazed at one another without speaking, our thoughts and feelings caressing each other saying it all silently. We both knew how blessed we were to have finally found each other in this world. On the beach that afternoon he had said to me as we lay talking, 'You knew I existed, you just didn't know where' and now I raised my glass in a toast. 'To Stinger, my beautiful Master.'

He carefully touched his glass to mine so as not to spill a drop of our good fortune. 'To my most treasured slave… no, to my slave, my most treasured possession.' He must have seen the shadow of disappointment cross my ardent gaze, because he added softly, the look in his own eyes telling me it was what he had meant to say all along, 'To Missa, the love of my life.'

I smiled. 'To us.'

I was blissfully unaware of how much those martinis and oysters cost. When it occurred to me to ask a few days later, I was appalled to discover the bill had been approximately sixty-five dollars, yet it was true when my Master stated it had been worth every penny.

The only thing marring my happiness even while electrifying my imagination more deeply than I cared to admit was the thought of occasionally expanding our sexual horizons to include other people. My Master had been corresponding with a couple on Swinger's Date Club he wished for us to meet casually somewhere to see if there was any chemistry between us. To protect their privacy I will call this couple Tom and Nancy (their real names aren't anymore fancy). My Master had e-mailed me some photographs and I had not been impressed with either one of them, but he believed they might prove compatible with us and I trusted his judgment more than my own skittishness when it came to Swinging. For this reason – not to mention the fact that I was training to be his slave and therefore had to do anything he said – I agreed it couldn't hurt to meet them. My Master had told them we usually went to Haulover on Sundays, so it wasn't much of a coincidence when we ran into them on the beach the following weekend. Stinger heard someone call his name as we were walking along the water, and it turned out to be Tom and Nancy, who had recognized us from our photographs, for we had since put up a profile on the site ourselves.

Nancy was an older woman, and in my opinion she looked it. I did not consider her worthy of my Master's attentions and it distressed me he apparently found her attractive. When I told him as much in private, he explained his tastes had developed over the years and he could now find women who were not overtly beautiful desirable on certain levels, because for him sensuality in a person is much more than just superficially pleasing proportions. He also said it really wasn't all that important what the other woman looked liked; the point was the erotic experience of having sex around, and occasionally with, other people. It was the excitement of fucking other people with me that turned him on, not any particular woman. Intellectually, I understood, but emotionally I was distressed he could even entertain the thought of fucking Nancy, much less desire to do so. I suppose you could say she had a handsome face, but I found her sun-browned skin unappealingly leathery, and I had set a much higher standard for my Master in my fantasies. Her best feature was her long blonde hair cascading in suspiciously perfect curls down her back. But in an effort to be a good slave, I told myself the fact that I was not attracted to Nancy in the least was the result of my not being bi-sexual, and I was willing to put my own judgment aside in favor of my Master's since he was more experienced in these matters. I hoped when the time came I would be inspired by the erotic dance of Swinging with another couple, the actual steps of which I had yet to learn. In this case, I was blindly following my Master's lead, and he later admitted he should have paid more attention to my physical reaction to these particular people. Being a scientist enables him to take a rather detached, almost abstract view of things, and his fixed goal at the time was for us to get over the hurdle of doing another couple so we could move on with our relationship and my training. If he had not been quite so eager, and I had not been so inexperienced, I believe we would have waited for another more inspiring foursome. Also confusing the matter somewhat was the fact that Tom and Nancy were extremely nice and refreshingly intelligent people we enjoyed talking to. My Master and I have since learned it is not necessary for us to befriend individuals to enjoy Swinging with them, but at the time it seemed like a good idea to find a man and a woman we could relate to on most, if not all, levels, friends to go out with and friends to stay in with. It was a nice theory, but in my opinion – and fortunately my Master always listens to my opinion whether he feels it is valid or not since the last thing he wants, as he has often said, is a slave who's a doormat – it is better to be close friends with a couple you are not intimate with since I would inevitably become jealous if there was another woman my Master was fucking regularly besides me, not to mention that the thrill of a sexual encounter with total strangers would be lost after more than a handful of assignations.

Tom was thin to the point of emaciation. There was nothing about his tall, bony body that aroused my delicious sexual submissiveness. He had long hair pulled back in a ponytail like my Master, but it was curly and coarse, nowhere near as sleek and noble looking. I think if a man is to have long hair it should be soft and shiny. I had never had a pleasant conversation with people while entirely naked, and I found the experience somewhat uncomfortable, perhaps because I didn't find either one of their bodies appealing, and because I had reservations about exposing what at the time I still perceived as my own physical imperfections. It was a relief when my Master and I at last walked back to our own towel, where I made the mistake of keeping my doubts mainly to myself and we concluded an intimate relationship with Tom and Nancy seemed promising since they too, unlike most other Swingers, were into fetish wear and bondage. I was vaguely hoping when the time came that Tom assuming a forceful personality in tandem with my Master's beautifully commanding aura would turn me on enough that I could transcend what might only prove to be superficial physical preferences. A Ft. Lauderdale fetish clothing store aptly named The Fetish Factory regularly held full dress up parties in different venues. The following Saturday night an event was scheduled at the Aqua Lounge and the Playboy channel's Sexcetera show would be there to film the action. Tom and Nancy had asked us if we wanted to go, and my Master and I had accepted the invitation.

7 Needing A Push To Swing

On the way to his weekly Thursday pool game with friends, Master and I spotted a shop called Something Sexy and made a brief stop. The small space was filled with the usual rainbow-colored dildos evoking an x-rated version of the wizard's Oz full of big-breasted Dorothy's spreading their red high-heels wide for the vibrating magic of plastic cocks, rather like the Tin Man gratefully accepted a clock for a heart. Every box boasted a picture of the traditional sexy bimbo whose expression clearly stated 'There's no place like my pussy… there's no place like my pussy…' We were hunting for fetish clothing because I literally didn't have a thing to wear to the party at the Aqua Lounge only two days away. My Master would be resplendent in an antique tuxedo from the Victorian era that had never been worn by the young man it was made for. Its intended owner was eighteen-years-old when he died, the same age as my Master when his mother found it in the attic of the house whose contents she had bought at auction. For decades the finished tux had lain in a box wrapped in the tailor's virgin paper before fate finally had it fitted for my Master.

I really didn't expect to find something suitable to wear at a common porno shop. The sexy garments hanging near the door were mere fragments of cheap material sewn together with less care than my old Barbie dresses. I wouldn't have bought any of the pieces on display for my dolls much less for myself.

'Missa, look at this,' came my Master's voice from the other side of the store, and I saw he had discovered a small section of shiny black vinyl items that looked promising. 'What do you think?' He held up a skimpy bodice that looked and felt like very fine leather.

'It's interesting,' I agreed, eyeing it skeptically. 'But I'd have to try it on...'

'Go ahead, we have time.'

'But...'

He handed it to me. 'Just let me know if you need any help.'

I did need help; I couldn't even figure out which side was up and if it laced in back or in the front. I then needed my Master to pull on the strings while I sucked in my tummy and held it in place over my breasts. The brief bodice – half sticky oil spill and half delicate spider's web – fit me like a perverse charm.

'I like it,' my Master declared, smiling down at my bulging cleavage. 'What do you think?' he asked me again, as if my uncertain opinion could possibly matter more to me than his obvious approval.

'I like it,' I admitted, gazing at my wickedly sexy torso in the mirror. The bodice rose into two vampire-like peaks barely covering my tightly squeezed and uplifted breasts, and my creamy cleavage was enticingly visible through the web of black strings holding the solid shadow tightly closed around my pale, almost luminous skin.

'If you like it, I'll get it for you,' my Master told me.

I have since lost track of how many times I have heard him say those wonderful words, but at the time I was still feeling guilty about how much money he was spending lately. 'That's okay, I'll buy it.'

'It's not a problem, Missa. If you like it, I'd be happy to buy it for you.'

'I know, Master, but I'd like to get this myself.'

'All right, as long as you realize it's not a problem, it's up to you.'

The bodice and its accompanying black thong were so small they easily fit in my purse along with the black stockings I bought to go with it. I had a black lace garter belt at home I could wear beneath it, the six-inch heel black shoes plus the long black gloves my Master had purchased for me on South Beach, and it turns out that was all I needed. My black leather collar was the finishing touch.

The night of the fetish party, I spent a considerable amount of time in the doll's house bathroom applying my make-up, which was heavy on dark-gray eye shadow, black eyeliner and an orange-red shade of lipstick my Master had bought me. I even went so far as to dab some silver glitter at the outer corners of my eyes. I hadn't had so much fun since I was a kid dressing up for Halloween. I had always chosen sexy costumes – gypsy, Egyptian princess, belly dancer, etc. – and tonight the only thing frightening about my attire was how little there was of it.

'Master, I can't go out like this...' I stood in the door of the bathroom looking down at myself incredulously. 'Can I?'

'Why not? You look unbelievable.'

'I'm half naked!'

'Mm!' He caught me in his arms, but then quickly released me so as not to disturb my bodice's delicate webbing or get make-up on his white collar.

'You look beautiful too, Master,' I said fervently. His glorious hair flowing over his broad shoulders in the vintage tux, he looked every bit a lord and master, and I could scarcely believe he was my lord and Master.

'Thank you, Missa.' He clipped the end of a black leather leash onto the ring at the front of my collar. 'Shall we go, my slave?'

'I can't go out like this!' I exclaimed. 'I have to put something on until we get... I mean, may I put something on to ride in the jeep, Master?'

'Well...' He regarded me soberly for a moment but there was a smile in his eyes. 'I suppose you should.' He sighed, unclipping the leash.

'Thank you, Master!' I carefully slipped a loose black dress on over the bodice, garter belt, thong and stockings I was wearing, not bothering to remove the long black gloves that gave my ensemble an elegant touch. I had sheathed my arms and legs in shadow while exposing flesh that was normally hidden, including my entire backside and the precious black purse of my pussy, the tops of my thighs and so much cleavage you could almost see my nipples from certain angles. I was glad of the concealing dress during the drive to Tom and Nancy's house even as I kept admiring the faux diamond bracelet glimmering like stars around the mysteriously ensouled darkness of my wrist. It reminded me of a poem I had written years ago I tried to remember now as my Master drove...

A baby smiling in a car window at night and
two lovers rolling over and over together
like the wheels of whirling galaxies
obeying destiny's force that seems not to
exist in the crawling world of the clock.
Yet minute by minute, thought by thought
dream by dream two hands
are meant to meet in midnight's merging,
all events wound with an inner twist
of my wrist, time set in my diamond bracelets
made of stars wound forever around his neck.

I was thinking about everything except Swinging; I still couldn't wrap my brain around the fact that we were supposedly planning to have sex with Tom and Nancy tonight. For once in my life, my imagination failed me, but only because I let it. It made me feel somewhat safe that we were all going out together as opposed to staying in, and I reasoned that by the time we got back from the club, it might be too late and we might all be too tired to do anything. Or so I hoped deep down while I did my best to avoid the thought altogether, which probably explains why I felt the ominous beginnings of a headache throbbing in my temples as we pulled up into the couple's driveway. I rarely ever suffer from headaches, but I'm not surprised one attacked me that night as a physical manifestation of the intense effort I was making not to think about what I believed my Master expected of me later.

Nancy might occasionally be into a little pain, but she and her skinny Dom were definitely not hurting for money. They lived in a spacious two-story house complete with a wall-sized fish tank. The lighting was dim, which my aching head appreciated, yet it put the rest of me on edge. I painted a smile on my face as Nancy gave my Master and me a tour of the place. I was not at all impressed with the décor, which contained too many faux animal skins and glass-and-metal tables that for some reason always look cheap no matter how much they cost. The spacious living room was so dark all I could really see were the colorful tropical fish swimming lethargically back and forth in the tank. Tom disappeared into the kitchen in search of wine. Nancy perched on the edge of a divan and watched as I obeyed my Master's command and slipped off my dress to reveal the little I was wearing beneath it.

'Beautiful,' she said, reaching out with both hands to caress my naked hips.

I figuratively steadied myself on my Master's expression, seeking direction from him while at the same time imploring him with my eyes not to make me do anything I didn't want to. Fortunately, Tom returned with the wine and I was able to take refuge behind a small glass moat while we all conversed politely. Nancy was wearing a form-fitting yellow latex dress that was effectively transparent and Tom was clad all in black. On a well-built man, the slits in his shirt would have been sexy, but on him the effect was almost macabre; he evoked a cadaver risen from the grave covered with decomposing shreds of cloth. Obviously my perceptions were negatively exaggerated by how profoundly I resented pretending to desire sexual relations with a man who completely turned me off. I loved my Master too much to resent him for putting me in this totally uncomfortable position, since I had let him do so in the first place by not properly communicating my misgivings, hence the headache taking possession of my forehead and temples like a hot iron band while I remained aloof as a princess. I didn't mind being the center of attention as long as no one but my Master expected me to reciprocate.

The party was up in Ft. Lauderdale, and Stinger, Tom and Nancy (I wasn't saying much) agreed it didn't make sense to drive up separately, and since there was no question of taking the more uncomfortable jeep, my Master and I slipped into the backseat of their spacious car. Naturally, this meant we would all end up back here together afterwards, and I was glad I had begged a glass of water plus two Advils before we left as this inescapable fact intensified my headache.

For over forty-five minutes, I sat with my half naked side reassuringly soldered against my Master's warm tuxedo clutching his hand and wishing the luminous green numbers in the dashboard clock would stop stabbing into my brain. My Master kept giving me concerned glances while sustaining a pleasant conversation with our hosts, who were too polite to remark on the fact that I wasn't being very sociable.

'How are you feeling?' Stinger asked me more than once.

'A little better.' The painkiller was kicking in, alleviating the throbbing in my temples, and knowing we were headed towards a public place was also helping relieve some of my emotional distress. I was able to tell myself that whatever happened later would take place in another dimension where I would feel differently about everything after a few drinks, good music and my Master's inspiring romantic attention.

We arrived fashionably late at the Aqua Lounge. The parking lot was already full of cars, including a long black limo. Only the loving presence of my Master gave me the courage to step out into the cool night air wearing next to nothing. In fact, the gloves, heels, stockings and bodice only seemed to accentuate my nakedness. I was willingly exposing myself to hundreds of strangers' eyes as well as a television camera, yet unbelievably enough I did not feel at all shy. When my Master snapped the leash on my collar, the universe seemed to click into place at last and I felt myself walking into the life I had always fantasized about as I took my first few tentative steps across the black asphalt. The crippling high-heels forced me to walk slowly just behind my Master, who looked so powerfully elegant in the vintage tux I would have willingly fallen to my knees right then and there and worshipped his cock in front of the whole world. I also felt protectively flanked by Tom and Nancy, their admiration an invisible carpet I was treading across the parking lot. A handful of people dressed entirely in black stood at the entrance to the club, yet they all looked beautifully different as a result of the cut and material of their outfits, their make-up and hairstyles. Although they looked at me, they didn't stare at me, as I had feared they would, and whatever qualms I had about appearing this way in public were forever brushed away by their casual smiles. Now all I felt was a strangely pure pride and happiness to be lead around on a leash by my magnificent Master so everyone could see what a beautiful slave was all his.

Finally making it past the crush of bodies in the elevator and foyer, we entered the club. It was not as crowded as the parking lot had indicated it would be, but Nancy assured us dozens more people would show up during the course of the night. We had arrived just in time to secure a comfortable couch in an intimate alcove just beyond one of the bars with a good view of two 'play' areas. A tritely sexy waitress indicative of Playboy's purported presence on the premises took our drink orders, and I settled back between my Master and Nancy. Tom was exiled to a chair across from us. Feeling intensely alive as well as blessedly safe in the crook of my Master's arm, listening to the pounding alternative music and watching the people milling before us, it was as though I had died and gone to heaven even though it looked more like the traditional idea of purgatory and hell.

'Lots of eye candy here,' my Master whispered in my ear.

'Why can't everyone dress this way all the time?' I whispered back fervently.

He shrugged philosophically, smiling his smile.

Almost everyone was wearing black, every style and texture of black imaginable, although the men seemed limited to two types – the tight leather or vinyl look and a more elegant vampiric style. My Master fell into the latter category in his antique Tux, which was genuine Goth. For the girls there was the requisite crippling footwear of extreme high-heeled shoes or boots, and I spotted more than one platinum purple wig, nevertheless, the feminine sex had more thematic looks to choose from. There was no question of me feeling jealous of anyone tonight; I had never felt so beautiful and so sexy. I would have preferred to be alone with my Master, but there was something titillating about sitting between him and another relatively attractive woman who was behaving very much like a man towards me. My Master's hand was on my left thigh, Nancy's hand rested on the other, and then fingers began crossing boundaries like circuits pleasantly shocking me with how daring we were all being. As she reached out and touched Stinger, I had no choice but to turn my head and kiss her – a yielding, undemanding experience that would have left me cold if my Master hadn't been watching, because I was doing it to turn him on. I immediately turned to kiss him for much longer, and suffered a rush akin to touching a live wire when I surfaced to the sight of his hand slipping up Nancy's dress through a convenient slit in the latex sheath. I felt at once strangely stunned and electrified watching him intimately caress another woman's sex while she reached down and pressed her hand against my own pussy. They took turns kissing me, and then they kissed each other right in front of my face. I caught my breath, loving the sight of my Master's profile kissing someone other than me. His features struck me as more nobly handsome than ever engaged in an intimate act he was so good at. Knowing how wonderfully stimulating it was to kiss him I could savor what she was experiencing even as I had the pleasure of seeing what he looked like doing it. The only thing I didn't like was that his eyes were closed so he wasn't looking at me, and this upset me intensely wondering if he had temporarily forgotten about me. It was a foolish fear, as his eyes and his smile told me a second later when he turned his face towards me again. He also didn't need to tell me how hard it got him to share my body with another woman; his excitement was as real and vital to me as the earth's atmosphere rousing storms of feelings inside me.

'It's like having my own personal Cleopatra,' Nancy declared softly.

Even though I had heard this compliment dozens of times before, it still made my blood purr, and increasingly swept up in this languid dance of the senses, I found myself leaning towards Tom where he sat exiled from the action. He met me half way, our tongues started playing, and right away I felt frustrated by his slow, insipid kiss. I trusted my Master was watching me kiss another man for him, so I was very upset when I glanced back at him and saw that he seemed to be concentrating entirely on Nancy. I promptly sat back, wedging myself between them, and smiled gratefully up at the waitress who finally arrived with our drinks.

I was happy when Nancy went and sat on her husband's lap and I had Stinger all to myself again. I thrived on the way his arm tightened possessively around my shoulders every time he glanced down at my cleavage, and the rest of me. Nevertheless, I could not contain an outraged outburst.

'You weren't even watching me!' I whispered furiously.

'What do you mean?' He looked confused. 'I haven't taken my eyes off you all night.'

'Do you think I wanted to kiss him?' I hissed. 'I was doing it to turn you on and you weren't even looking!' I was not making much of an effort to fight the black hole of jealousy sucking me into its crushingly painful reality. 'You were kissing her, not watching me!'

'I was aware of you the whole time, Missa,' he said firmly. 'Even if I looked away for a moment, it didn't mean I stopped being aware of you and what you were doing... what we were doing together. I told you, it's all about us, dear.'

'Even when your eyes are closed and you're kissing and caressing her, not touching me or looking at me in any way, it's still all about us?'

'Yes, because I know you're looking at me, watching me and reacting.'

'Hmm.'

'Missa?'

I stared fixedly into space. 'Yes?'

'Look at me.'

I obeyed.

'Do you have any idea how beautiful you are and how much I love you?'

'Mm...' I could never look into his eyes without melting against him, and now I gratefully let go of my self-inflicted torment and held on to the happiness inspired by my faith in our love.

As the night wore on, we were photographed more than once, and a week later the pictures were posted on The Fetish Factory's website. My favorite is a shot of me pinned between Nancy, her back to the camera as her invisible hands fondle me, and my Master, who is standing just behind me. My breasts are exposed and my eyes are blissfully closed as he passionately buries his face in my hair. When I saw the image, I loved the intense expression carving out his profile so much that I made this erotic triptych the wallpaper on my computer for weeks afterwards.

We walked around the club a few times, an increasingly slow and difficult task as more and more people continued arriving. Soon it was standing-room-only, so we explored the small space while Tom and Nancy held on to our highly coveted couch, and vise versa. There were 'scenes' being played in alcoves and on a handful of 'stages' set up on the main floor that consisted of both female and male slaves being beaten by their masters and mistresses with a variety of implements, including floggers, paddles and whips. Some submissives were tied to iron crosses, others were bound elaborately with rope, and a group of three lovely girls in tight red corsets that left their breasts and bottoms vulnerably exposed had their wrists attached to straps hanging above them. They were forced to bend slightly at the waist and take whatever punishment two male Dom's meted out to them, even flaming torches dancing swiftly over their buttocks and the backs of their thighs. The Playboy camera was concentrating on this scene, unfolding just beyond our private alcove, but I was interested in the more subtle action taking place right beside our couch. A Dominatrix was perched on a cushion facing away from us as her young slave-boy wearing black boots, tight black vinyl pants and a chain around his neck devotedly rubbed her back. He kept giving me surreptitious glances as he massaged his mistress, and finally I couldn't resist reaching out and caressing his hard naked back as we exchanged a secret smile.

My Master squeezed my thigh. 'Very good, Missa,' he said softly, obviously pleased by my initiative.

When one of my favorite Garbage songs started playing, it inspired me to get up and dance. Nancy quickly slid into my spot so Tom could sit beside her, and as I savored the intense sensuality of moving my body to good music, alternately facing the couch and away from it, three pairs of hands and three sets of lips caressed my naked ass gyrating invitingly in their hungry faces. The next day, I asked my Master if he had been listening to the lyrics I love so much, and he replied, 'No, I was too busy trying to figure out how to lick your pussy while you danced.'

During the long drive back to Miami, my Master played with my breasts almost the whole way. He rubbed my nipples between his thumb and forefinger gently and repeatedly, rubbing and tugging softly, rubbing and tugging until I felt hypnotized with pleasure. Then he handed Nancy his camera so she could photograph me bending over his lap sucking his big hard cock, and I love the way my long faux diamond earrings and bracelet glimmer around the hot shaft of his erection in the pictures.

The moment I had dreaded all night arrived almost as soon as we walked into the dark house. I think Stinger asked to used the bathroom, and although I'm sure there was one on the first floor, Nancy led him upstairs, naturally I followed him, and suddenly we were all in the master suite sitting on the edge of a big round bed covered with a faux leopard-skin spread. I totally resented the way my Master and I had been manipulated upstairs. I had never let a man do this to me on the first date, and I wondered angrily why I was letting a couple do it now to my precious and nearly virginal relationship with Stinger. He agreed with me later that it wasn't right the way they corralled us upstairs like that, yet he didn't seem bothered by their behavior at the time. I sat as close to him as possible (if I had been a cat all my claws would have been sunk into the shirt over his chest) and my turbulent aura made it obvious I was not inclined to let go of him to start sensually purring around someone else.

'Missa's a little scared,' my Master explained.

'I'm not scared,' I hissed, suddenly furious with him for not understanding the problem – that neither of these people turned me on even remotely enough to want to have sex with them. I don't remember what he whispered to me. Maybe he offered me the chance to leave, but I don't think he did; I think he told me to relax, gently but relentlessly insisting I lie back on the bed and relax... 'Just relax, Missa, trust me, it'll be all right, just relax...'

The next thing I knew, my Master was sucking one of my nipples, Tom was gently licking the other, and Nancy had swiftly positioned herself on the bed between my legs and was eagerly licking my pussy. I raised my head curiously off the pillow to study the scene of my body being worshipped from all angles, moaning since I knew it was expected of me, but really because I was disappointed by how little pleasure I actually experienced. A woman's light and agile tongue working energetically between my thighs did absolutely nothing for me in any sense, which came as no surprise. All I felt was dread at being expected to reciprocate, so when she lay down on her back beside me, I concentrated desperately on her pierced nipples. Playing with one while watching my Master suckle the other was slightly titillating, and I suffered a flash of hope that with another more tempting woman it would be a whole different ball game. I can't say I savored the sensation of a thin hard ring against my tongue surrounded by flaccid skin, the overall texture of which did not inspire me to caress it. Yet more than anything I wanted to please my Master, so I dutifully positioned myself between her legs and prepared to lick pussy for the first time in my life. Apparently, just seeing my mouth so close to another woman's sex seriously turned my Master on because he knelt on the bed and started fucking me violently from behind. I gasped with pleasure as he entered me, then moaned and closed my eyes as he literally thrust my face between Nancy's thighs. I shoved myself back defiantly, and tentatively licked her little labia, which didn't seem to taste or smell like anything.

'I've never done this before,' I confessed.

'I'm honored,' she said, gazing expectantly down the length of her body at me.

I licked her small cunt again a few more times, but I knew I was incapable of making any real effort to please her, so I stopped going through the motions and encouraged my Master to take over. It was the first time I ever saw him eating another woman, and the sight of his beautiful profile had the usual effect on me as I watched his lips and tongue skillfully evoking her appreciative moans. I would have been content to hand him a condom and watch him fucking her so I could relax secure in the knowledge that I was pleasing him for a variety of reasons, and I was so determined to give him what he wanted that it seriously annoyed me Nancy was not cooperating by being more interested in me.

She sat up suddenly. 'Just let me watch for a while,' she said rather impatiently.

Tom, who was still fully clothed where he knelt impotently at the edge of the action, moved towards me willingly, and I suffered a faint thrill thinking I was about to experience my first double penetration.

'Actually,' my Master pulled me into the safety of his arms, 'I think that's what Missa wanted to do.'

I knew he was protecting me, but the truth was that letting two men fuck me would have been much easier for me than pretending I enjoyed licking pussy.

Nancy got off the bed abruptly and switched on a bright light. 'This isn't working,' she stated bluntly.

I could have kissed her.

Tom promptly got up as well. It was obvious his wife called all the shots.

My Master and I remained on the bed. The relief I felt intensified my deep desire to please him, so when he positioned me on my hands and knees and fucked me passionately and possessively from behind while the other couple watched as though mesmerized it felt better than anything else had all night.

Afterwards, we sat around drinking hot tea while Tom, Nancy and Stinger made polite conversation and I brooded. I got the impression Nancy blamed me for the evening's failure, which made me angry because in reality we had been maneuvered up into bed without any foreplay whatsoever. We had also made it perfectly clear from the beginning that I was not bisexual. In my opinion, she was to blame for the way she had essentially tried to force us to immediately meet all her expectations. I did not appreciate it in the least, but I did not say anything until my Master and I were finally alone in his jeep. As we discussed the experience, my indignation was aggravated by the profound frustration that filled me whenever I failed to please my Master completely, and by his quiet, almost emotionless voice.

Hours later, we were still talking where we lay on my bed in the doll's house. My Master was, in his relentless scientific way, dealing with the emotional natural disaster of my resentment towards him as a result of the night's events. He said it would only happen again and again until we got to the root of the problem. He told me he was not sure I really desired to do anything he said, and that it would be unhealthy for me to obey his commands if there was even the slightest chance I would resent him for it afterwards. I desperately tried to explain this wouldn't happen if I wasn't physically repelled by whoever he commanded me to have sex with in the future, but he just stared fixedly up at the ceiling, so deep in thought he was silent for minutes at a time, which stoked my despair as I waited for him to guide me out of the emotional labyrinth I was hopelessly lost in. When he stated that my failure to properly communicate my misgivings to him was only part of the problem, a revelation dawned in the depths of my exhaustion.

'The problem is that even though I say all I desire to do is please you, I'm still really only thinking of pleasing myself,' I began slowly, working it out as I spoke. 'I only really want you to command me to do things I want to do myself... and yet if I obey you by fucking another man that turns me on, I'm really only obeying my own impulse and desire, and it's only about pleasing myself the way I did before I met you... it wouldn't be about us being together even while having sex with other people... it wouldn't be about my being excited because I was obeying you, and about being turned on by the knowledge that I was exciting you with my submission... I mean, if it's really all about loving you more than anyone or anything else and longing to please you, it shouldn't matter if the man attached to the penis fucking me for your extended pleasure is my type or not because it's all abut being turned on by you, by the mysterious thrill of obeying you, my beloved Master, without question. It's all about the excitement of watching you, and of you watching me, and it doesn't matter who we're using for that, not really.'

My Master let me know I had hit the nail right on the head when he quietly but firmly commanded me to assume the sleen position, and kneeling on the bed behind me began remorselessly pushing the head of his erection into my tight sphincter, making it clear he planned to punish me for my transgressions by not using any lubrication. Yet consciously fully accepting my absolute submissiveness to him aroused me so much that my ring slid fervently down his hard cock, joining us deeply and completely.

Hours later, I left my Master sleeping peacefully in my bed as I slipped on a sundress and black leather flip-flops to walk Merlin. I'll never forget opening the front door and stepping out into the brilliant sunlight of a late March morning in Miami. My neighbor across the street was washing his car while broadcasting Salsa from the speakers, and the brisk sensual beat followed me down the sidewalk as wonder lightened my steps. On that glorious day I felt alive in a whole new world free of the selfish weight of my ego. Love suffused my soul as light filled my eyes, the vivid vibrant colors all around me hot sensual kisses against my elated awareness of the vital truth that dawned on me in the gray moments just before sunrise. Obeying my beautiful Master was not a means to an end; it was an end in itself. I truly loved Stinger as I had never loved another man, and so I could never really desire another man except as a way of pleasing my Master whenever he happened to be in the mood to expand our sensual horizons with other bodies. Walking Merlin on that ideally warm morning, I finally grasped what he meant when he said, 'There's Us, and then there's the rest of the world' and I knew it wasn't just a thrilling game we were playing, it was true – I was his slave.

8 Slave Rings And Rules

I am kneeling in front of my Master sucking his cock with my ass thrust up in the air looking particularly inviting in a tight black vinyl mini dress that laces in back. My head is moving up and down in his lap where he sits on a comfortable black leather couch. My eyes are closed, but my pussy is very much aware of the people around us, especially of the man sitting directly behind me. I can feel the touch of his lust on my hips as I move them subtly back and forth in rhythm with my lips. This little scene is unfolding in the back room of Club Kink. I love sucking my Master's dick. I could never have imagined a penis would ever taste and feel so good to me, and it just keeps getting better; how much I love his erection just keeps growing. I'm a much better cock-sucker now than I was when I first met Stinger, yet it's a mistake to think you're not always learning.

'Very good, Missa, that's enough for now,' my Master said, smiling down at me as he helped me off my knees and back onto the couch beside him. He admired the cleavage created by my dress, which he bought me and which zips conveniently open all the way down in front.

The man on the couch across from ours got up and approached us. 'Excuse me, but could I presume to offer you a foot massage?' he asked me respectfully.

'No thank you,' I replied, smiling.

As the man walked away without insisting, Stinger commented, 'He obviously doesn't understand the first thing about Master and slave etiquette.

'What do you mean?'

'He should have asked me for permission to give you a foot rub, not addressed you directly. When a slave is with her Master, you never talk to her without his permission, much less offer to do anything to her.'

I didn't know how it was possible, but every moment I spent with Stinger just got me more and more turned on, and as always the possibility that he would give another man permission to do things to me was at once exciting and terrifying. We got up and wandered restlessly down out of the back room. Club Kink was as small as most of its patrons were large. We had driven all the way up to Pompano Beach, where apparently obesity was a major fetish. The club was decorated with women reminiscent of thirty-thousand-year-old figurines, except their rolls of fat were draped in long flowing black lace-trimmed garments evocative of tablecloths salvaged from Gothic castle's banquet halls. And at least two or three of these macabre mother goddesses were escorted by a slender man who was obviously in thrall to her generous curves. I tried to imagine what it was they saw in a woman who needed their assistance just to stand up, and concluded her physical helplessness formed part of a perverse equation of attraction in which how much there was of her was directly proportionate to how little chance there was of her ever betraying or leaving him. Perhaps he liked watching his dick sink deep into folds of flesh rippling and surging like warm waves around him, drowning him in a primordial mass of matter absorbing his energizing shaft. Whatever the attraction, these creatures seemed proud of their bulk rather than embarrassed by it, a defiant negative of the conventional picture.

It was obvious to my Master and me the moment we entered the club that we had come to the wrong place to meet people from our own sensual system. Club Kink was an alien world populated mainly by extremely fat and/or extremely ugly people, with only a handful of exceptions. And tossed into this aesthetically wicked brew were a few decrepit middle-aged men in T-shirts who looked as though they had wandered in from the strip bar next door. We agreed we were never coming back, and then proceeded to try and enjoy ourselves. At one point, my Master pointed out a cable hanging down out of the shadows. We had been wondering how the full-figured women of Club Kink could possibly be suspended; they weighed so much it would take a giant man to pull them up. We got our answer in the form of a winch hanging from the ceiling, the kind Stinger informed me is used to lift cars and engine blocks and other extremely heavy things.

I felt more beautiful than ever walking beside my Master in my black vinyl mini dress, six-inch heels and faux violet fur. We circled the bar, curiously exploring the disappointingly limited space, while on the "stage" an older Dom, his long silver hair tied back in a ponytail, professionally disciplined a slave whose plump posterior quivered beneath each lash.

'Hello.' A slender man, wearing a long-sleeved black "pirate's" shirt over tight black leather pants and boots that were considerably more attractive than he was, intercepted my Master and me during one of our idle orbits of the bar in search of any action that might miraculously materialize. 'Would you like to have a taste of my Violent Wand?' the stranger asked me, holding up a luminous violet shaft almost the same color as my fur.

I was immediately intrigued, violet being my favorite color as well as my safe word, and my Master and I smiled at each other happily because something interesting appeared to be happening. The man introduced himself (I will call him John) and revealed his suitcase of goodies – excitingly wicked-looking phallic objects all powered by some strange electricity.

'What does it do?' I queried, studying the violet wand in fascination.

'Here, let me show you.' He brought the wand down near my naked thigh and looked at my Master. 'May I?'

'Would you like to try it, Missa?' Stinger asked me.

'Yes, Master.'

His pleasant smile deepening, John gently applied the wand to my inner thigh, stroking it up and down slowly. 'How's that?' he murmured, caution and eagerness shiningly balanced in his eyes.

A deep, pleasant warmth penetrated my flesh, and almost at once I was craving the sensation higher up in my cleft. 'It's very nice, I like it...' Leaning against my Master, I spread my legs a little wider, and without words, John and I clearly communicated with each other as he gently began inserting the glowing violet shaft into my pussy. It was exquisite feeling the warm, subliminally vibrating tip of the slender electric dildo parting my labial lips as it began penetrating me. It slid in deeper, but I wanted more, and John gave it to me slowly, staring up at my face the whole time to study my reaction. I could tell he was torn between fear of going too far and how thoroughly he was enjoying giving me what I wanted. By now we had a captive audience in the form of several couples sitting at the bar, and I think I enjoyed their focused attention, which contained the mysterious heat of their desires, as much as I did the energy pulsing between my thighs. Being fucked by a violet wand would have been nice any time, but it felt even better in public with my Master bracing me protectively and possessively against him as another man thrust the charged rod in and out of my pussy with his permission. I was disappointed when the wand finally slipped out of me, but then I was happy to see it was only because John wanted to try another one of his toys on my willing body. The attachment he pulled out was red-hot and shaped like a flame with a dangerous-looking tip he said would seriously delight my nipples.

My Master whispered in my ear, 'Are you okay, Missa?'

'Oh yes,' I breathed, and he reached forward and unzipped my dress in front to expose my breasts. I glanced down at them, and was proud of how beautifully firm and round they were, an ideal blend of softness and firmness as my nipples tightened and lengthened, eager to be the center of attention. I held my breath as the devilish red flame hovered over one of my aureoles, and then gasped as red lightning forked out of the burning tip into my nipple.

I moaned, and John immediately subjected my other nipple to the same hot, sharp lick of electricity that felt shockingly good, like being bitten and licked in the same instant. The deep, nipping warmth penetrated my skin, sending hot surges of excitement down into my belly and from there into my smoldering sex. I couldn't get enough of the crackling red lightning flashing into the swelling hills of my breasts, crowned with rock-hard nipples that acted like receptive rods inviting a storm of agonizingly arousing sensation into my flesh. I arched my back and thrust my bosom out in shameless pleasure, languorously submitting to the burning, snake-like licks of the wicked wand as it traveled slowly down my body to my navel, where the delicious heat pooled and concentrated almost intolerably.

'Oh yes,' I whispered, urging John to thrust the tip of the wand's red head deeper into my belly's vulnerable heart, so I could masochistically relish the painful pleasure as it stabbed me with sharp, unrelenting surges of power. Ice was melting in drinks sitting on the bar as everyone sat transfixed by the show, and one woman exclaimed 'Wow, you're my idol!' as John finally, reluctantly, pulled the wand away.

My Master proudly began zipping my dress up again.

'Wait,' John declared quietly, and changed the head attached to his wand yet again. 'Kiss her,' he urged, resting the new rod against my thigh.

Stinger bent his head towards my breasts, and instantly exquisite electricity snaked between his lips and my nipple. We moaned with mingled excitement as he suckled me for a moment before raising his mouth to mine, and now everyone could see the subliminal sparks that always flashed between us when we kissed.

John and his magic wands were definitely the highlight of Club Kink, and for the rest of the evening he prowled around us, at one point exchanging his suitcase of kinky toys for a large camera and asking my Master for permission to photograph me. At that moment I happened to be standing on top of a chair, precariously perched there on my six-inch heels by my Master, who had also unzipped my dress all the way so that I was effectively naked. I was on display to the entire club as I danced for his pleasure, bracing myself on an exposed beam over my head. All I was wearing beneath my dress was the skimpiest black vinyl thong imaginable, and I relished the hunger in John's eyes as he gazed up at my softly curving body. I almost felt sorry for him when my Master politely but firmly denied him the satisfaction of photographing me, apparently feeling John had enjoyed himself with me enough for one night. His masterful possessiveness thrilled me, inspiring my body's sexily undulating response to the pounding music as he stood smiling up at me, ready to catch me should I fall. I couldn't believe I was standing nearly naked on top of a chair in front of an entire club. I had never done anything so shamelessly extroverted in my life and I enjoyed myself immensely, perfectly safe to bask in my own desirability because my Master was there to protect me even as he enjoyed showing off what was his.

The next morning there was blood on my white sheets, which explained the vague discomfort I had been aware of in my belly-button as I slept. Apparently, I had overindulged in the red wand because I discovered burn marks trailing down my skin from between my breasts down to my navel, which the night before had felt bottomless with desire for the hot energy stabbing it. I was more surprised than anything because my skin had looked completely unmarked afterwards. My Master photographed the evidence of the wand's hot kisses after gently treating them for me, and I considered the temporary discomfort more than worth the pleasure I had experienced, an attitude that prepared me for my next big step as a sex slave.

At Haulover beach, I had noticed and admired the way piercings glinted in the sunlight. Silver rings adorning the over-sized aureoles of silicon-stuffed bosoms did nothing for me, however, the way they glinted in the delicate nipples of real breasts I found extremely erotic. I often wore jewelry to Haulover because it intensified the sensual pleasure of being naked. The cool touch of silver around my ankles and hips and caressing the sides of my neck enhanced my awareness of my soft warm flesh. It also imbued my mortal skin with the metal's magically supple timelessness, forged and shaped in heat like the feelings of my heart. When I wore jewelry to the nude beach I felt profoundly elegant, as though I was proclaiming my belief in ensouled flesh and love's eternal desire as opposed to merely glorifying the doomed beast of my carnality. It is my driving passion to understand the why of anything I find enjoyable, and this is how I explain the simple fact that I enjoyed adorning my naked body in public and feeling the jewelry's cool caress against my warm skin.

There was one young slender woman in particular whose nipple rings shining in the sunlight made me suspect there was another dimension of sensations my own stiff lovely peaks were meant to penetrate; a whole other higher realm of erotic stimulation my breasts had been made to experience.

My Master listened to me express my sentiments on the matter, and after the third or fourth time I brought it up he said casually, 'Maybe you should get your nipples pierced, Missa.' He had waited just long enough to make the suggestion, until I had stoked my own interest enough not to flinch at the thought.

'But do you know how much that would hurt,' I protested. There were many things I never would have considered doing before I met Stinger, things I never thought I wanted to do and then discovered I did, and having any part of my body pierced was one of them. Yet here I was, of my own free will, musing out loud, 'Maybe I should get my nipples pierced.' Nancy had had both her nipples and her clit pierced, and she said the latter especially had been more than worth the instant of pain for all the pleasure it had given her since then. The consensus seemed to be that pierced nipples were even more sensitive and hence heightened sexual excitement. Whether this was myth or fact, I was eager to find out because I had never been easy to arouse and I figured I could use all the help I could get. I had known my Master less than two months, so I can be excused for not yet realizing that just being with him was going to loosen me up inside in wonderful ways. Now all I have to do is think about him fucking me, or imagine his dick sliding in and out of another lucky pussy, or picture any of the fantasies we've made come true together and others we still have, and I get so turned on it almost hurts.

My Master said that if I got my nipples pierced these would be my slave rings and that I would wear them always as a constant reminder that I belonged to him, and this was more than incentive enough for me to take the piercing plunge.

The evening of April fool's found my Master and me in the lobby of Tattoos by Lou in South Miami. I was more thrilled by the thought that I would be receiving my slave rings that night than nervous about the initially painful process, which I hadn't really let myself dwell on. After all, what were a few seconds of pain compared to a lifetime of happiness as Stinger's slave. I wanted these rings with which we would be visibly betrothed to each other as Master and slave more than anything, so it was with an almost supernatural calm that I found myself in the piercing chair.

The man doing me had a very reassuring, professionally casual demeanor. My Master sat on a stool beside me, and held one of my hands firmly in his, as Drew exposed my breasts and began sanitizing my aureoles with a cotton swab. In his quiet, calming tone, he declared my nipples had positively been made to be pierced. They were so long and thick, he said, they wouldn't give him any trouble at all. I was proud and pleased to hear this, and I sensed my Master was more nervous than I was. He had been unusually sarcastic in the waiting room as we flipped through a magazine together, and when I commented on this he admitted it was his defense mechanism against anxiety. I don't remember if Drew told me to take a deep breath and hold it; I really don't care to dwell on those moments. I closed my eyes when I saw him position the tip of a long needle against one side of my right nipple, which suddenly seemed to suck the whole world into it in the form of a hot, penetrating, indescribable pain. I survived by holding on to my Master's hand for all I was worth, and then it was over and there was only the throbbing memory of a sensation that overflowed the borders of my memory it was so excruciatingly intense. I cursed the mysterious duality of the universe at that moment and the fact that I had two nipples, because now that I knew how much it really hurt, I had no desire to repeat the experience. But of course there was no question of not going through with it and just having one lovely silver ball-ring. So once again I clung blindly to my Master, and even though it didn't seem possible, the second piercing was even more excruciating, perhaps because it was my left nipple and that side of my body has always been weaker and more sensitive since I'm right-handed.

My nipples burned and throbbed afterwards, but as this discomfort was nothing compared to the torture of being stabbed by a needle, I wasn't really aware of it until we were back in the jeep. The feather-soft touch of the loose white tank-top I was wearing was almost too much to bear.

Two Advils, and two scotch on the rocks, later, I was feeling much better. My Master and I were seated at the bar of the now defunct Bushwacker Lounge, formerly located on the border between Miami and Coral Gables. We were talking to Tim, one of the bartenders.

'Missa just got her nipples pierced,' Stinger informed him very much like a proud father. 'Why don't you show him, Missa?'

I glanced around the bar. It was full of men, but they were all looking up at the TV screen watching a game.

'They won't see,' Tim assured me, and I really didn't care whether anyone saw or not as I carefully lifted my white top, exposing my freshly wounded nipples to the dark bar, proud of the brand new silver crescents shining around them like planetary rings in the magical universe I had lived in since I met Stinger.

Tim clearly appreciated the sight, and told the story of that night for months afterwards. He loved describing how a woman exposed her freshly pierced breasts to him in a bar full of men, none of whom noticed what he alone had the privilege of seeing because they were all wasting their time watching a game on TV.

The hardest thing about the next couple of weeks was not being able to sleep on my stomach. I had never realized how important it was for me to be able to toss and turn freely at night. After getting my nipples pierced I could only lie on my back, or very gingerly on my sides, taking great care not to disturb my slave rings. For the first few days my nipples were so sensitive that just touching my rings, and moving them painstakingly back and forth to clean them, caused me a minor agony I was able to deal with only because I knew it was only temporary. I cut holes in one of my old sports bras and went around the house with my breasts supported but my aureoles completely exposed, and at night when I was out with my Master, I lived on painkillers and in the lightest, loosest shirts possible. Needless to say, my breasts were completely off limits to him, or at least my nipples were, a fact he didn't much like but that he put up with patiently. He was wonderfully kind and supportive, which helped me get through those days when I was acutely aware of my every movement and everything and everyone that came near me posed a threat.

During this relatively quiet week or two of recovery, one sunny afternoon my Master e-mailed me my Slave Rules. No electronic message I had ever received before had made me so happy. He had found a document over twenty pages long outlining in minute detail the way a slave should behave towards her Master. This was not merely a list of her physical duties; it described a whole way of being. Each specific rule was numbered, and in his e-mail Stinger instructed me to read them over carefully, make whatever modifications I deemed necessary, and then e-mail the form back to him for his final approval. I eliminated a whole section that referred to a Master possessing more than one slave, and other sections describing slaves who were not on my level (in that they were happy to be mindless doormats) and together my Master and I drafted this concentrated version of my Slave Rules:

1 I love and adore my Master.
2 I love and adore my Master's body.
3 I love my Master's cock and I love making it hard.
4 Master fills me with wonder. The mere thought of Him and just hearing His voice make me happy.
5 I will do whatever Master says.
6 I am Master's most prized possession.
7 I shall wear my Master's collar with pride as a symbol of my complete submission to Him.
8 I trust my Master implicitly and know he wants only the best for me and would never do anything to harm me.
9 I will be absolutely faithful to my Master and never have sex with another man or woman unless he desires it.
10 I must strive to be a truly sensual being and find every aspect of life sensually pleasurable, from the most menial chore to the intense pleasure of sexually serving my Master.
11 I will always tell Master exactly what I am thinking and feeling and keep nothing from him.
12 I will respond to Master's questions promptly and in

detail, never holding back any part of myself.

13 My greatest joy in life is giving Master pleasure. If he is happy, then everything is all right.

14 I must remember to thank my Master for both the pleasure and punishments I receive, for I am blessed by his discipline, which is an expression of his love for me.

15 Master's will is my will.

16 I am always ready to serve and please my Master, and to this end I will keep myself fit and beautiful and happy, as befits Master's one-and-only slave. Everything I do must in some way please my Master.

17 I will always wear the slave rings my Master gave me on both my nipples as an expression of my absolute love and submission to Him.

18 When my Master comes home at night, I will greet him wearing only one of my collars and high-heels, nothing else, unless I wish to add stockings and a belt to my slave's uniform.

19 My greatest pleasure in life is knowing that I have truly pleased my Master, and I will strive to do so whenever possible. My greatest pain in life is knowing that I have displeased my Master, and I cannot be truly happy again until I have been punished for it.

20 I will learn everything my Master desires me to learn and I will never interrupt him while he is speaking. I always have much to learn in order to be the best and most beautiful slave possible.

21 I can use the safe word my Master gave me whenever I truly feel the need to except when I am being punished.

22 I must strive to overcome all my doubts and fears trusting that Master respects my feelings and knows my limits and will never push me too far, too fast. Only through absolute submission to Him can I show my Master how much I love him and be truly happy myself. I could never be truly happy or truly be myself without Him.

9 Smoothing Rough Spots In Velvet

With my nipples as freshly pierced as my heart by love and desire for my beautiful Master, I accompanied him to Lipstick, our first stop on an abbreviated tour of Miami's strip bars. It was my first time in one, and while Stinger delighted in taking yet another of my activity virginities, I was excited by how many I had to give him. We sat at the oval bar (where my Master told me he had written an important paper one night on a napkin until the sun rose and the club closed) facing the short runway stage watching a stream of girls "dance" and strip before us. Tanning booths and black lights washed their skin as free of flaws as a baby's while cursing them with demonic bone-white teeth and fingernails. At least ninety percent of them had bleached their hair blonde and stuffed their breasts with silicone. They danced for two songs each, gradually stripping off what little strategically designed clothing they were wearing while strutting back and forth from pole to pole, and then perfunctorily slipped everything back on and circled the bar for tips. My Master handed me a dollar bill every time a girl came by, and smilingly watched as I slipped it into her thong. My knuckles grazing a variety of hips left me jealously amazed by how soft their skin was, until I touched myself in the same way later and experienced the same silky and inviting sensation. I still didn't want to admit to my growing desire to caress other women's bodies. It seemed to me that would be admitting my own figure was somehow lacking, which was silly and unattractively catty of me. But I couldn't help being overcome by a powerful primeval jealousy my first time at a strip club, even as I grudgingly admired the girls' skill with extreme high-heels and metal poles. I was unable to take my eyes off them except to glance at my Master's face, anxiously witnessing his reaction to the seemingly endless flow of fuckable flesh. There was no denying most of the strippers had desirable bodies, which when completely naked made it easy to ignore their often unappealing faces.

The knowledge that my handsome Master could, if he wanted to, have many of these women and hundreds more like them, drove home to me like never before the importance of personality and soul, because it was me he was with and it was me he loved. With my thighs clamped together on the barstool, I felt magical as a mermaid in a sea of lesser fish as one pussy after another gaped lewdly open before us. The sight would have left me cold but for the power my Master has to melt my resistance, composed of scale-sharp fears, and open my legs and my mind to elements I never would have dreamed of inhabiting. Part of me wanted to be jealous but somehow found that it couldn't. On the contrary, I felt strangely empowered sitting with Stinger at the bar of a strip club. The place made me think of a temple now crudely secular, but still faintly evocative of a more sacred age when priestesses embodied the Goddess as they worshipped her sensual mysteries. The phallic metal poles dancers cling to are all that's left of mystical columns, yet at least they enable me to please my Master with a host of figures and pussies, my soul the metaphysical female principle itself and my body one special manifestation of a universal force.

On another night we visited to a real dive aptly named Bare Necessities. The place was dark and bleak and the strippers were barely attractive enough to satisfy even the basest need. We left without having a drink.

On the way home from pool on another occasion, we stopped at a place along the highway whose name I can't remember. Unlike Lipstick's endless supply of tanned blonde bimbos, this club boasted only five girls who each danced alone for a long time on an elevated platform inside the box-shaped bar. It's a good thing I had the demonic pet of my jealousy on a conceptually short leash (I say pet because we all grow perversely fond of the behavioural patterns we're brought up with even if they constantly sink their teeth into us and cause us nothing but pain, until we find the courage to shoot them in the head once and for all) because a blonde-haired angel took the stage who was my complete physical opposite, making it impossible to compete with her. Feeling perfectly happy and secure in the crook of my Master's arm and affection – we always sat close together, kissing and talking – I let myself enjoy this girl's slender, almost innocent-looking loveliness the way I imagined a man would. I experienced a deep aesthetic pleasure caressing her naked body with my eyes that was an end in itself for me even as I enjoyed the stimulation of sensing Stinger's natural male urge to stick his dick in her. I could hardly blame him; If I had had a cock, I would have wanted to fuck her myself. Because she and I were so different, it was like matter and anti-matter canceling each other out and suddenly plunging me into a purely sensual dimension blessedly free of jealousy.

Of course, I was expressing all these thoughts and feelings to my Master, whose understanding and lucidity never fail to help me make sense of things. Now he said, as the golden-haired nymph gyrated lackadaisically towards us, 'I want you to do exactly what I'm about to do, Missa, so watch carefully.' He stood up, sat on the bar facing away from the stage, then placing a dollar bill between his teeth, he leaned back, arching his spine to place it directly between the dancer's receptively cupped breasts. She giggled literally in the face of his acrobatics, and then waited patiently, smiling beatifically as I accepted a dollar from him and repeated the performance a bit more gracefully. It was a simple feat and yet it left me reeling. I had never experienced a sensation so silky-soft and delicious as a pair of soft breasts engulfing my features for a blissful instant as the stripper caught the dirty old paper between her clean young mounds. I could understand now how the feel of a woman's skin would be enough to drive a man mad if all he could ever have of it was teasing glimpses like that. As my Master commented, 'Strip clubs are just torture if you don't have a girl friend.'

'If you have a girl friend, you shouldn't need to come to a strip club,' I retorted mildly.

'That's true,' he agreed, 'but there's lots of things we enjoy doing we don't need to do.'

'Hmm.'

Later on, as all the dancers took the stage just before closing, the lovely one broke the spell cast by her Nordic good looks by talking. Her coy little act was to shudder slightly and hug herself as she complained about how cold it was in the club while she and her fellow co-workers made a few last rounds for cash. Her flat mid-western accent and obvious acting were completely disenchanting.

'Suddenly I can really appreciate the invention of the gag,' I remarked.

My Master laughed and kissed me and told me how much he loved me, three of my favorite things in the world. We stopped going to strip clubs for a while after that, and then visited a couple more before returning to Lipstick. It ended up being our last time there, and just as we were about to leave, my Master casually told me to take my dress off and walk out of the club naked. Needless to say, I resisted, shocked and appalled by the command as well as scared of being arrested for indecent exposure. Granted, the place was full of naked women, but they all had a license to reveal their private parts in public and I didn't. Good slave that I am I wasn't wearing a bra or panties beneath my short violet dress, which inevitably came off, because parading myself to a club-full of strangers for a few moments was easier for me than enduring even a second of my Master's displeasure. So I quickly pulled my dress up over my head, handed it to him, and began weaving between bar stools and a mirrored wall, making my way to the door wearing only black high-heels and my precious new nipple rings. I don't know how many people saw me since I avoided glancing at anyone and my Master later admitted he was too busy looking at me to notice, but a woman followed me out into the lobby where I quickly slipped my dress back on. She stared at me with a wide-eyed amazement I found quite gratifying as I heard another woman exclaim, 'All right!'

I've come to the conclusion that it's very hard for a woman to be able to truly appreciate her own unique beauty if all the myriad conflicting ideas of desirability accumulated through the ages are not filtered and focused through a man's loving gaze. As anyone who watches the History Channel knows, what is considered a sexy body in the present day is not the same as in countless other hot and bothered moments in time, cooled now into frozen pictures of vanished emotional and psychological temperaments. Changes in diet and nutrition, the prolongation of physical existence and a variety of other factors are constantly affecting what individual cultures perceive as an aesthetically pleasing figure. And then there is every individual's ever-changing history in the pages of all the mirrors we catch glimpses of ourselves in during our lifetime, a heavy tome indeed. Good proportions are to beauty and sensuality what the skeleton is to living flesh – it's important but it's not everything. The look in my Master's eyes gives the image I have of myself a vital sensual depth dangerously lacking in this world of disembodied images coming at us from every direction.

The first grave sin I committed as a budding slave was born out of vanity. My Master had set me the task of developing the roll of film we had shot at Haulover and in a couple of other places. I did so, and went to pick the prints up one afternoon before he came over. Flipping through them, my self-esteem suffered a terrible blow when I saw my naked body captured in full sunlight. I knew I didn't really look exactly like that; it was the angle and the lighting, etc. that were so unflattering, yet I was disgusted and horrified by the thought of my Master seeing me like this, so I hid the photos away. When he came over later, I cringed when he asked me if I had had the pictures developed.

'Yes,' I replied, 'but I didn't get a chance to pick them up today.'

He continued placidly perusing the New Times as the equivalent of a nuclear explosion took place in my psyche and laid waste to the paradise I had lived in with Stinger since we met in a horrible flash – I had lied to him! I sat staring at his contentedly smiling face in abject misery unable to believe I had told him a flat-out lie. I had never even dreamed of lying to him before; not even the smallest fib had crossed my lips. I knew I had to tell him, but I dreaded it, so I just sat there compounding my misdeed with every second I let tick by that felt like blood pouring out of the small but vital wound I had made in our passionately trusting relationship.

'Master...'

He gave me his full, unsuspecting attention.

'Master, I lied to you...'

His eyes widened slightly, but he remained silent, waiting for my confession.

'I did pick up the pictures today, I just didn't want... I just didn't want you to see some of them. I look so awful! And yet it's nothing compared to how I feel now... I can't believe I lied to you!' I slipped off my chair and sank to my knees before him. 'Please forgive me, Master!' I buried my face in his lap. 'It'll never happen again, I swear it, never! It feels so terrible to keep anything from you. It's the most terrible feeling in the world!' I went on in this vain, until calmly accepting my apology he asked me what I thought he should do about this small yet very serious transgression. 'You should punish me, Master,' I replied quietly but fervently. 'I want you to punish me. You have to, so I never forget how much it hurt me to lie to you.' I meant every word, so much so that the next day I sent him this e-mail at work:

> *I need you to punish me with severe physical pain for my transgression last night, Master. I feel you should mark me so I can carry around for a few days a reminder of how deeply it wounded my soul to lie to you, whether the lie was insignificant or not.*

My Master set the date and time of my punishment for the following Monday evening. I remember I had just seen the cover of my new book, which was due out in April, and I was elated. I was not looking forward to being punished, but I was not dreading it, either. In my mind whatever physical pain my Master chose to inflict upon me could not hurt anywhere near as much as the existential emptiness I had experienced after lying to him. Merlin and I were driving over to his apartment tonight, and still high from my publisher's e-mail, I slipped on a short, tight, sleeveless yellow dress that in my eyes resembled an abbreviated ancient Egyptian gown, and white high-heeled sandals with straps linked by small golden hoops evocative of the Mycenaean style in Greece. Around my neck I wound a string of bud-shaped golden metal beads long enough to cross three times over my chest, and added a touch of color that also completed the queenly-collar look with two delicate necklaces made of green and violet beads. The weather has always been my hairstylist, and the cool dry temperature outside had provided me with an appropriate Egyptian look by making my black hair and bangs sleek and straight.

Driving to my Master's place always felt like a joyous adventure intensified by Merlin's dancing excitement when he realized he was coming with me. My hands were full of bags containing clothes, dog supplies and human treats when I knocked on my Master's door. He greeted me warmly, as he always does, but there was a seriously sober look in his eyes that pierced the bubble of my writer's euphoria and reminded me that I was actually going to be punished tonight; I wasn't just going to sit comfortably down to describe the experience, not yet. I set my bags down at once as my Master indicated I should do, and gladly filled my arms with him instead, the only thing I really needed, as he held me close.

'You look beautiful, Missa,' he said, 'and I'm very proud of you, but you're still being punished tonight.'

'Yes, Master, of course, I want to be,' I replied truthfully.

'Take off your clothes,' he commanded, moving purposefully away from me, and I noticed that a corner of his living room had been sinisterly prepared for my chastisement. I was not just being spanked tonight;

his home gym boasted a cushioning towel on the seat, and coils of rope told me I was to be bound and suspended in an appropriately exposed and vulnerable position. Yet what distressed me was being told to undress. It was like being forced to shed my personality, which was particularly difficult to do in a moment when I was feeling so pleased with myself. I slipped off my dress reluctantly and then just stood there.

'Take everything off, Missa.'

'Even my jewelry?'

He paused in the midst of some arcane preparation to stare at me. 'Did you hear me?'

I quickly divested myself of beads and watch and earrings and sandals, until I was left wearing only my skin and the black hair falling softly over my shoulders. I was no longer the smugly happy MIP who had written a book soon to be published, I was Missa, who didn't really care about anything except the man I had just stripped for, the man it had hurt me so much inside to tell even the smallest lie to, the man I wanted to belong to absolutely, with no clothes or thoughts getting in the way of the mysteriously pure and profound bond between us.

My Master seated me on the towel he had kindly provided for my exposed pussy, and then tied me up in such a way that I was stretched taut, with my back and buttocks presented for punishment. And last but not least, he blindfolded and gagged me. This was punishment, which meant I was not allowed to use my safe word. I had to trust my Master to know my limits and respect them. I can't picture the exact position he put me in; my usually clear and vivid memory fails me here. I recall only vivid fragments of my first, and I am glad to say as yet only major, punishment, for I have never again lied to my Master. I know it hurt, but I had braced myself for that, and I could handle it, at first. I was not prepared for the number and variety of implements he used on me, and the differing, although equally searing, quality of the agony they radiated through my flesh. I don't actually remember what they all were; I have had to ask my Master to list the items for me, which included one of his leather sandals, a small riding crop, a wooden hairbrush, a split bamboo cane and his heavy black leather belt. I distinctly recall all these instruments of torture now, yet before he told me all I really remembered was a featureless cloud of pain in which each item provided uniquely cruel flashes of agony. This was serious punishment, and much as it hurt, part of me relished it. I had always wondered what it would be like, and now I knew it was more terrible than I could ever have imagined, unendurable really. I writhed and moaned and broke out in a sweat desperately seeking the mythical silver lining of ecstasy in the increasingly hot and humid cloud of misery enveloping all my nerve-endings... and I think I must have glimpsed it somewhere along the way somewhere between the hairbrush and the split bamboo cane because suddenly, after an exquisitely agonizing lick from my Master's belt that raised a serious welt on my hip, it was all over suddenly, much sooner than I had expected it to be. My Master says my chastisement lasted quite a long time and the reason it seemed to pass so quickly for me is because I went into some kind of profoundly submissive trance. I still can't quite believe this as I don't remember drifting into an altered state, and yet it's true my memory of the event is strangely brief, punctuated by excruciating highlights when I seemed to 'wake' up to the actual agony from a deeper, darker realm temporarily inhabited by my overwhelmed senses. The split bamboo cane striking the naked soles of my feet was one such searing second, and finally there was the cruel lick of my Master's heavy belt, which fully roused me from my mysterious stupor to the sweet knowledge that it was all over as I felt him freeing my wrists.

He removed the gag and the blindfold and helped me gently up into his arms, where he held my slick, flushed body for a wonderfully long time. Later he said to me, 'I love so many things about you, Missa, for example the way you trembled for about ten minutes after I punished you' but at the time he led me silently into his bedroom and made me assume the sleen position on the floor in the dark.

'I'm going to fuck your ass now, Missa,' he warned me, and I moaned, dread and gratitude soldered into one glorious collar of obedience around my mind as my body felt more his than ever. My Master had by no means been inordinately cruel with his punishment – he had only subjected to me as much as he knew I could take and that my transgression deserved – yet all the uncertain or rebellious thoughts and feelings I often experienced when utterly submitting to him had been completely beaten out of me, so that all I knew was the strangely bottomless happiness and pleasure of really and truly belonging to him and wanting to give him whatever he desired. When the engorged head of his erection thrust into the dark little heart of my anal whorl, and began remorselessly sliding into the tight hot space between my burning cheeks, I felt nothing but an overwhelming pleasure as he breached my sphincter and sank all the way inside me. The weight of his body against my buttocks was exquisite as he thrust his cock into my bowels and took me fast and hard and deep, subliminally stimulating my clit as he rammed his rending hard-on into me mercilessly. I suspect it's true I was in an altered state, because for the first time in my life I came without having to touch myself. I was miraculously carried away by the pulsing power of my Master's orgasm making me feel so full of him I could hardly stand how much I loved the hot selfish rush of his spunk baptizing the darkest recesses of my being.

Going to Miami Velvet was like going to a badly run temple. I would have preferred a sacred sensual atmosphere as opposed to the bawdy, used car salesman hedonism blasted by the DJ, and the occasional contests involving wildly simulated acts of intimacy that made me appreciate why the Catholic church is one of the best things that ever happened to sex. Mystery and the danger of the forbidden, an emotional struggle with the dark yet latently divine seed of eroticism, passions deepened by a belief in ensouled flesh... these are all aphrodisiacs in my psyche even though I'm not a practicing Christian anymore, which explains why the atmosphere at Velvet completely turned me off. But annoyingly profane as it was, it was also one of the few places my Master and I could go to worship. I was still struggling with the profound implications of Swinging, but the fact is I was drawn to it like a moth to a flame. Stinger and I had our sensual wings singed more than once at sex clubs, mainly because I'm not bi-sexual and playing with a woman doesn't turn me on anywhere near as much as watching my Master play with her, and most of the people we encountered weren't willing to go all the way. Or I should say most of the women weren't willing to indulge in a full swap, and their partners naturally respected their wishes, undoubtedly considering themselves lucky to be there in the first place.

Our next few trips to Velvet are a sensual collage in my mind, and it's much more pleasurable to remember them this way than it is trying to fit the experiences back into the framework of the actual visits in which they occurred, nights inevitably punctuated by a few unappealing, and several frustrating, moments. This way I will always recall with pleasure a handful of vivid encounters cresting in sensual waves outside the otherwise featureless flow of time, living paintings untainted by my inevitable physical exhaustion at the end of each night. My Master's intense virility was a double-edged sword in that the marathon of serving him wore me out completely as I sucked his cock over and over again, and he fucked my cunt countless times before coming for the third or fourth explosive time deep in my ass.

I believe it was on our third Saturday at Velvet that we ran into Mina and her husband again, Mina, owner of the first pussy other than my own I first saw my Master wrap around his dick, protected by shiny latex from actually making contact with her innermost skin. This had been before we declared our love for each other, and I was glad of the opportunity to see how I felt about it this time watching him. Every time I thought about the memory it excited me, but I had learned the hard way that fantasies are not as complex as reality, and I suspected I had a long way to go before I could create a relaxed, comfortable bridge between them. I was still tensely wearing the knowledge that Stinger loved me and only me like a life jacket, afraid his slightest glance or caress (not to mention thrust) in another direction would plunge me into my own tumultuous emotions, where the current bred into me by a romantic Catholic upbringing went completely against Swinging. I was afraid I would once again have to struggle to keep my heart from sinking into a despair so deep I could hardly breathe as I watched my beloved Stinger penetrating another woman. I had suffered this terrible numbing of my soul the first time I watched him fucking Mina, and I dreaded it even as I hoped I had made some vital progress since then.

I remember the four of us sitting on a couch upstairs, my Master sandwiched between Mina and me, her handsome black husband perched on the cushion beside me. He told me I was beautiful, really beautiful, and tentatively caressed my leg. I was wearing black stockings, a black lace garter belt, six-inch black heels, my nipple rings and matching silver hoop earrings. Mina was naked as a beached fish and soft and pale everywhere. My Master had one arm spread across the top of the couch, and even as his right hand stroked my thighs, soothing me by reaffirming our bond, I watched the fingers of his left hand idly caress Mina's shoulder as we all talked. The sight both bothered and excited me in the double-edged way I was becoming familiar with even while trying to learn how to handle it. I think she was touching me too, and in order to please my Master, I caressed her as well, briefly. Her skin was pleasantly tender and nicely unblemished. She was a bit too plump for my taste, but on the other hand I was glad she wasn't more attractive, which made it easier for me to believe my Master when he assured me he had no desire to fuck her, or any other girl, in particular, because it was all about sharing sensual experiences with me.

I was anxious to get things going to test myself, so I was glad when we all got up and walked to the back room, where the management had made a slight effort to please their more kinky patrons by furnishing the small space with a black iron cross, and a contraption resembling something between a modern weight bench and Medieval stocks my Master indicated he wanted me to position myself across. My knees were comfortably supported as I spread myself face-down across the higher central section of the black leather cushions, and my Master raised the top part of the wooden frame so I could comfortably rest my wrists and necks in the slots before he brought it back down carefully and locked me in place. Mina and her husband stood by, clearly relishing the show as my Master then stepped behind me, shed his robe and thrust his erection into my pussy, which was perfectly offered up to him in this position at the same convenient height as his pumping hips. He fucked me like this for a few minutes while I hung my head and moaned, the feel of his hard-on stabbing me intensified by the enjoyment two other people were taking in our pleasure. I think the scenario must have excited me because I was hot and wet, and submissively open to the moment when my Master abruptly pulled out of me, and casually offered another man use of my helplessly bound body. I don't remember his exact words; the gist of it is that he offered him a turn with me, and Mina's husband didn't hesitate to snatch up the proffered condom and opportunity.

I watched my Master walk around my prone figure to the mattress in front of me as I felt another man take his place behind me. Mina had already positioned herself across the black sheets, lying on her belly eagerly waiting to feel Stinger inside her again doggie style. Part of me could scarcely believe what was happening even as I heard myself say to her, 'You want his big dick inside you again, don't you?'

'Mm, yes,' she admitted as my Master knelt behind her, quickly slipping on a condom.

I felt her husband gently caressing me. 'Are you all right?' he asked me.

'Yes,' I assured him, hiding my impatience as I watched my Master grab another woman's hips and lift them up around his rigid dick as another man penetrated me, but much more tentatively. I was glad when for a few moments he fucked me hard and fast and his thrusts felt good enough to excite me with the sight of my Master ramming himself into another pussy with a relentless, concentrated energy a lot of men aren't capable of, including Mina's husband, who almost at once softened to impotent dimensions inside me. Feeling sorry for her more than for myself I gasped, 'You love having his big, hard dick inside you, don't you!' and she moaned again in helpless agreement as Stinger banged her. Apparently fucking me was exciting the gentle black man so much he paradoxically couldn't stay hard. I was disappointed when he slipped out of me because now I was left alone with nothing to feel except uncomfortable in my imprisoned position, and with nothing to do except watch another woman getting what I wanted. It was a strain to hold my head up so I could keep observing the spectacle of my beautiful Master violently fucking someone else as I waited for him to look over at me watching him, yet he seemed utterly intent on packing his erection into Mina's lucky pussy and didn't seem to be concerned about making eye contact with me at all, as if I wasn't even there. I hung my head in despair as my helpless position became intolerable in the face of his indifference to the fact that I wasn't feeling anything now that the man he had handed me over to had literally left my pussy out in the cold. I don't remember what I said, I just know I raised my head again and begged him to stop.

He pulled out of Mina at once, abandoning her as he immediately stood up and devoted himself to me with a tender concern that made me regret my panic attack, but not enough that I wasn't happy he was all mine again as he released me from the stocks and helped me up off the bench. Mina and her husband were all smiling patience in the face of my tumultuous feelings, because they were aware of the fact that I was a relative newcomer to Swinging, and later we all ended up together again in another room lying in intimate languor on a large mattress gazing at up our reflections in the ceiling. The sensual tableau appealed to me, and I found the black man's hard, slender body aesthetically pleasing both to my eyes and my sense of touch even though I didn't really desire to feel him inside me. What I really wanted was to get Mina to suck my Master's cock, and as we two girls kissed and held on to each other while being fucked fervently from behind by our partners, I gradually helped Stinger position his magnificent erection directly over both our faces. I wordlessly urged her to open her mouth and accept him, but at the last moment she turned away and devoted herself to her husband, who seemed reluctant to stop caressing my body even as he pumped into hers.

Later, when I explained to my Master that I had panicked in the back room because he wasn't meeting my eyes, he told me he had been looking at me almost the whole time, that in fact both he and Mina had been looking at me as they fucked. He had a vivid movie in his mind of looking over at me, and being aware of the fact that it was hard for me to keep my head up so I could see him, but he was letting me try. This had not been my perception of the event, but it was true I hadn't been wearing my glasses, which I've come to realize I don't just need for driving anymore so maybe I should seriously consider contacts. My Master said there was no reason for me to be upset, that I had done very well, and I was happy he was pleased even though I knew I could do better in the future and desperately wanted another chance to prove it to him.

The Velvet collage begins in a corner of the large back room upstairs with me sucking my Master before turning obediently around on the dark red sheet so he could fuck my pussy from behind. There were no mirrors except on the ceiling so I couldn't see him, only feel how much it pleased him to be there, flanked by other naked undulating bodies as he thrust his almost painfully hard dick deep into my submissively crouched form. He was energized by the subliminal touch of people's eyes on us as he looked around him boldly, and I didn't need to witness it now to know there was a soft smile on his lips above his rock-hard penis. Most of the time I hung my head, hiding shyly behind my long hair like a Prima Donna on stage ignoring her audience, because in my opinion no man could hold a candle to Stinger and I was the luckiest girl in the club to be on the receiving end of his beautiful cock. But occasionally there was a couple it pleased me to look at, and as I watched a girl being fucked from behind by her handsome partner like a mirror reflection of us, my detached aesthetic appreciation warmed up into a melting excitement as the sight mysteriously doubled the pleasure I took in my Master's penetrations. She and I had not started out facing each other, but the passionately pumping hips of our partners swiftly positioned us directly across from each other on the public mattress. I was now face-to-face with an attractive woman whose figure was fuller and heavier than mine, and whose straight brown hair brushed against my more wildly curling black mane as we kissed, obeying the wordless desire being driven into us. I looked up, and saw her lover flash a secretly triumphant smile I had no problem imagining being returned by my Master, and it aroused me to know I was pleasing them both as I kissed her again.

A woman's mouth felt intriguingly different from a man's, softer and smaller, and yet while her tongue was more delicate it seemed even more demandingly playful. And included in the novel experience for me was the strangely sweet stimulation of moaning breathlessly together in response to the hard-ons stabbing us. It wasn't easy holding my body and head up as my Master banged me with increasing fervour, and when he suddenly pulled out of me, I collapsed beside her. It was wonderful feeling as though I momentarily had two bodies with which to please him; it doubled how sensual and beautiful I felt. Also exquisite was the contrast between his hard body pressing urgently up against me from behind, and her soft, yielding breasts and skin languidly merging with mine as we continued kissing. I didn't, however, like the sensation of her long nails as she fingered my pussy, so I was glad when a man's hand slipped between my thighs and took over for her. I couldn't tell who was finger-fucking my hot cunt, but I suspected it wasn't my Master and that he was busy experiencing another woman's slick depths as I lay sandwiched between them. Our four bodies had obeyed an inexorable sensual choreography that enabled my tongue to effortlessly dance with three others in turn. All I had to do was turn my head to the right and it was my Master's beloved lips that opened over mine. Then when I turned my head to the left, I could kiss the girl again for a while, before she raised her face over mine and I watched her profile merging with Stinger's before closing my eyes and letting another man's tongue thrust into my mouth as his hard fingers dipped in and out of me even more hungrily, hurting me a little, yet the discomfort was also delicious. Glancing up at the mirrored ceiling in between kisses, I began feeling lost in an ideal dream of intertwined limbs crowned by beautiful faces wearing rapt expressions evocative of an erotic Renaissance painting come to life on the blood-red sheets of Velvet that night. The magical tableau ended when the girl asked me in a conspiratorial whisper if I wanted to help her go down on her lover, and I declined the offer, having no desire to suck a strange cock without protection.

In between playing with each other and with other people, I danced for my Master whenever, and wherever, he indicated, including on an elevated platform complete with a stripper's pole where I enjoyed lifting my high-heeled foot onto the railing and giving passers by a glimpse of my naked pussy, which to my surprised disappointment was enthusiastically admired by more women than men.

Upstairs again on another night at Velvet, we walked into one of the smaller rooms. I was wearing what remained of my Catholic school girl outfit – a very short grey-and-white plaid skirt, a Gothic silver cross hanging from a black string between my naked breasts, white knee-high socks and shiny black vinyl extreme high-heels. The lighting was not at all subtle and I could see myself clearly in a side mirror as I bent over to brace myself on the group mattress, which was full of naked people. I could not help admiring my long legs, and the way my pierced breasts trembled as my Master let his white robe fall to the floor and penetrated me, bringing my face uncomfortably close to another girl's gaping pussy. She was lying on her back with her spread legs hanging off the bed as she blew her partner where he knelt beside her face. I met his eyes, and suffered the thrill of being fucked by my beloved Master while another man watched. He was young and handsome, and as we looked at each other my pleasure deepened beneath his appealingly intense stare. I had no experience whatsoever to speak of with any female sexual organ besides my own, yet even I could tell the meticulously shaved vulva before me was quite pretty with its healthy, rosy hue and delicate labial lips framing the thankfully dry centre leading into her body. I knew it would please my Master if I licked the girl's pussy, so I did, curiously, and was encouraged by an eager nod from her lover to taste her again, this time less tentatively, because really there was nothing not to like about her soft, clean skin. She could not have been very excited because she wasn't at all wet, which was fine with me because I do not have an appetite for women's juices, and I was glad when her partner leaned over her body and met my lips with his as I raised my head from her pussy. I relished kissing him as Stinger rammed me encouragingly from behind, and I began fantasizing about a full swap, so that I was agreeable when my Master pulled out of me, grasped the girl's ankles and raised her spread legs as if to penetrate her. She shied away at once, anxiously protesting to her partner in Spanish, who pulled her safely up into his arms. (I knew Stinger had not actually intended to fuck her since he had not put on a condom, and he later confirmed that he had been playing with her to test her reaction.) I was furious with the girl for daring not to want him, which I found impossible to believe, and I seriously resented being teased as I felt we had been. My Master took it in stride, slipping his robe calmly back on while I snatched mine up off the floor angrily and stalked out of the room as best I could in my crippling shoes. I was intensely disappointed that one of the few attractive couples at the club was not into a full swap, which in my mind was the only way to fully please my Master the way I longed to. I kept forgetting that I didn't need to suffer this sort of pressure since it's true that just being there with me pleased him immensely no matter what happened. Later on, we passed this same couple coming up the stairs as we were on our way down. As she led her lover contentedly by the hand, he and I shared a hot, sarcastically brief kiss behind her back that said it all.

On another night my Master and I encountered a wonderfully vocal young woman in the back room as she was being passionately worshipped by her boyfriend, who couldn't seem to choose between eating her out and penetrating her, so he kept switching back and forth to her wildly responsive delight. 'Si, mi reina, si' he kept saying, calling her his queen. I liked her breasts, which I discovered were as firm as they were full when I reached over and caressed them with one hand, bracing myself with the other as my Master fucked me from behind again. La Reina's cries and moans of pleasure grew even louder when I added my attentions to those of her lover, who did not complain, but who also didn't seem too happy to be sharing her, especially when she turned eagerly into my arms and began kissing and fondling me. Her enthusiasm was more delightful than her groping efforts to finger my pussy, which I gently discouraged, but feeling how much I was pleasing my Master, I continued caressing her without restraint, as I had never before touched another woman, intrigued by the novel experience of searching for her clitoris with my fingertips and sensing when I had found it by her body's response as she arched her back and cried out even more loudly. My own pleasure deepened as though I was touching myself, and I must admit I enjoyed sucking her nipples and fingering her labial lips as her boyfriend ate her. There was nothing not to like about the experience even though I myself was nowhere near to coming. She was making such a racket that a girl who was obviously her friend, but whose partner had a lot less stamina, chided her for her wanton display, but La Reina blithely ignored her as she basked in the attention being showered on her by her boyfriend and me. And I made sure my Master was able to reach around me and briefly feel up her writhing body, during which he pounded into me with such force it was all I could do to hold myself up. When she had finally had enough, La Reina rose with silent dignity. Holding her boyfriend's hand, she bent over to kiss me and stroke my hair, then she led him out of the room as I leaned gratefully back in my Master's arms to rest...

Until he decided it was time to fuck my ass. I didn't mind at all, in fact, my smouldering pussy was glad his relentless erection was thrusting and pulsing and swelling somewhere else inside me. It seems every time my Master fucks my ass I love it more than the last, and that night the pleasure was excruciating as I saw a woman watching us enviously. She clearly wished Stinger's big dick was sliding in and out between her fleshly cheeks, and it turned me on to feel even more like the lucky one than I usually did when he possessed me. Not even the girl being done by three guys at once with porno movie precision a mattress away was anywhere near as lucky as I was. She kept interrupting the action to give her partners instructions, which in my opinion defeated the excitingly dangerous edge of a gang-bang, but then I lost sight of her as my Master finally came violently inside me, burying me in the mattress as his cum flooded my rectum right there in front of everyone.

10 Power In Being Together

My Master made preliminary contact with a couple on Swinger's Date Club he considered promising and instructed me to get in touch with them as well. I will call this couple Alan and Gloria. The former responded to my e-mail right away with their phone number, and when I dialled it one sunny morning, he answered. We only spoke briefly, however, as he was getting ready to meet a ship coming into port (which made me curious as to what he did for a living) but later on that day he called me back, and after a few minutes put his girlfriend on the line. Gloria and I soon found common ground in our distaste for Swing clubs in general. We were both anxious to explore the more intimate venue of getting together with another couple in private, where we would have more control over the environment and the atmosphere. I let my Master know I thought Alan and Gloria a promising pair, and he gave me permission to make a date with them somewhere. Alan was constantly in and out of town, but I finally pinned him down and we agreed to meet one Tuesday night at Mac's Club Deuce in South Beach.

My Master and I arrived early, and I was enjoying sipping my scotch on the rocks and being alone with him. He was telling me about an infamous couple from the roaring twenties who wrote a book entitled Living Well Is The Best Revenge. They believed one of the ten qualities that defines a beautifully successful relationship between a man and a woman is the ability to have sex with other people and feel even more in love with each other as a result. I didn't see it clearly at the time, but in retrospect I realize my Master was on a mission; he wanted to get us over this particular milestone as soon as possible. And I was equally determined to conquer the dragon of jealousy, that still kept painfully burning me even as I sought to fully enter the ultimate kingdom of my fantasies where true love lives in harmony with wicked sensual abandon. The green beast scorched my nerves a little now when Alan and Gloria walked into the bar, but then went up in a puff of surprise when I saw how handsome Alan was. After Tom, he qualified as a brunette Apollo in my grateful eyes, although in truth his looks were as boringly unremarkable as a Ken doll's. Gloria's hair was cut almost as short as her lover's, but her face was cute enough, and her slender, naturally full-breasted figure appealed to me as the sort of body I felt worthy of my Master's attentions.

I don't recall a word of the conversation that ensued as Gloria sat down beside me at the bar and Alan took the stool on her other side, all I remember is the pleasantly charged relief that surrounded us like a cloud hovering over the mythical realm of carefree Swinging. As couples, we seemed to have pretty much the same philosophy and rules concerning the Lifestyle. My Master and I clicked with them on more levels than we had with Tom and Nancy, and they obviously felt the same way about us because we promptly made a date for Friday night. If I had to suffer another cock inside me, I definitely preferred it be attached to a relatively attractive man. It also gratified me that even though Gloria was quite handsome, and her body met the standards I had set for my Master in my fantasies, she could not be described as beautiful like me. Maybe other women don't have catty thoughts like these when Swinging, but I did at the time, not having yet mysteriously absorbed the fact into all my blood cells that no other woman can compare to me in Stinger's eyes no matter what she looks like just as no man compares to him in mine.

That Friday night, my Master parked his jeep at the edge of a park in South Beach and we walked a few blocks to the building where the couple we were planning to fuck was waiting for us. Alan had turned out to be a ship's captain, and when he wasn't away at sea he stayed in Gloria's apartment. We passed through a black wrought iron gate and traversed a narrow walkway to a blue door boasting the right numbers but that was strangely ajar. People in Miami don't usually leave their front doors wide open to intruders, and for a few moments we were at a loss as to what to do when no one responded to our greeting. This had to be the place, but we hesitated to walk in uninvited. Eventually, Stinger decided it was the only course of action open to us, and we stepped into the living room. Because I was with him, it was titillating fun violating a girl's private space, closely studying her possessions like the embodiment of her thoughts and feelings lying vulnerably open to us. We searched for evidence that this was the right apartment as we wandered around the small room, and several photographs of what looked like Gloria with her family confirmed this was indeed her place of residence. We thought we heard voices coming from beyond the hallway that opened onto a bathroom and a bedroom beyond it, yet there still didn't seem to be anyone around, so we sat down on the futon couch to wait. Stinger casually flipped through a newspaper while I sat as close to him as possible, clutching my black leather condom-filled purse trying to control the dark bloom of my annoyance, which was inevitably sprouting weeds of anxiety. I had expected the couple to walk back in through the front door when they returned from their inexplicably urgent errand, so it was a surprise when Gloria suddenly appeared from the direction of the bedroom, although admittedly she was much more astonished to find us reclining comfortably in her living room. We all had a good laugh about it as Alan also appeared a second later, and we discovered where the voices had been coming from when they lead us to a small private patio opening up off the bedroom.

They offered us balloon glasses of red wine, and as the sun set beyond the ivy covered brick wall we sat and talked about politics and the environment, science and literature, discussing everything except sex. It was just like being on a first date, and after a while I was bored to distraction wondering how on earth this polite scenario was going to translate into a hot erotic encounter only a few hours later. At first I enjoyed the intellectual conversation, but after a while I lost interest in what I felt was increasingly inane banter and began resenting how much time my Master and I were being forced to waste with these strangers just because we wanted to use them sexually. I began to see the virtue of Swing clubs, where there is no need to get to know anyone before you play with them, and I was very glad when we finally left the by now dark patio, where the only sensual activity had been slapping my bare thighs to kill mosquitoes primarily attracted to my Cuban blood.

We strolled leisurely down Washington Avenue towards Lincoln road, where we were planning to have dinner. Set free from the endless conversation, I was enjoying my wine buzz, as well as having my Master mostly to myself again as we walked with one arm around each other window shopping, and giving in to the slightest temptation to enter the stores. Gloria had wrapped an old lady-like shawl over her tight tank top and was walking more swiftly ahead of the group, with Alan torn between keeping up with her and talking back at us. I had already begun to sense her tension, and either her lover was ignoring the signs or he was too insensitive to notice them. But Stinger and I were having fun as we took our sweet time shopping. I even tried on a black vinyl mini skirt we saw on a mannequin, and my Master approved of it so much he bought it for me.

'You just missed the beautiful sight of Missa trying on her new black mini skirt,' he informed the couple waiting for us outside.

Gloria quickly turned her back on us again and kept walking, her back straight as a figurehead's leading the way through the exotic sea of life rushing down Washington Avenue on a Friday night, and her captain walked obediently at her side even though he would clearly have preferred to steer the course more slowly with us.

We dined on Lincoln road at Sushi Siam, a special place for me not only because of the excellent Sushi but because my Master and I went there on one of our first dates. Enjoying more wine, this time white, seated outside in the perfectly temperate night, beside my beautiful Stinger, beneath a tree and beside a fountain, with currents of people flowing constantly by, I was feeling no pain, and did not doubt the evening would turn out just as my Master and I desired. Alan kept bringing up BDSM, and using our relationship to try and communicate his desire to Gloria of travelling farther down that path. So far they had only taken baby steps together – she had let herself be tied up on more than one occasion – but that was as far as they had gone, and the truth is she did not look particularly turned on by the conversation whenever it came up. She kept talking about her new job and all its trials and tribulations, and wouldn't stop talking. Even after dinner was over and it was clearly time to either get down to business or say goodnight, she looked like she had hours of talk left inside her, and sure enough, she suggested we all go to a bar where one of her acquaintances was working that night. She proceeded to describe how beautiful this girl was, confirming my impression that she was more than just bi-curious, and Alan finally lost his patience. He echoed Stinger's and my thoughts exactly when he said it was too late to go to a bar because by the time we all got back to her place we'd be too tired to do anything. He was all for heading straight back home, and even though she obviously would have preferred to keep postponing what was to come, she was outnumbered three-to-one.

Back at the apartment, however, she herded us out onto the patio again for yet more wine and conversation. By now I had determined Alan could never be the Master in this relationship even if Gloria deigned to be physically submissive to him on occasion. He was a spineless creature, but he had a handsome face and an agreeable disposition, and I desired something greater than just the feel of his dick in my pussy, which I already knew would not make much of an impression anyway. I longed to fulfill my Master's desire that we smoothly and successfully have sex with another couple, which would empower us and enable us to move on with our relationship unhindered by the pressing need to overcome this obstacle in my confidence and training as his slave. I suffered one blindly jealous moment when Gloria's short skirt hiked up her slender thighs as she shifted in her chair and my Master said, 'Mm' watching her. In that moment I almost hated him for daring to openly desire another woman in my presence, and in the next moment I realized the grave mistake I was making that has been made by so many women throughout the ages. I might as well also be jealous of any delectable dish that made him say 'Mm' when it was set before him in a restaurant, just as she was making her body available to him through the venue of

Swinging. I was very glad, and not at all surprised, when in his polite but irresistible way my Master took over. He kept the conversation going even as he got up to illustrate a subject Alan kept bringing up – bondage – with the rope he had conveniently brought with him.

As I smilingly complied, my Master began tying me to the chair I was sitting in while Alan eagerly convinced a reluctant Gloria to at least let him bind her arms to her own seat. I don't remember how Stinger secured me to the cloth-and-iron piece of garden furniture, but I do know my legs were invitingly spread wide open, and of course I wasn't wearing any panties. Within minutes, and without seeming to make an effort, my Master rendered me immobile. All I could do was raise my head when he bent over to kiss me, and moan with pleasure at his touch as he opened my shirt to expose my breasts. Alan eyed my pierced nipples hungrily, as Gloria whined and complained about how uncomfortable she was and demanded to be untied at once. Her boyfriend complied, more intent now on tasting what was there for the taking, and he got up to tentatively suckle my nipples as Gloria vanished inside, ostensibly to procure another bottle of wine. Meanwhile, I felt a delicious peace submitting to my Master's will as he watched another man fondling my helplessly bound body. The jagged tensions in Alan and Gloria's relationship made my bond with Stinger feel even more smoothly and beautifully profound. We were completely together, our thoughts and desires flowing as one along the ever-shifting shore of each moment in a way that effortlessly took over the evening as the other couple was caught up in the undertow of our love for each other, for we were determined to use their bodies for our pleasure. Only moments later, my Master untied me and we all finally made it into the bedroom, where we succeeded in washing Gloria's nervously chattering body onto the soft white shore of her bed.

My arms were still tied behind my back as my Master had me crouch beside him where he sat on the edge of the mattress and suck his cock, which he had pulled out of the black slacks he was wearing beneath a long-sleeved white button-down shirt. He looked devastatingly elegant as I glanced up and saw him leaning down to kiss Gloria, who was lying in the middle of the queen-size bed with Alan going down on her. It hurt me to watch my Master French-kissing another woman even as the sight turned me on in that double-edge way that cut me to the quick. He gave her a long, lingering kiss before turning his smiling attention back to me, for which I was breathlessly grateful as I fervently swallowed him whole again. But even though he made it clear I was pleasing him, he still leaned towards Gloria to kiss her again, and I felt both excited by and resentful of the fact that my arms were tied behind my back, making it impossible for me to caress his chest or his thighs or his hair flowing freely down his back. All I could touch of him was his dick with my tongue and my lips. Meanwhile, Gloria was having both her mouth and her pussy kissed, and I beseeched my Master with my eyes the next time he looked at me to do something about this gross imbalance, since I felt I deserved to have just as much attention paid to me (or more) as the annoying Gloria. I think Alan had his hand up my black skirt and was stroking my bare ass, but I scarcely noticed as my Master stood up and quickly undressed. I moaned with happiness when he got on the bed in a way that told me he was going to fuck me from behind, which meant pinning my face down against the mattress since my hands were still bound and could not support me.

I'm always happy when my Master is inside me, whether people are watching or not, and as he rammed into me I was oblivious to everything else. Then he pulled my head up by the hair as he fucked me so I could see that Alan had made Gloria take off all her clothes and tied her wrists over her head; he had pinned her down and she was forced to suffer the flow of the action whatever course it took. I thought about kissing her, knowing the sight would please my Master, but I couldn't bring myself to make intimate contact with the mouth that had produced so much annoying chatter. Alan fucked her in the missionary position for a few minutes, but she complained to him in a whisper, and he pulled out of her. He had followed Stinger's lead and stripped down to his erection, which could not hope to compare with my Master's. Kneeling on Gloria's other side, Alan leaned over her as if to kiss me, but instead he teased me, pulling his lips back just as they were about to touch mine. I found the game more annoying than exciting, and when he finally kissed me it was nothing remarkable (as I had known it wouldn't be) but that was irrelevant since I was with my Master and I knew I was pleasing him, and this is always what turns me on no matter the circumstances. When he pulled out of me and freed my arms, commanding me to take off my shirt, I knew it was time for him to fuck Gloria and for Alan to take his place behind me, which he promptly did, accepting the condom my Master handed him. I held myself on my hands and knees for another man even as all my attention remained focused on my Master's cock, also sheathed in plastic now, as he positioned his body over Gloria's and penetrated her, slipping into her with disappointing swiftness because I would have liked to savour the torturous sight of his hard-on gradually becoming submerged in another pussy. It was a slightly pleasant sensation when Alan entered me, but the truth is when I think back on all the men that my Master has allowed to fuck me, it's as though they were never there. Whatever pleasure their rigid, pumping penis's gave me was only the superficially sweet icing on the rich dark cake of how much it aroused me to watch my Master's hips working between another girl's thighs knowing how good his big, thick dick must feel to her as I got wetter and wetter gloating over the fact that only I was always blessed with what they could merely enjoy for a little while. The fact that Swinging can be a transcendent experience doesn't mean it can't also sometimes possess an excitingly cruel edge. Stinger was looking at me almost the whole time he was fucking Gloria, whom he occasionally deigned to kiss as he thrust his erection energetically up into her totally submissive body. I was aware that Alan was fucking me as violently as he could, yet he was scarcely making an impression on me except to add a profound spice to the kisses my Master and I kept sharing directly over Gloria's face. Her lips were parted as she panted in ecstasy beneath his virile onslaught, and there was a vaguely amazed look in her eyes I could understand feeling her boyfriend already coming. His much smaller cock pulsed for a few deeply enjoyable seconds inside me before sliding limply out of my hot cunt, which was ready for a feast after this small and unremarkable appetizer. I was intensely gratified when my Master abruptly pulled out of Gloria and whipped off the condom.

'Hey!' she cried before she could stop herself.

'Sorry, but Missa needs me,' he said, implying she could blame Alan for her loss since he had not done a good enough job of keeping me satisfied.

I lay happily down on my back and spread my legs for his beloved erection as Alan started going down on Gloria again, but apparently the loss of my Master's cock was too deep a wound to be satisfied by the bandage of her boyfriend's lips because once more she started complaining. She always seemed to be muttering at him with a hostility that made me respect him less and less for putting up with it. My Master came violently in my pussy, blithely ignoring the fact that Gloria obviously resented him for pulling out of her just as she was about to climax.

'I'm sorry,' he said to her afterwards, 'but I knew Missa wanted me to come inside her.' This, he later told me, was the excuse he gave her for indifferently pulling out of her, and I had to admire his polite consideration for her feelings.

Alan untied her so she could get up and use the bathroom, and while she was gone (a long, long time that made it obvious she was busy trying to relieve herself of hang-ups and anxiety) the three of us decided it would be fun to fulfil my fantasy of a double penetration. When Gloria returned, Alan promptly positioned himself beside me without consulting her, eager to go for it.

'What are you doing?' she demanded. He told her, and she flew off the handle saying we had had no right to decide anything while she was gone, etc. etc., which was true, but she had brought it upon herself by disappearing for an inordinate amount of time that was nothing short of rude. After their argument, she disappeared again, during which time my Master and Alan entertained themselves by agreeing it would be fun to tie one of us girls up. They decided it would be Gloria, and at that point I threw my own quiet but intense fit prompted by a beauty pageant-style jealousy that they had chosen her to be the bondage girl. Fortunately, my Master is very sensitive to my moods, and he nipped my irrational hysteria in the bud by taking me gently aside. When I confessed how undesirable and left out their discussion had made me feel, he assured me I was being silly (which of course part of me already knew but needed to hear him say anyway) and explained the reason they had selected Gloria to tie down was because she was insecure and nervous and not having a choice in matters might help calm her down, which of course I understood. I came to my senses right away, unlike Gloria, who when she finally returned kept simmering and sputtering angrily like a neglected teapot. Her attitude made it impossible for anyone to get in the mood to do anything, so apart from a few photographs Stinger took with one of his digital cameras, that was it for the night.

'I got the feeling when I was kissing her,' my Master said to me later when we were in his jeep on our way home, 'that she hadn't been kissed like that in a long time.'

'I feel sorry for her,' I told him. 'I mean, she gets to be kissed by you and to feel you inside her and then she has to go back to Alan, whose dick is so much smaller...'

'It's not that much smaller,' my Master protested humbly.

'Yes, it is,' I insisted fervently, 'and he comes in less than five minutes!'

He reached over and rested his hand on my thigh. 'That's because he was fucking you, Missa.'

'Meow...' I leaned over and caressed his shoulder with my cheek. 'So far,' I murmured, 'all the other men I've had inside me just make me appreciate your cock even more, Master.'

'You're so sweet, dear.'

'But it's the truth.'

He glanced at me again as he caressed my leg. 'I know.'

'But not everyone who Swings can feel that way, you know?'

'Yes, but they're not us, and it's not our problem, and it's not all about size anyway.'

I smiled to myself. 'Yes, Master, whatever you say.'

After a moment he added lightly, 'Size matters, huh?'

'Yes,' I laughed, 'it does.'

I said to my Master on the beach that Sunday, 'I've realized that Swinging short-circuits all the things that can go wrong in a relationship and makes them work in your favor instead. Jealousy is transformed into excitement' and the next day I made the following entry in my journal:

> *I cannot stop seeing my Master kissing Gloria and then fucking her. He kissed me while he was fucking her and while Alan was*

fucking me from behind. We were so together the whole time; it really was an extension of our sensuality. I could feel the power we had, while Gloria and Alan kept bickering. I felt no anxiety, no jealousy, just beautifully, sensually relaxed as my Master was tying me up out on the porch. Every time I think about that night I get so turned on it's hard to concentrate. When we made love afterwards at home, it was so unbelievably good and intense, and the next morning I climaxed twice as he fucked me from behind; it was so easy. I lost count of how many times we fucked this weekend; we were in a heightened state of arousal and more into each other than ever. I was even more into kissing him than usual – I got lost in his kisses – after watchinghim kissing Gloria while sitting on the edge of the bed in his white shirt facing me, but in those moments turned away from me.

The intimate setting was so much more erotic, so much more relaxed and therefore exciting, and the way he fucked Gloria was different from the way he fucked Nina at Miami Velvet. 'I'm glad you noticed that,' he said. The touch of tenderness and respect he showed Gloria made the act of fucking her even more of a turn on for me to watch because, really, that's all he was doing was fucking her, using her for our pleasure, not just our pleasure in the moment but also afterwards when we were alone together again. Swinging with another couple was like a drug that made me high all weekend; it was anincredibly potent aphrodisiac. When my Master penetrated me during one of the many times we fucked afterwards, I saw him entering Gloria, saw how he looked doing it, and somehow I felt what was happening "objectively" knowing another woman had been in my same position and experienced what I was experiencing... but only for a teasingly brief time, not all the time, not always, as I have the privilege and joy of doing.

I imagine that watching my Master fuck other women will restore and preserve the exciting objectivity that is otherwise only there in the beginning of a relationship. Because even as we become closer and closer, I won't make the mistake of confusing him with me, an illusion of comfortable sameness that can lead to taking for granted and dull the sharp and creative edge of desire. The dangers of proximity can be conquered if the 'the Swinging Sword' is wielded properly. When my Master has been inside another woman his mysteriously arousing separateness from me is restored, and sensually it's even more exciting between us than after we just met because on all other levels our intimacy just gets deeper, making sex more and more intense instead of less so.

I would love to watch my Master thrust his beautiful erection between Gloria's lips, gagging her endless anxious chatter as he fucks her mouth. I want to watch her sucking him and trying her best to please him with her lips and her tongue while kneeling before him, and then I want to go and kneel behind him and lick his ass, so he can feel my warm, wet tongue rimming him while he thrusts his dick into another girl's warm, wet mouth.

Then I would love for my Master to order me to sit on Alan's cock and brace myself on his chest so he can kneel behind me and fuck me in the ass as another man fucks my pussy.

Finally, I would love my Master to fuck Gloria long and hard, like her own man can never fuck her. It would turn me on so much to watch him start off gently, facing her and kissing her, completely melting her around him, and then gradually start fucking her harder and faster, totally selfishly. I want to watch him ramming into her knowing how good it feels and sensing how much she's loving it even as it hurts her a little, maybe because he's so long and

> *thick and she's not used to it, but mainly because she knows he's just using her pussy and that she may never feel him again because I'm the one he loves not her. I want to watch my Master turn her over onto her hands and knees and come inside her from behind while he looks into my eyes and I feel him mysteriously inside me even as another woman feels him inside her.*

I sent this entry to my Master at work via e-mail and he replied with this message:

> *I really love you. Your diary entries are lovely. I am sitting here not able to think about anything else right now. Thanks for confirming with Wisperwood. Did you call the other two places that I sent? I'm looking forward to seeing you. What is the schedule with your father?*
> *Love, Stinger*

My Master and I were planning to move in together and were already looking for an apartment. It was the end of May and his lease expired at the beginning of August, yet we didn't want to wait that long if he could get out of it without losing too much money. I was free to leave the doll's house whenever I wanted. I couldn't wait.

Alan and Gloria were eager to see us again, or at least Alan was because he kept calling me, and finally my Master and I decided to give them another chance. Perhaps Gloria wouldn't be so nervous and uptight the second time we got together, and maybe Alan would miraculously discover some staying power. I was more than skeptical, but I loved how together being with them had made Stinger and me feel, and I selfishly wanted another opportunity to make certain scenarios come true. I seriously doubted Gloria would submit to all the things I wanted her to do for my Master's pleasure, but it was worth a shot since the fantasies were burning a hole in my psyche.

No longer considering them worthy of a Friday or Saturday night, we met them one evening during the week at Ray's On The Water. The place was wildly popular with the after-work crowd and therefore expensive, but personally I didn't see the appeal. It was hot and humid and mostly standing-room-only, none of which I appreciated in my high-heeled black leather boots. I was wearing them beneath a loose black mini-skirt that flared attractively out of a form-fitting black velvet, short-sleeved button-down shirt. Even my hair was black, which made the splash of color on my lips, and around my hips in the form of a belt made of multi-colored glass ovals linked on a chain, even more dramatic. We were early and they were late, but at least we managed to scavenge seats at the bar. As the sun set over the water, I sipped a large martini and basked in my Master's love and attention, mysteriously intensified by the presence of another man obviously lusting after me, and of another woman doing her best to hide what an impression Stinger had made inside her the other night. With the darkness rose a deliciously cool breeze, and eventually it wafted our alcohol-lightened bodies a few blocks away to Tobacco Road. Normally admission is twenty-dollars on the nights live bands are playing, but the man at the door greeted my Master warmly and waved us inside.

'Hey, why do you get in for free?' Alan demanded in astonishment.

'Because I'm me,' my Master replied, and it was one of the highlights of the night.

Gloria was suffering from cold sores in her mouth, which I thought made her quite unappealing. We were standing upstairs against a wall listening to a deafeningly loud band play while sipping more drinks, and

I was getting bored and impatient. Leaning back against my Master, I savored his boldly intimate caresses as smugly as a cat, so that all my nerve endings hissed in disbelief and disgust when I glanced over my shoulder and saw him slip his index finger between Gloria's lips. Part of me perceived it as an arousing, elegant gesture that sensually linked the four of us with each other, but all I could think about was that a minute ago that same finger had been inside my pussy, where I had no intention of letting it go again. I stiffened against him, and was coldly non-responsive when he asked me what was wrong. It wasn't until he started becoming angry with me for not explaining my abrupt change of mood that I told him what my problem was. He left for the bathroom (I assumed to wash his hands) justifiably annoyed with me for not confiding in him calmly and maturely, but I hadn't been able to control my reaction. A hot, unexpected spark of jealousy, combined with my fear of catching something unpleasant in the serpent-riddled paradise of Swinging, ignited an emotional storm inside me I weathered as quickly as I could awaiting his to return. Regretting my childish, foot-stomping attitude, I steered myself back into a calm, clearer state of mind again. My Master is a scientist and perhaps it is knowing exactly how different germs operate that enables him to have a more relaxed attitude than my less informed imagination enables me to adopt. I think he simply forgot about Gloria's cold sores because he did not make a large mental note of them when she mentioned them the way I did. The point is, I should have communicated my feelings to him right away, sincerely and respectfully, not thrown a jealous tantrum designed to turn all his attention back to me again and keep it there in a negatively unattractive instead of a positively desirable way.

Alan wanted us all to go back to their place, and even though Gloria seemed increasingly tense, she shrugged and went along with the suggestion. We returned to our respective vehicles, but once there my Master told me it was entirely up to me whether or not we drove to South Beach or went somewhere else because he personally didn't care one way or the other. Talking about it in the parking lot, we agreed it was probably going to be a waste of time trying to have some real fun with this couple – who clearly had a lot of problems in their relationship that Swinging magnified painfully – but I stubbornly, childishly, refused to put away my fantasies until the next time we had an opportunity to play them out. I was filled with despair at the thought of having to go back to Velvet, and we didn't have another potentially promising couple lined up, so I told my Master I wanted to go to South Beach. He insisted I shouldn't feel pressured to want to do anything, and I assured him the only pressure I felt came from within me. I longed to prove to myself that the beautiful togetherness we had experienced the other night had been real and would happen again, ideally every time we chose to have sex with another couple. I also didn't want to lose the one opportunity I had at that moment in time to please my Master, so we drove to the beach.

When we arrived at Gloria's apartment, the door was unlocked. We let ourselves in and discovered not only that she and Alan were already naked, but that they were one orgasm ahead of us. She had effortlessly succeeded in getting her helplessly excited boyfriend to fuck her before we arrived, wanting him all to herself, and her insecure possessiveness set the tone for the night. Watching me suck Stinger's cock on the living room couch quickly got Alan hard again, but even when we all adjourned into the bedroom, Gloria clung to him and wouldn't let go, insisting coyly but adamantly that he fuck her and her alone. Smiling at each other, my Master and I decided to simply enjoy the voyeuristic and exhibitionist elements the night had to offer. At one point, Alan asked me if I liked taking it up the ass, and as Gloria protested she was going to let him try it sometime, I silently assumed the sleen position. My Master fucked me up the ass good and hard, and I let the intently watching couple hear how much I loved it. We left the apartment feeling even more empowered by our love for each other than the last time as Gloria talked us to the door, chattering inanely she was so relieved we were leaving. Alan was unusually quiet and sullen, undoubtedly annoyed he had let himself be cheated out of a potentially much more enjoyable evening. After that night he kept sending me e-mails suggesting we all get together again sometime, and inviting himself and Gloria to the next fetish party Stinger and I planned to attend, but I just rolled my eyes and hit delete as my Master had gladly given me permission to do, and we never saw them again.

11 The Myth And Truth Of Monogamy

I saw a photograph of Mitch and Michelle on their profile. I thought he looked interesting, and my impression was confirmed when I read what he had to say about Swinging. I promptly copied his words in my journal, which I cannot reproduce here, but their gist is that he and his partner always remained within touching distance of each other when they were having sex with another couple, and their closeness and focus on each other naturally appealed to me.

My Master and I met Mitch and Michelle one evening at a bar in South Beach evocative of a cheap nineteen-fifties science fiction film. The bar stools were painted silver, the cushions on the benches were silver, the small round flying saucer tables were silver, even the walls were silver, the designer clearly having suffered a lobotomy of the imagination. Michelle was more attractive than her photographs. She had come straight from work and was wearing an elegant black pantsuit that set off her long legs, big breasts and shoulder-length black hair. I thought Mitch disappointingly slender since I like broad shoulders and strong (although not overly muscular) arms and legs on a man, and in my opinion his handsome face was too soft, with lips a woman would have been proud of. Nevertheless, he would do, and after a drink at the bar, we all adjourned to an atmospherically dark back room lined with comfortable couches conducive to more intimate conversation.

I sat between my Master and Michelle, and I could feel his approval as she boldly caressed one of my bare thighs. She was obviously more interested in me than in Stinger, and I was at once relieved and disappointed and worried, because I could not possibly reciprocate her sexual attraction to another woman. But it was obviously pleasing my Master to watch her fondling me, and it was his arousal that magically stoked my own and enabled me to experience a ghost of pleasure. Then she abruptly leaned past me to kiss him, and I wasn't sure how I felt. Things were happening much more quickly than I had expected; I wasn't prepared for the pace she was setting and that Stinger was happily going along with. Mitch spoke so softly I could barely hear him, but when I did, I definitely liked what he was saying, which helped make up for his partner's disconcerting aggressiveness. Until he brought up the subject of condoms, that is, and how much he and Michelle disliked them and desired to find a couple they could develop a long-term relationship with in which the need to practice safe sex would not be a concern. I kept casting smiling glances at my Master in growing alarm as Mitch explained that, in their opinion, a layer of plastic destroyed the sensual intimacy of intercourse. Then Michelle bluntly stated they had just both been recently tested for AIDS, and everything else, and proudly announced they were clean. I don't remember Stinger's exact words, all I know is that to my intense relief he made it clear to our passionate new friends that we always used condoms during intercourse with other people. 'At least for now,' he added, holding out the promise of a more satisfyingly carnal future should our association with them develop and deepen enough for us to consider such a dangerous plunge.

Before we left the bar, Michelle and I went up to the bathroom together, and after we washed our hands she grabbed me by the hips just as a man would and pulled me to her, leaving me no choice but to slip my arms around her neck and return her ardent smile with a politely bemused one of my own.

'I think we're going to be very good friends,' she murmured. 'Don't you?'

'Yes,' I said, seeing no reason to disagree as I enjoyed the novelty of the experience but felt nothing else.

We left the bathroom hand-in-hand and it made me happy to catch my Master smiling at the picture we made from where he and Mitch were waiting for us, and they weren't the only men whose eyes followed us all the way to the door. Beside Michelle's masculine pantsuit, I felt deliciously feminine in white high-heeled sandals and a baby-blue mini skirt that buttoned down the front. Above it I was in a white button-down shirt with half sleeves and a cleavage that belied the business-like collar and tailored cut.

Less than fifteen minutes later I was barefoot and submissively unbuttoning my blouse while three sets of hands vied to make short work of my skirt, barely giving me time to wistfully drape my delicate garments over the rough railing of a lifeguard house overlooking a ghostly-white stretch of beach and the heaving black waters of the Atlantic sea. The sun had set along with my hope of spending a romantic evening alone with my Master. I didn't really want to be there, but my body was helplessly caught between three strong erotic currents washing over me in the form of a mouth sucking on my pierced nipples and a tongue surging between the rippling folds of my smoothly shaved labia, while another tongue slipped between the lips on my face. It was my beloved Master kissing me while Mitch intently devoted himself to my breasts and Michelle energetically licked my pussy in between teasingly blowing both men. I'll never forget the way my Master smiled at me as I looked down to watch her gripping his erection in one hand and her boyfriend's in the other as she sucked one cock then another. We all huddled fervently and furtively together in an effort to avoid being seen by any passersby on the beach, who would have gotten quite a shocking treat if they had chanced to look up at the lifeguard shack where four people were drowning all their thoughts and frustrations in a rush of senses and sensations...

At least I knew this was the theory, but my mind was never completely submerged in the experience. All that clinging flesh got uncomfortably hot and sticky in the humid atmosphere, and made me feel I had been unexpectedly shoved off the edge of a civilized evening into waves of sexual energy where I was forced to cling to rigid cocks for dear life, while submerging my face between swelling breasts, all the while diving into cavernous mouths as though my tongue was just a playfully wild dolphin. Yet there were moments when I found myself surrendering to the flow, like when I sucked Mitch's dick glancing up at my Master, who was smiling down at me in between kissing and fondling Michelle's big tits. Our sensual sea was definitely polluted with silicon, and I didn't relish the unfamiliar feel and flavor of another man's hard penis sliding down my tongue and filling my mouth as though it belonged there, but I was compelled to let it dive between my lips and threaten to choke me before I breathlessly turned my face towards my Master's much more fulfilling erection. Until tonight his was the only cock I had tasted since we met, and I was slightly astonished by my actions now, but I guess I was grateful to Mitch for inspiring me infinitely more than Tom and Alan ever had. And there was something quite gratifying about crouching between two men bracing myself on their hard-ons as I alternated my oral skills between them, wondering at how different these two fine examples of semen-slick dicks felt and tasted. There was nothing unpleasant about Mitch's more slender but still gratifyingly long manhood, yet every time I came back to him it was like having to lick and swallow vanilla ice cream mixed in with the chocolate I loved so much more, because the flavor of my Master's cock is like nothing else in the world.

'Good girl,' said Michelle, her Cretan goddess breasts bulging out of her modern businesswoman's outfit. 'If I had known what was going to happen, I would have worn something else,' she added afterwards, when I was still the only one who was naked as we finally prepared to leave the lifeguard stand where my sexual energy was completely washed up for the moment. I was seriously looking forward to eating some nourishing food now and relaxing in a comfortable air conditioned restaurant. I had enjoyed certain parts of the experience, but mainly it was how happy my Master looked with me, and with life in general, that made it all feel worthwhile as he tenderly slipped my shirt back on while Mitch solicitously buttoned my skirt, also a good excuse to keep touching and caressing me. He was the perfect passionate gentleman, and my Master and I did not need to discuss it out loud to agree they were the ideal couple for us to Swing with successfully in every way. Before we walked down the steps and onto the beach again, we all agreed to meet again tomorrow night at a hotel near the airport Mitch knew about that rented rooms by the hour which were perfectly clean but also boasted mirrors on the ceiling and heart-shaped Jacuzzis. I was pleased they sounded comfortable at least.

We slipped our shoes back on when we reached the sidewalk, and my Master and I led the way down the narrow concrete path towards the little silver diner we had in mind. I spotted a penny on the way, and a mischievous impulse prompted me to keep my legs straight as I bent over at the waist to pick it up and make a wish (as I always do) thereby exposing my naked assets to the couple walking behind us. I had overheard them complimenting my curvaceous figure, and it was Michelle who rushed up eagerly behind me and spanked my ass with a resounding smack. My Master loves it when I do naughty things like that, and basking in his appreciation now as he slipped his arm with loving possessiveness around me, I knew there were many more fun moments to be had in life if only MIP would relax instead of always being tense and afraid and let Missa come out and play. But it was almost exactly a year later before Missa's attitude was fully entrenched in my psyche and part of my mind and heart 24/7.

We were to rendezvous with Mitch and Michelle in the parking lot of a restaurant near the hotel. My Master and I arrived some time before them and sat waiting in the jeep intently observing every car that pulled in.

'Do you feel like you're on some secret mission?' he asked me.

'Mm,' I replied, not really sure how I felt. This clandestine meeting strictly for the purposes of sex was exciting on a certain level, but I wasn't aroused. The thought of fucking another couple was only an abstract goal for me in the sense that I already knew from experience it would turn me on to watch my Master, and to be watched by him, and that I would feel even closer to him afterwards than I already did. It was not about desiring the other two people involved. Naturally, I had discussed how I felt about it with my Master, because the only thing that truly displeases him is when I keep something from him, and after one of our many conversations on the subject (which took MIP a very long time to deal with mentally and emotionally even while Missa understood it perfectly) I made this entry in my journal:

With couples it's partly about being able to see each other from a distance as we cannot do when we're fucking each other, the stimulating memory of which enhances our own intimacy. It excites him to watch me being taken knowing I am doing it to please him, knowing I belong to him and other men can only taste me. It excites him to feel another woman's pussy while seeing my body penetrated. I know it turned him on (because he told me) to see how much sexier I was than Michelle...

Meeting Stinger is like finally finding the right spaceship and together taking off into the universe surfing waves of energy and life, pausing on temporary shores then moving on. Swinging intensifies our intimacy astronomically...

It's the soul that loves, and if it's true, as I believe, that it shapes our flesh, my pussy was made for Stinger's cock, so I don't ever need to be concerned that he'll find a pussy he likes better than mine. Also, a pussy is just a pussy and a dick is just a dick, and what we have is light years beyond mere physiological facts...

There was nothing unpleasantly seedy about the hotel room we all filed into, the men elegant in button-down shirts and us two girls stepping carefully in our come fuck me shoes. There was a mirror on the headboard of the king-size bed, and the ceiling above it was tiled with mirrors. Opening off the room there was a red heart-shaped Jacuzzi, and when Mitch switched on the large screen television a porno movie was in heated progress. No one protested when he turned it off indifferently; we had all the makings of our own adult film right there in the flesh. My Master and I had brought a bottle of red wine, which he proceeded to uncork as I headed for the stereo with the tape I had recorded that afternoon (while happily packing boxes because my Master and I were moving in together soon). The tape contained all my favorite songs by The

Crystal Method, Curve, Garbage, Filter, etc. I had hoped they would prove inspiring when the time came for me to go with the sensual flow.

Mitch had dressed Michelle for the occasion in a black French Maid's outfit that showed off her fake breasts and made her look cheaply voluptuous. I was wearing a tight black mini skirt, a tight red low-cut sleeveless shirt, my multi-colored hip belt and red stiletto heels. Mitch made it clear how much he liked the tastefully sexy outfit by caressing my hips and pressing me against him, even as Stinger's hands silently admired Michelle's lace garters and black stockings. But she seemed more interested in getting my opinion of how she looked, so I dutifully cupped and kissed her big tits, moaning appreciatively, but the truth is her body didn't turn me on in the least. Then, as we all inevitably converged on the bed, came that terrible moment when I realized I was actually going to have to share Stinger with another woman and divide my attentions between him and two other people, which I really had no desire to do. I held back, still holding a glass of wine like a shield in my hand. My Master noticed my sudden reticence, but this time he responded to it with controlled impatience instead of tender understanding. I knew he was tired of dealing with my last minute panic attacks, which bore no relation to how relaxed and positive I always was when entering these situations. Bracing myself, I rode the wave of my tumultuous emotions instead of letting my thoughts start flailing tensely around in them, and setting my wine glass down I took my position on the edge of the bed.

It is interesting in retrospect what tableaus unfold right away of their own accord. Mitch sat beside me as Michelle promptly sank to her hand and knees before me, thrust her face between my thighs, and began licking my unprotected pussy. I watched with a sinking feeling as my Master knelt behind her, and when he lowered his head and began eating her out from behind, there was nothing for me to do but close my eyes and bend over the erection Mitch had pulled out of his pants for me. At one point I glanced up at his face as I sucked him, and he later confessed to me in a private telephone conversation (which I of course told my Master all about later) that the way I met his eyes blew his mind. 'Here was this beautiful woman I really didn't know at all sucking my dick,' he said, 'and looking up into my eyes... it was just incredible.' At the time, however, he didn't say anything, and full as my mouth was, it was nothing compared to the despair that filled my soul when every time I came up for air I saw that my Master still had his beautiful features buried in Michelle's pussy. At least I assumed he was tonguing her cunt and not her asshole, I sincerely hoped so! My only comfort was the feel of one of his hands gripping my leg and maintaining a sensual connection between us while the woman he was licking in turn licked me. I wish I could say Michelle's cunnilingus pleased me, but the truth is it made scarcely any impression on my nerve endings. Almost from the beginning, I wanted out of this position where all I could feel of my Master was his hand on my leg as I was sandwiched between two other bodies I didn't desire as I did his. Losing sight of his face and eyes mysteriously cut off the blood supply to my sex, which didn't begin responding to the erotically charged atmosphere until he rose from behind Michelle's very lucky pussy. It seemed to me he had blessed her with his oral attentions for much too long considering all the attention she had seemed to pay him she was so intent on exploring my cunt. I also couldn't help resenting how much he had seemed to enjoy feasting on another woman's sex lips and juices, whereas I had sucked Mitch down mainly because I was expected to, and it filled me with despair that my pussy wasn't the only one Stinger truly relished plunging his face into the way I really only enjoyed going down on him. What I still failed to realize is that it was the whole experience that was turning him on so much, not the particular charms of Michelle's labia. I could have allowed the sight of him hungrily eating her out to turn me on rather than upset me, connected as I was to the irresistible current of his pleasure by way of his hand gripping my leg and sustaining our profoundly arousing connection with each other. But I was still learning how to wire my mind so my thoughts remained excitingly positive, rather than negatively shorting out because they were still unable to handle the intense charge of group sex. In another conversation we had about Swinging, my Master said this to me, and I wrote it down in my journal so I would never forget it:

I love you. I command you never to forget how much I love you. Whatever we do together enhances our relationship and can never be degrading if it's done out of love. You have to learn to make lemonade out of lemons, Missa. There are two issues here. When will you realize jealousy can be turned into excitement right away in the moment, not just afterwards? And when will you realize that if you're pleasing your Master everything is all right?

I was definitely pleasing my Master that night, and after we all moved on to the bed together things went much more smoothly and enjoyably for me. I was quickly stripped down to my hip belt, the men took everything off, and only Michelle kept her crotchless French maid's bodice on as I found myself relaxing into Missa and, astonishingly enough to MIP, directing the action. I said I thought it was time to live out my fantasy of a double penetration, but I chose to let Michelle (who had already experienced the pleasure of two cocks inside her) go first. My Master lay on his back so she could straddle him, then Mitch positioned himself behind her and entered her anally. I watched curiously as she rode Stinger and her lover thrust his more slender rod between her ass cheeks. At first I knelt on the mattress beside the intently occupied bodies, but then I got up to circle the bed voyeuristically. My Master followed me with his eyes in between smiling encouragingly up at Michelle, who was breathlessly determined to come with the aid of the little vibrating egg she was holding against her clitoris. In my opinion, she was concentrating more on this mechanical aid and her desire for an orgasm than on the men penetrating her, which I thought was a waste, since a climax can be had anytime but a double penetration is a special treat in and of itself.

At last she gave up, exhausted by her efforts, and we took a short break while the men rested up. I went to turn the tape over (I wasn't really listening to it but it was a stimulating backdrop) and Mitch followed me. It pleased me to entertain my Master, who lay back against some pillows watching the scene unfolding in front of the black screen of another man caressing my naked body, then pressing me up against him from behind and slowly bending me forward in a passionate mime of what was to come. I made absolutely sure Mitch slipped on a condom before I crawled back on the bed and happily impaled myself on my Master's deliciously stiff dick. Then, as in my daydreams, another hard cock penetrated me at the same time, slipping up into the tight space of my ass more swiftly than I would have liked. Fortunately, this second erection was not as thick as my Master's, yet for some reason its penetrations became excruciatingly unpleasant after a while. Yet I was completely filled with cock and I loved it, and my Master's beautiful smile and whispered encouragements were aphrodisiacs making my soul glow with a fulfillment that in turn suffused my flesh. Michelle circled the bed taking photographs of my first double penetration with Stinger's digital camera. I have a lovely graphic record of the event which my Master and I later agreed could have been better, but it was still great fun. The problem was that Mitch's hard-on just didn't feel good in my anus. It should have been my Master's erection in my ass; my rectal muscles have grown familiar with, and deeply fond of, his cock. Also, plastic becomes abrasive after a few strokes, something a hot juicing pussy is better able to handle. Mitch pounded into me relentlessly, making me more aware of his rending erection than of my Master's thicker shaft pulsing in and out of my naturally slick sex, but at least I was able to look down into his eyes and kiss him whenever I wanted to. Unlike Michelle, I wasn't trying to come. It would have been impossible with Mitch's energetic backdoor thrusts overwhelming my clit's much more subtle sensitivity, but it was a highly satisfying experience anyway.

After that I don't recall exactly what happened. The next thing I remember is lying on my back in the middle of the bed, with Mitch kneeling between my legs and easing his long cock slowly in and out of my wet pussy as I stroked my clit furiously. I was going to come, despite the fact that my Master seemed very far away where he stood pounding into Michelle from behind as she braced herself on the edge of the bed. He was fucking her so violently that she collapsed across the mattress just as I climaxed so intensely, I had to close my eyes to endure the blinding explosion of pleasure between my thighs. I reluctantly lost sight of my Master climbing onto the bed behind the moaning Michelle, but gladly shut out the vision of Mitch towering proudly over me believing it was his penis that was giving me so much pleasure. I felt a touch of guilt and loss at having enjoyed an orgasm with another man inside me, then I experienced a heady caress of hope as my Master asked me over Michelle's prone body, 'Did you just come, Missa?' I hoped he would be just a little bit upset and jealous since I had still never seen him ejaculate inside another woman (albeit into a condom and not actually saturating her cunt with his cum) but he just looked at me with a smile in his eyes when I replied, 'Yes' and kept happily sliding his erection in and out of another woman, who definitely sounded as though she loved the feel of his big, thrusting penis.

Meanwhile, Mitch braced himself on his arms to penetrate my yielding pussy more deeply, obviously prepared to keep fucking me for a long time, but I was already seriously missing my Master. It seemed to me the full swap had gone on long enough, and it suddenly filled me with despair that I appeared to be the only one who felt that way.

'Stinger, I need you,' I moaned, and blessedly a moment later we were in each others arms and he was pounding into me, filling my grateful body with his beloved cock, which felt better than ever after Mitch's teasingly slender organ sheathed in lifeless plastic like the dildo it was to me. My Master came fiercely inside me, but the evening was far from over.

We adjourned to the heart-shaped Jacuzzi for a wine break, laughing as the foaming water nearly overflowed when we turned on the jets. There was room for all of us, but Michelle stepped out almost at once to play with Stinger's digital camera again, and I have a lovely shot of me half perched on Mitch's lap, my glistening body just floating over the water in the direction of my smiling Master as he finger fucks me beneath the bubbles, the back of his head to the camera but his profile reflected in a mirror. Michelle said something as she finished taking pictures, then suddenly I had both men to myself for a while when she failed to return, and it pleased me in a selfish way I don't care to be ashamed of that she did not appear to be missed as both Mitch and Stinger delighted in playing with me. I heard the shower running and guessed what had happened, yet like a greedy child I refrained from explaining the situation to the two rock-hard males completely at my disposal. Michelle finally reappeared wrapped in a white towel, and Mitch had some serious explaining to do. No one had heard her request that we all go shower together, and when we failed to show up in the bathroom, she believed we were all deliberately snubbing her. I could have felt bad about having kept silent (my intuition had told me when I heard water running that she expected us to join her) but on the other hand it was Mitch's responsibility to attend to his partner's words and feelings, not to mention her presence, at all times, not mine. I didn't blame her for being upset, but it was her lover's fault in the end; he should not have been so indifferent to her absence. In fact, it was Stinger who at one point asked him, 'Where's Michelle?' which annoyed a catty part of me even while deepening my love and respect for him.

Hurt feelings eventually soothed by loving concern, we dried off and returned to the bed, where I got wet again helping Michelle suck Mitch's dick. Then, much more pleasurable for me, we took turns slipping my Master's cock into our mouths, before I decided to lick his smoothly shaved balls while I let another woman's lips and tongue work on his shaft. It was a feast of fulfillment for me being able to share the work of worshipping him as I experienced just as much satisfaction with only half the effort. Yet I would have to wait to really have fun that way with another girl, because Michelle was more into licking my pussy and I didn't have the heart to tell her she was wasting her time.

Intensely relaxed, we enjoyed gazing up at our reflections in the ceiling, striking languid painting-like poses my Master captured with his camera. We came away with dozens of striking photographs of that night. I for one was happy we did not swap partners again, but instead fucked our own lovers while watching the action from every conceivable angle. I had another orgasm, only this one was much more special because I climaxed at the same time as my Master with him inside me. He was taking me from behind, and we were holding each other's eyes in the mirror as we came, losing sight of the other couple engaged in the same position. Later, Stinger told me how much it turned him on to look at both Michelle and me being fucked on our hands and knees and to think how much more beautiful I was.

I was sure the night was finally over after that – it was nearly midnight and we had arrived shortly before nine – but both men got hard yet again and I found myself wearily, but happily, lying on my belly on the bed sucking my Master dick while Mitch licked my slit, lapping soothingly at my labia while Stinger included Michelle in the action by reaching over to finger her clitoris. She was not very responsive, however; like me, she was exhausted, and fortunately not like me, she had to be at work early the next morning, so understandably she wanted to go home and get some sleep. I shared her sentiment that it was time the evening came to an end (I dreaded the possibility of another full swap which I no longer had the energy to handle in any sense) but the men were enjoying themselves too much to be rushed off the bed. Mitch went to the bathroom, and when he returned, he smacked my Master's ass with a hairbrush. He and Michelle laughed uproariously, and Stinger didn't seem to mind, but I was shocked by the unexpected gesture. I discovered later in another private phone conversation with Mitch that he was flirting with the idea of behaving bi-sexually with Michelle's encouragement. She wanted to see him fucked by a man and vice versa, and for this reason, amongst several others – including that I was clearly not bi-sexual enough for her tastes – we never got together with them again. And after our encounter with them, I began to feel that finding another couple we could do things with socially as well as sexually on a regular basis was not a desirable objective. The excitement of being intimate with total strangers would be lost, and I would not be able to tolerate knowing there was another woman my Master was fucking regularly. It seems to me that after two or three liaisons the thrilling edge would be dulled by familiarity, and personalities like gravity would destroy the sensually transcendent experience. If you get to know people too well you inevitably cease to merely have sex with them and venture dangerously into the realm of love making, which is the sacred domain of two people who share a truly special bond with each other. I've discussed this with my Master and given it a lot of thought, and I wrote what I concluded in my journal:

The myth and truth of monogamy is this: You can be in a monogamous relationship, in the sense that you only make love to one special person, even if you occasionally enjoy spicing up your intimacy by having sex with other people together, which is still mysteriously making love to each other using different bodies.

The four of us finally made it out of the hotel room into the moistly warm embrace of a June night in Miami, but before we all got into our respective vehicles we paused to kiss goodbye. I went along with the romantic farewell even though I wasn't into it; I had no desire to submit to the tonguing Mitch gave me while Michelle embraced Stinger. I had suffered the same reaction the night before when we parted on South Beach in a dark doorway, hugging and kissing each other's partners like the old loving friends we were not. We had only just met these people a few hours ago, they were complete strangers to us, and I saw no reason for individual displays of affection, during which my Master felt completely lost to me, just because we had all played together. Of course, if I had enjoyed Mitch's tongue in my mouth I might not have minded so much, but like handshakes all kisses are different, and overly moist languid ones are never appealing. I am enjoying a little revenge here with this derogatory comment because during one of the times Mitch called me when he was alone (in my opinion a violation of Swinging etiquette) he confessed that his condom started coming apart when he was fucking my ass. My Master and I had already noticed in one of the photographs of my first double penetration that Mitch's rubber had ridden down so low he didn't appear to be wearing one, but we had both watched him slip it on so we weren't concerned. This belated revelation that our protection had been compromised made me angry with Mitch for having kept the problem from us at the time. When I told my Master about it I was very upset, but he calmly reassured me. He said he had not noticed anything amiss, and that Mitch was probably exaggerating the bad condition of the latex so I would believe we had already had unprotected sex together. Stinger's reasoning made sense, because Mitch had also remarked during our conversation that since we had all had unprotected oral sex there was no reason not to have rubber-free intercourse as well. I promptly explained to him what my Master had taught me, that oral sex and intercourse are two very different things and dangerous to a greatly varying degree. After this disturbing talk with Mitch, which contained the revelation about Michelle's desire to watch him being submissive to another man, my Master and I were turned off from ever wanting to see them again.

I was exhausted by the end of our night in a hotel room with another couple, but elated to be alone with my Master again having at last completely made it over this particular hurdle in my training.

'I'm so proud of you, Missa,' he said as we pulled out of the parking lot, his hand resting on my thigh. 'Now let's go home.' And soon it would mean just that; soon we would be driving to our place, the dreamed of, longed for, space where I could fully live as Stinger's devoted slave 24/7.

12 The Fetish Factor

It's almost impossible for me to describe how relaxed and peaceful and even more totally and happily in love with each other Stinger and I feel the day after a night spent fucking in the presence of, and maybe with, other people. I would not trade the beautiful feeling of closeness and contentment with each other and the world that my Master and I experience after a night of Swinging for anything. We find it much more fulfilling than simply going to a club and sitting around drinking in between dancing and walking around aimlessly. Unfortunately, that's all you can do at S&M clubs, and my Master and I are not alone in our frustration that the Lifestyle and BDSM rarely merge into a totally fulfilling whole. Saturday nights when we didn't have other plants, and weren't in the mood for Velvet, we attended fetish parties hopeful our bodies might become a bridge between the worlds leading to all sorts of exciting possibilities.

The Fetish Factory, a Ft. Lauderdale based BDSM clothing and accessories store, regularly held parties in varying venues. The first one we attended was at the Aqua Lounge with Tom and Nancy, and we were curious to see what the event would be like in the much larger space of the Millennium Nightclub. The new space my Master and I had moved into in Wisperwood was also much larger than either of our previous apartments. It's hard to properly discipline a slave when she is not living with you 24/7, but now my Master continued my training in earnest. I was ecstatic we would always be going home together, and that all our resources were combined so I could begin pleasing him as I longed to, not just sexually but in every aspect of life. I wanted to provide him with a lovely, comfortable home, gourmet meals every night, clean towels and clothes all neatly arranged in the closet, healthy lunches for his office, everything. My organizational skills and love of good food made these tasks come so naturally to me they seemed effortless, like cosmic presents I was fortunate enough to work at unwrapping everyday, for inside everything was how much I loved this man and myself and the life we were growing together. I take great satisfaction in making everything as pleasurable as possible for us, leaving him free to concentrate on his work and on me, his most treasured possession. I was a rough gem when I first met my Master he has gradually been shaping to fit the setting of his desires, and everyday I feel my being shines a little more purely and brightly with the priceless truth of how much I love him and just what that means in the scheme of things. It means I have become truly myself like never before by accepting the fact that I desire whatever he does. This is a beastly paradox, and during my training as a slave I learned you have to make it past this terrifying threshold in your mind to truly make any progress. Believe me, it isn't easy re-writing society's programming, which is wired to your thoughts and emotions in maddeningly complex ways. In essence, you have to learn to outwit your own brain if you're ever going to change.

A series of fetish parties punctuated the intensifying discipline in our new home. The Millennium Nightclub was a large venue indeed, with two bars and a spacious dance floor and several movie screens, but it was still disappointing. There was an abundance of eye-candy, several 'scenes' being played out during the course of the night, dancers on pedestals wearing skin-tight black latex cat-suits, and fetish flicks promoting the expensive kinky clothes, shoes and accessories for sale at The Fetish Factory. The films never stopped playing, but no one else did, so that my Master and I actually shocked people when he leaned back against a wall and commanded me to kneel before him and lick his balls through his black vinyl pants. I obeyed him eagerly, because for some reason it seriously excited me to feel the full firmness of his crotch against my tongue coated by the cool, slick, shiny material. We had grown accustomed to Swing clubs and it was very frustrating not being able to really play with each other in public.

Nevertheless, another Saturday night found us back at the tiny Aqua Lounge, where we ran into John again, wielder of the infamous Violet Wand, who invited us to a private fetish party he was throwing at his house. We also met two other Masters and their slaves, and it was relatively interesting to talk with them. One Master had been a dominant for years, and his skill with floggers was impressive. Stinger and I sat on a couch comfortably facing an iron cross to which this Master had bound his slave. She was clad entirely in white lace – bra, panties, garters and stockings – and as he 'beat' her I was entranced by the performance as I observed her body gradually slumping in mindless ecstasy, until only the restraints seemed to be holding her up. I found the swift twisting of his wrists hypnotic as he used two floggers on her at once to keep up a relentless, smacking rhythm that made my pussy hot and wet just watching. He had to help his slave to her knees when he was finished with her, and it was beautiful to see the way he caressed her hair and held her close as she clung to his leg. I knew I had just witnessed something genuine, and was intensely curious to see if I could actually fall into a trance-like state as she had. Like me, this slave was not a pain slut, in the sense that her Master did not use whips or canes or other intensely cruel implements on her that left serious marks; her skin was flushed after the event but still smooth and intact. I almost wished Stinger had not declined her Master's offer to flog me as a lesson on how to do it properly. On the other hand, I really didn't want another man beating me. This Master's slave would kneel and kiss his ringed fingers whenever she returned from the bar with a drink for him, and I could tell Stinger admired her ritual deference. We ourselves had not come up with so formal a greeting. My Master had simply told me I was always to meet him when he returned home wearing my official collar (or any other jewelry expressive of a collar) high heels and nothing else. I was to greet him this way everyday without fail, and to my surprised dismay I soon learned this was easier said than done. Sometimes I just didn't feel like being naked, not because I was cold but because, I now realize, I wanted to hide my body from my own eyes. My self esteem fluctuated like the graph of an earthquake. Some days I was not pleased with the size of my breasts. On another day I hated my little round tummy, etc. etc. Looking down at your body is not the most flattering perspective, and it took me months to realize that no matter how critical I was of my own figure, my Master always thought I was beautiful. Learning to see myself through his eyes has been a vital key to my sensual relaxation and liberation. 'No woman is completely happy with her body, Missa,' he has told me on more than one occasion, 'but I'm certainly happy with yours and that's what's important.'

I'm afraid I was a very sloppy slave at first, mainly because the feminist part of my brain could not tolerate the term 'slave' or truly take it seriously. I was constantly rebelling in little ways for which my Master punished me patiently but firmly. Very often I would slip something on without his permission only a few moments after he returned home, as though greeting him naked was only a perfunctory chore that once performed I could sweep under the carpet because it didn't really mean anything. My attitude was all wrong at times; the slightest comment or incident would set off a combative tone in me disguised as my God-given right to express my opinion, but it was really impatience and mistrust. At last I got it through my head that my Master was not trying to suppress my opinion on things, he simply wanted me to learn to express them respectfully, and to understand when it was actually important to do so, which is a far cry from just being tense and petulant all the time. Never before in my life had I met a person whose judgment I trusted as much, or more, than my own, and it took me a long time to surrender this tense control I had always needed to have over everything to protect myself. Now my Master takes care of me. It pains me to remember how often I underestimated him by unconsciously expecting him to behave as other men had in the past, which inevitably meant disappointing and hurting me in the end. It is truly dismaying to look back and see just how long it took my psyche to claw out of the wreckage of past associations into the open and luminous relationship I have with Stinger. There were more parts of my emotional being that had been hurt, nearly crushed, than I had believed, and they all needed time to heal beneath the patient application of my Master's genuinely deep love and respect for me. It took me a little over a year, but finally the beautiful Missa my Master saw in me from the beginning became fully entrenched in MIP's psyche 24/7. It was far from easy getting to the point inside me where I was able to make this entry in my journal, but it was more than worth the effort:

I was thinking that I missed being regularly tied up and flogged when I realized that if my Master was forced to bind me and beat me all the time in order to keep me in line he would be serving me and I would be a useless slave to him. The purpose of the initial period of literal training was to impress upon me the fact that my will is always subject to his now because I belong to him absolutely. I have learned to trust him to always know what is best for us, so I hold myself in whatever position he puts me in since ropes and cuffs only symbolize the power his desires have over me, and the emotional pain of displeasing him by failing to serve him gracefully – without flinching no matter what frightening commands he inflicts upon me – is mysteriously deeper than any physical pain can ever be. I am bound to my Master 24/7 in that pleasing him in any way possible is all I really think about. For me happiness is being with him; I believe I was made to feel his hard cock in my body and his love in my soul even when he is deep in another woman's hole for his fulfilment is indistinguishable from my own.

My Master and I attended the private fetish party in John's home. I thought the lighting left a lot to be desired – plain-old electricity as opposed to atmospheric candles and torches that would help fill the room with enigmatically interesting shadows. Instead there were just a bunch of normal people sitting or standing around talking, the only difference being they were wearing fetish clothing. The whole affair was disappointing. My Master and I had cherished the secret hope that since it was a private home some of the guests might choose to indulge in public sex as well as floggings, but it never happened. There were some decidedly interesting and revelatory moments though. I was wearing my black vinyl dress with a faux violet fur, extreme high-heels and of course my collar. I loved it when my Master led me around on a leash, forcing me to follow a few steps behind him, which gave me the opportunity to admire the long hair flowing down his back and his tight ass in black vinyl pants. It made me so happy to know he was proudly showing me off to everyone as his possession, for a beautiful woman's absolute love and submission is a priceless treasure only a true man can handle. For a while, I knelt on the floor at his feet in a traditional display of Master and slave etiquette, but most of the time he let me sit beside him on the comfortable black leather couch, from which we observed another Master beating his slave beside us. She was naked except for a tiny thong panty (disappointingly enough she had also taken off her extreme high-heels) and she was clearly relishing the hot pain rushing through her gorgeous body. Her full breasts quivered beneath every blow while her tight ass absorbed them stoically and her reddish hair tumbled around her face, but it wasn't necessary to see her expression to gauge her reaction to her Master's increasingly violent assault. It seemed to me he was becoming much too hard on her, pulling out different-sized paddles he slammed down across her flushed cheeks with such force she collapsed against the cushions. She promptly pushed herself back up, but it became increasingly difficult for her to do so as the pain and heat climaxed inside her. She was falling into that mysterious trance I kept observing and yet still doubting. Soon she began swooning after every blow and he had to slip an arm around her to hold her up, until he finally had mercy on her and stopped.

The Master and his ritually deferential slave from the Aqua Lounge were there, and I enjoyed watching his performance with the floggers again. BDSM can be an expensive pleasure, however. All the Doms at the party carried their whips and riding crops and floggers in black containers ranging from custom-made mini closets to converted golf club cases. It struck me as a bit preposterous how many different kinds of floggers and other implements of pleasurable torture our host possessed, all proudly displayed in a life-size case in a back room containing nothing else except a raised black-leather platform reminiscent of a doctor's office. My Master closed the door, and we played alone in there for a while. He commanded me to lean over the table with my panties softly shackling my ankles to expose my ass. As a former editor of erotic BDSM novels I always cut out the word 'dripping' in relation to a pussy, but that night I discovered the incredible fact that a pussy actually can drip as I felt mine doing just that in response to the rhythmic, slapping beat of a variety of floggers, critically interspersed with the softly soothing caress of feathers and furs. Even when the material being used bit into my skin and really hurt, the stimulation was so inexorably deep I was never more ready for my Master's dick than when he thrust into me from behind and fucked me urgently for a few moments. I experienced it as a terrible loss when he pulled out of me, but it was true we were crossing a line and we didn't want to overtly disrespect our host and his wife.

Out in the spacious living room, my Master continued testing out different floggers on me, this time with the added stimulus of an audience as I bent over and braced myself on a chair, willingly submitting to the stinging, burning, hauntingly arousing, assault. It was then I experienced my first taste of that trance-like state I kept skeptically witnessing:

I learned at the private fetish party Saturday night that B&D is much more than being rendered physically helpless; it is a trance-like state where my beloved Master truly does master not just my flesh but my whole being. My mind has never been so quiet as during a flogging, and the peace I felt afterwards was both profoundly relaxed and infinitely excited.

I also learned that a pussy really can drip, as mine did.

I learned that I have much to learn and a beautiful state of being to look forward to as Stinger's slave, as Missa leaving behind MIP.

I hated being apart from my Master, but of course we both had work to do, yet some days were more endless than others, and I was happy to realize he could feel the same way when just before we moved in together he sent me this e-mail from his office:

> *'I couldn't stop thinking about you all day, so I went home and finished the floggers and it was better.'*

My Master is very skilled with his hands in every sense, and also extremely intelligent, which means he can make whatever he wants to if it's small enough not to require a workshop. We both agreed the Fetish Factory and other BDSM stores charged ridiculous prices for their clothes and accoutrements, so he made himself a series of floggers with materials we purchased at Michaels and Home Depot. To me they're beautiful not only because they look and feel good, but because my Master made them so they're an extension of him as no store-bought flogger ever could be. They hang in our bedroom now from a metal tool rack and look fabulous.

To say that I love living with my Master is an understatement of astronomical proportions even though I have suffered some painfully frightening moments in my efforts to forge a whole new self in the core of my being, the nature of which I have discovered is my intense love for him. My timelessly romantic imagination already knew what I have had to struggle to incorporate into the mental and emotional being of a woman shaped by all the conflicting perceptions of the late twentieth century. Life isn't necessarily easy even when your blissfully happy, but if you really desire to change yourself inside so that the profoundly beautiful aspects of your soul can shine bright enough to wash out all the imperfections of your limited rational persona, it can be done. Because something else experience has taught me is that nothing happens in life unless you really want it.

There were so many special moments in Wisperwood it's impossible for me to remember them all, but some of the things my Master did to me there stand out in my mind so I'll describe them here... a few strands in a web of love and lust whose corners are lost in the beginning of time...

There was the night my Master made me position myself on the ottoman on all fours with my back arched as deeply as possible, then slipped a riding crop in my mouth and commanded me to bite down on it and sustain that pose while he proceeded to fuck me hard from behind. I somehow managed to absorb the force of his thrusts without my arms giving out, and for some reason the need to hold myself perfectly still for him caused his driving cock to make even more of an impression inside me than usual, maybe because I couldn't move my hips to try and alleviate the rending fullness of his penetrations, or to slightly shift the area of stimulation somewhere else in my pussy and vulva. His hips slammed relentlessly into my statuesque flesh taking it exactly as I got it and, of course, loving it. After he came inside me, he made me keep the riding crop in my mouth while I sustained my pose as though nothing had happened so he could admire me, then finally he pulled the rigid stick out from between my lips and said, 'Well done, Missa.'

There was the night he punished me for insulting him. Did I really call him an arrogant bastard?! We were in the jeep on our way to some party or other and casually discussing evolution vs. Creationists. Suffice it to say that I express myself much more eloquently when I'm writing than when I'm conversing, and I think that we often hear what we expect and fear rather than what is actually being said to us. In the end it turns out we were in agreement – evolution is a fact, but no one can say whether or not there is a divine spark behind life – yet before that happened, because I misunderstood his argument, I called him an arrogant bastard, to my immediate and absolute dismay. I apologized with tears in my eyes, and in fact I couldn't stop crying every time I thought about it all the next day. I did not have to ask to be punished; I deserved and expected and wanted to be severely punished. So my Master set the date and time, and when it arrived he bound me carefully but severely in a position that exposed my soft cheeks to the paddle he had made, and which I hated because it hurt far worse than anything else he ever used on me. This paddle was strictly for punishment, and I can vouch for its effectiveness. But the pain of having insulted and disrespected him was still somehow far worse, and I endured a series of cruel hot smacks across my ass that brought tears of agony to my eyes without protest. The paddle my Master forged is so hard it makes me excruciatingly aware of the bones in my buttocks in a place where I usually feel there is plenty of cushioning flesh. My Master gave me as many blows as I could tolerate, yet I would not have moved a muscle to escape them even if he had not tied me in place. My relief when the punishment finally ceased was so great, I half sobbed with gratitude when he plunged into my slick hot cunt from behind and began violently fucking the burning memory of my pain away into a pleasure so deep, it went beyond the superficially enjoyable sensations of my clitoris. Then he removed the ropes binding me, and helping me to my feet led me to his bathroom. I had no idea what he intended when he commanded me to kneel in front of him in the bathtub, but when he gripped his cock in his hand I opened my mouth to suck him. 'No,' he said, which would have seriously confused me if I had been thinking straight, which I wasn't… I loved the trance-like state I fell into whenever my Master beat me and then used my body for his pleasure… I gasped, overwhelmed by equal measures of shock and excitement as the hot stream of his urine suddenly hit my chest, and flowed down my body as he slowly peed all over my breasts and shoulders. He had never done this before and I couldn't believe how good and natural it felt; it made me feel warm and wonderful to kneel beneath the fountain of my beloved Master's urine, and I had to admit it was the perfect culmination to my punishment for calling him an arrogant bastard. (On another occasion, strictly for pleasure, he had me kneel in the tub again while he peed all over my face as I kept my eyes and mouth closed relishing the hot pulses of his piss baptizing my features.)

There were the countless times when he performed my anal training kneeling behind me where I crouched in the sleen position on my bed so I could watch him in one of the many mirrors he had put up in our bedroom. No words can describe how beautiful he looked to me while he was fucking my ass, how much I loved the expression on his face mysteriously lubricating my sphincter, so that after the initial slow and careful penetration he was able to slide his thickening cock in and out of me faster and harder, until he was pounding into my tight hole, his penis growing and expanding as he approached his climax stabbing me full of his pleasure so I thought I would die it felt so terribly good. I am proud to say that recently my Master was able to fuck my ass twice in one night, minutes after shooting his first load into my rectum, and I don't know why but I seem to love it more every time.

There was the evening he made me lie naked on my back in the middle of his king-size water bed, then spread my legs and tied them over my head so he could go down on me. My hands were free to caress my breasts or rest on his head, but there was nothing I could do to escape his tongue. No man has ever pleased me so much this way as my Master always does. It's as though he senses my body's most subtle responses to his licks and probes, and so knows exactly where to go and when, as well as how long to concentrate his efforts in one place before moving on. It was always hard for me to come through oral sex until I met Stinger, and I can still hardly believe how swiftly he is able to coax a climax out of me this way. That evening his lips and tongue were effective enough, so when he brought his fingers into play, gradually working them into my slick pussy more swiftly and deeply, the pleasure was almost too much for me. My hips writhed against the bed and I pushed his face into my cleft as my flesh screamed for release, yet he deliberately kept me on the edge. When he at last had mercy on me and focused his hunger on my clitoris, I suffered what I can honestly say was the most intense orgasm of my life. The excruciatingly intense ecstasy lasted a long, long time as I came and came in his mouth feeling as though I was dying and my body was catching a blinding glimpse of heaven. Afterwards, I felt weak in the knees and wonderfully at peace, as though a good percentage of my thoughts had been burned away leaving only the relaxed perceptions of my deepest sensual self.

There were the countless times my Master impulsively opened his pants and fucked me after I sucked him for a while. I was constantly sinking to my knees in every room to practice my oral skills on his beloved penis, and to my delight I was apparently doing a good job of it because I always made him erect fast, and was rewarded for my efforts by being fucked hard in whatever position he desired.

There were the nights when he bent me over the back of the couch, naked except for my official collar and a pair of extreme high-heels, and flogged me for a long time before he fucked me from behind. There was no doubt left in my mind about the trance-like state I had witnessed other slaves falling into. I am seldom more at peace, my thoughts temporarily drowned in the hot wet depths of my pussy, than while my Master is beating me and caressing me and finally penetrating me; priming my body for his rampant erection with contrasting sensations that stimulate my nerve-endings to torch-like peaks in the haunting darkness of my submissive sensuality. It makes no rational sense whatsoever that being physically abused in a ritually controlled sense turns me on, but the fact is it does. My sex gets so hot and deep I feel as though my Master is plunging us back in time through his penetrations to a realm of ancient mysteries our modern brains have lost touch with but can still catch a glimpse of in the sub-culture of bondage and domination.

There were the times we fucked watching a porno movie in the bedroom, in which my Master had set up a second entertainment system designed strictly for erotic stimulation. There was always an X-rated movie in the VCR and mood music in the CD player.

There was the night he blindfolded me and made me obey the lightest touch of his riding crop, which punished me with biting licks if I failed to properly sense which way it wanted me to move.

There was the evening my Master told me to go find a blanket. When I returned with a big ivory-colored flannel blanket in my arms, he told me to stand before him where he sat on the loveseat and wrap it around my naked body as he watched. I obeyed, and then he told me to open it slowly. 'Mm,' he said, 'I love looking at you naked' and as he gazed at them, my curves felt even softer and warmer against the soft, cool blanket. 'Come here,' he commanded quietly, and sat me on his lap like a little girl with her daddy. I lay back contentedly, resting in his arm and against the arm of the couch, as he reached into the blanket and began playing with my pussy. He fingered my labia, firmly and steadily, almost roughly, teasing me with the presence of his bunched fingers at the entrance to my hot opening already aching to be penetrated. I felt happy and relaxed as a baby full of a bottomless yet also somehow innocent desire. He cradled me in his arms like that, half wrapped in the flannel blanket, for a long time while I basked in the tenderness of his love and the strength of his protection, for I knew my Master would always take care of me.

Then there were nights when we just went out to play pool with some of our friends. I usually liked to sit and watch since I had never played before and everyone else was very good at the game, and one evening made a particular impression on me:

Everything at the pool hall last night struck me as so alive and so sensual and I felt so blessed to be there out of my writer's shell… the sharp clicking of the balls, their vivid colors, the tides of sound, the mist of cigarette smoke… the shafts of the pool sticks and the cosmic beds of the green tables all spelled life to me, and I was so happy to be there and not sitting alone at home dreaming of a man like Stinger.

After I returned to the table from the bathroom, my Master walked up to me, slipped his arm around my waist, and kissing me asked, 'Where did you go? I missed you.'

I was sure it couldn't get any better than that, but then he did it again the next time I left and came back.

'Where do you keep going?' he said, holding me and kissing me again. 'I keep missing you.'

The last fetish party we attended in Florida was by far the most enjoyable. The venue was a strip club on other nights, and a series of very small rooms designed for lap dances were put to good use by couples like my Master and me. I was wearing my school girl outfit with my shirt open to expose my pierced nipples, between which dangled a fine silver chain hung with a tiny Gothic cross. As we wandered around the club I picked up a devoted follower in the form of a skinhead man who kept telling my Master how lucky he was whenever he passed us. I enjoyed dancing for my Master, and with him, and watching kinky performances including a slender woman in a black vinyl cat-suit with a strategically placed zipper and a latex-clad man eating her out on stage. I especially liked it when my Master locked me up in a narrow cage and then kissed me through the black wrought-iron bars. For some reason it was highly stimulating to have my body imprisoned while my tongue enjoyed the full freedom of wandering and exploring inside his mouth, dancing passionately and energetically with his. We did a lot of kissing that night, and I did a lot of sucking. My Master fucked me in one of the back rooms once or twice to a teasingly small but nevertheless stimulating audience, but they were fetish people, not Swingers, and disappointingly skittish. One couple even made it clear they did not want to be watched, which made me wonder why they were going at it in a little room open to the public. None of this stopped my Master, of course; I spent a good part of the night sitting in front of him clinging to his black vinyl pants as I sucked his dick. Towering over me, he grabbed my head and moved it upon and down over his penis, gently gagging me with his semi-soft length for a good thirty minutes. I wasn't wearing panties beneath my school girl skirt, and I could feel the hot touch of stranger's eyes on my pussy as I sat with my legs invitingly spread. I couldn't see anything except my Master's crotch, but he told me later that one man watched us the whole time, and afterwards in the bathroom said fervently, 'Thanks, man, you're a god!'

Semen shining like dissolved starlight on my lips, I thought, There's nothing like fleshing out your dreams and making them reality.

The night before his ten day plant collecting trip to Africa (which I spent weeks dreading because we had never yet been apart) my Master sent me this e-mail to open after he left, the subject Tasks in my absence:

Missa,
I will be away for ten days and I will miss you although I know that our love keeps us bound and together and that will override any

feelings of sadness or worry. You must always remember that all of the progress that you have made is yours and can never be taken away by anything. You are my one and only slave and I am very proud of you. Now it is time for you to run our household by yourself while I am travelling. I expect you to maintain the efficient and comfortable household that we have and to maintain a positive and productive attitude. You will also continue your training at all times. In this light I have outlined some specific tasks for you below.

1 You will ALWAYS wear your collar whenever you are in the house alone and awake.
2 You will wear your slave uniform for at least 4 hours per day.
3 You will perform some specific tasks listed below. You may schedule them as you wish.

Prepare 2 meals that you will again later prepare for me when I return. These will be sensual meals infused with sensual symbolism. You will write a brief description of each and email them to me on the days the meals are to be prepared after my return.
Take at least 48 photos of yourself for me. You may determine the costume lighting and venues. At least 2 should be outside.
You will call and speak on the telephone to at least 5 different people other than me. These are social calls, not business. One call should be to a person or couple that we have or potentially have a sexual interest in. You will write down all of the details of that conversation for me. This is not a command to have a sexual experience, only to discuss one that we may share.
You will explore the Internet for fellatio and hand stimulation techniques to use on my cock. You will become proficient in at least

one new technique and be ready to use it upon my return. You may practice on your dildos.
You will find a painless and non-damaging way to insert your but plug and dildo, one at a time, in both your anus and pussy and to hold them in each for 10 min. You may use condoms, lotions etc.
Finally, you will get to the airport to meet me upon my return. You need not have a ride, I can provide return transportation. You need only get yourself there.

I love you my dear slave Missa,

Stinger

A few endless days after he left, in which I kept hearing Shakespeare's Juliet in my head saying "for in a minute there are many days" I wrote in my journal:

Please, Lords, keep my Master safe for the sake of our love and all the beauty it is capable of… Stinger, my beautiful Master, going away for ten nights and nine days, has – like everything else we have done together – shown me how much we love each other and deepened our bond… I realize now MIP, creature of comfort and fear, is almost gone. It's all about loving and living, every moment, every day… This is the hardest task my Master has ever set me – to be without him for nearly two weeks.

I received an e-mail from my Master when he arrived in Africa:

Hi Beautiful,
We made it to Bulawayo and went out on a game drive at Matopos

park . We're staying in town tonight and going out to the ranch tomorrow. I love you and I miss you - thinking of you always.
Cheers,
Stinger

I spent a lot of time writing in my journal while my Master was gone, struggling with the demons of fear, terrified of losing him in a plane crash or some other meaningless accident so soon after meeting him:

You can never really know anything for sure. All you can really know is how much you love someone.

Living well, being in love and reflecting on the mystery of existence through creativity are more important than any specific activities or actual achievements.

I kept remembering the things my Master had said to me as I slept in his bed every night and did everything he had told me to do:

'I love you, Missa. I know you've heard it before, but you've never heard it the way I'm saying it to you now. And always remember that whatever we do is peripheral to how much I love you'...'We have each other. There's US, and there's the rest of the world.'

13 Dancing Another Dimension

Cuddling on the loveseat one night, I gazed up at Stinger's beautiful face and said, 'There must be an easier way to feed my Master.' Part of me felt very much like a lioness longing to bring him a fresh kill – a delectable young woman I could delight in watching him use for his pleasure along with me in a sensual feast. In an ideal world, no other man would ever have to be involved; he was the only man who could ever truly interest me, all others would inevitably be disappointing. But how exactly could I go about finding an attractive single woman willing to play with a couple? There was certainly no such creature wandering the carpeted paths of Miami Velvet, and my Master and I decided it was high time we tried another club. The most promising alternative was nearly an hour's drive away, but how tired we were of Velvet made the trek feel worth it.

Plato's Repeat was a much smaller venue, but right away I appreciated it's more tasteful black marble bar, leather couches, lamps and wooden dance floor, a décor evocative of a gentleman's club rather than a disco.

My Master and I chose to go there on a Sunday night our first time since it was free, and we felt like a relaxing evening together. It was BYOB, the food was free and we had a pool table all to ourselves in the tasteful lounge. We were sitting at the bar along with a handful of other people when I noticed a pretty young woman. I pointed out to my Master that she appeared to be alone, which might present a good opportunity for us, a possibility I found at once promising and frightening.

'Mm... I like the way you think, Missa.'

Part of me was energized by the hope of catching her for my Master, another part of me was nearly blinded by jealousy at the mere thought of helping the man I loved pick another woman up at a bar. I was torn between eyeing her covetously and angrily ignoring her.

'You know, Stinger,' I said tightly, 'a lot of people would see my agreeing to Swing with you as a way for you to cheat on me with my permission.'

He masterfully controlled his anger as he replied quietly, 'Missa, cheating on you would be a lot easier than this. If I wanted to cheat on you, I could easily do it, and you'd never know it. That's not what this is about.'

'You're right, I'm sorry.'

'We don't have to do anything. You're the one who keeps bringing up other women, not me. I love you, Missa. Even if it takes years until you feel you're ready for that, it doesn't matter. I love you. Don't you have any idea yet how much I love you and what you mean to me?'

They say three times is the charm; after hearing him say 'I love you' three times the paralyzing spell of my fear and jealousy were magically broken, and I was able to relax for the rest of the night, towards the end of which we went to play in the hot tub room. The single girl we had seen earlier had hooked up with a single guy, and they were kissing in the Jacuzzi. By now my Master and I were both naked beneath the white towels we discarded as I sank to my hands and knees on the cushions so he could penetrate me from behind. A handsome, powerfully built black man was also sitting in the water, and though he had obviously been stalking the other girl, he now turned all his attention on me. I felt my sensuality blooming beneath his penetrating stare and lifted myself up, pressing my body back against my Master so this other man could more fully admire my pierced breasts and the heavy Gothic cross hanging between them, the cold, hard feel of which mysteriously accentuated the soft nakedness of the rest of my body. My Master's hot thrusts combined with another man's coolly penetrating regard made me feel intensely beautiful and mysteriously bottomless, as though I could take as much hard cock as I got, and my excitement deepened as the single guy and girl in the hot tub stopped kissing to look at us. It was as though they were all mesmerized by the sight of Stinger and me fucking, and I experienced a rush of power upstaging the pretty girl who was obviously up for grabs with my unavailable yet irresistible presence. It was as though we were weaving a sexual spell...

Very soon the black man and the girl were talking, her original partner left out as my Master sat on the edge and I got into the tub to suck his cock for a while. I was very aware of the other woman's appealingly slim and pert-breasted body so near to mine in the water, and felt drawn towards it like a magnet I shyly resisted for a few minutes while I concentrated possessively on my Master's erection. But it was as though I was a dancer fighting choreography I longed to follow, and finally I just let myself do what I had been aching to... I reached over and very lightly caressed the girl's breasts where they bobbed just above the water. She had her eyes closed, as though she had sensed my desire to approach her and was making it easier for me, as well as for herself. She kept her eyes closed as I stroked her more boldly, startled by how much I enjoyed it, but I wasn't stopping to think; I was gladly surrendering to an exquisite current of desire and pleasure coming effortlessly together as a sense of grace and beauty we were all embodying as I began leading the sensual dance, and everyone followed everyone else in breathtaking rhythm. It's impossible for me to remember exactly how things happened, but it became obvious the girl had abandoned her initial partner in favor of the muscular black man, whose forceful eye contact with me soon translated into a slow, sensual kiss as I leaned over her body towards him while she made an effort to suck his big dick. I felt as though we were introducing ourselves without words and expressing very deep things about ourselves it would otherwise take years to learn as we kissed gently, almost reverently. Before this I had tentatively kissed her, and she had seemed even more of a novice to bisexual pleasures than I was, which I found appealing. Then my Master was sitting on the edge of the tub again and I had somehow hypnotized her into moving towards him with me, temporarily abandoning her partner. With her eyes closed again she let me slowly but inexorably float her body through the water towards my Master and slip the head of his penis between her lips.

'Oh yes,' he whispered, and even though his erection was much too big for her small mouth, I relished every second I watched her struggling to suck him down and please him with her tongue. My Master later described to me how the other two men watched him in astonishment, because not only had he come to the club with a beautiful woman, she had willingly recruited another girl to help her please him.

The four of us ended up out of the water on the cushions with the rejected guy watching from the tub in desperately hopeful frustration. My Master began fucking me from behind again, and the powerfully built black man penetrated his milk-white partner, who also knelt submissively on her hands and knees facing me. I kissed her and fondled her firm little breasts, but she was too overwhelmed by the big black dick sliding in and out of her tight little cunt to respond in kind. She kept mumbling dirty phrases like, 'Oh yeah, fuck my pussy with your big cock!' and I found myself lying on my back with my face beneath her breasts sucking hungrily on her nipples as my Master pounded into me. Once or twice I looked up and saw him cheek-to-cheek with the girl as their long hairs merged, both their features cast even more beautifully by the look of rapture on their faces as they kissed breathlessly.

'Oh Missa!' my Master gasped, collapsing against me as he climaxed deep inside me. I think the other man came at the same time, and the slow sensual dance that had built up to a passionate tempo pulsed to a profoundly satisfying end. Stinger rose and took my hand to help me up, but before we left I sank down into the hot tub again and kissed the young man who had been left out. 'You're sweet,' I told him, in that moment sincerely meaning it, although I suppose my gesture was rather cruel since for a split second he hoped it was his turn to have fun now.

My Master and I returned to our locker to dress, and walking past the bar on our way out, we saw the new couple we had played with standing together. She was still naked except for a sexy pair of white silk panties, and he had the requisite white towel wrapped around his lean hips. I experienced a rush of fondness for them, and they seemed to return the feeling as we all hugged affectionately. I'll call her Linn and her new friend Darren. She and I exchanged e-mail addresses before my Master and I left the club feeling wonderfully content. I was somewhat surprised, and very happy, that we had enjoyed each other so much without the need for a full swap, which my Master told me Darren had clearly been willing to go for, but he had thought it best not to indulge with a third man hovering around desperately wanting in on the action. I was disappointed to hear this was the reason we had stayed together, and sensing my reaction, he laid his hand on my thigh as we drove away.

'Besides, I was perfectly happy just to be with you, Missa,' he added. 'You were beautiful tonight, dear. You were every man's dream, and I loved fucking you knowing you were mine and that they all wanted you.'

At Plato's Repeat Sunday night, I finally truly broke through my mental barriers and fears and became Missa.

I have never felt so sexy and so relaxed and free of tension. I enjoyed every moment. It was like a slow-motion sensual dance with every movement naturally choreographed. Everything I did I did because it felt good. It was not a task, a chore, to please my Master; it was pure pleasure. I felt my power, a combination of my physical looks and the beauty of my soul, which is sensitive to others and their feelings and loves them. Swinging can be a way to connect with people that transcends society and the mind.

I felt so good yesterday on Monday. The experience turned off a tense, controlling part of me. It was like bathing in a purifying sensual sea in which I had nothing to be afraid of because Stinger truly loves me and protects me. He will never let sharks get to me, or dunk my head and feelings into something I don't want and force me to drown in it. He said he could see it in me, that look in my eyes. When I become Missa, I am in control, but in the relaxed beautiful way of dancing, and my Master and I follow each other's leads gracefully.

I mentally rebel at the thought of Swinging because you enter another sensual, fluid dimension where a part of you cannot go and is therefore frightened of. You touch upon another level of being that is at once lower, more animalistic, and higher, a pure expression of the soul's unbound sensuality.

I'll never forget the way my Master said, 'Oh Missa...' as he was coming inside me while I was lying with my face beneath the other girl's breasts. After that he told me, 'I loved fucking you there surrounded by people who all wanted to fuck you knowing you were all mine.'

At the bar earlier he told me fervently three times, 'I love you so much' and it was the charm that brought Missa to life.

I felt more relaxed and peaceful the day after our Sunday night at Plato's Repeat than I could ever remember being, and I was all for returning to our new club again the following weekend, this time on Saturday night. The place was crowded with couples, theoretically presenting all sorts of stimulating possibilities, but in reality I didn't see a single pair who moved me. It didn't matter, however, because Linn was there, by herself. After my Master and I had played with each other a good long time in a private room, as well as in the bigger play area – more interesting than Velvet's because it was surrounded by mirrors and the mattresses were elevated to different levels, providing for a better view of the action – we found ourselves in the hot tub room with our pretty new friend. We sat around the Jacuzzi modestly wrapped in our white towels, our feet in the water, talking. I waited for myself to become jealous, but it never happened. In fact, I felt so relaxed I left her alone with Stinger for a few minutes while I went to the bathroom.

When I returned, I sat between them again, and for a few more minutes pretended to be interested in hearing about her cat and her apartment, etc. Then I casually removed my towel and coaxed her into the water with me. My Master continued to sit placidly on the edge of the tub, but he was naked now too, and as I began sucking his cock, it didn't take me long to illicit Linn's help with my efforts. Even though she didn't have a clue what she was doing, I experienced a rush of triumphant happiness that I was giving my Master the pleasure of being served by two girls at once. We had an audience in the form of two older couples lounging around on the other side of the small room, but I was only peripherally aware of the women reflecting the action in the water by bending over their partners' laps; my entire being was concentrated on the goal of getting my Master's cock into Linn's hole. I remember murmuring encouragements to her as she protested weakly, telling me that she and Darren were becoming serious about each other and she didn't want to cheat on him, and I assured her he would want her to do this as I kept my Master's impressive erection temptingly in her face.

'He's so big...' she whispered, and I knew I had her. She could not resist the desire, the mysterious honor, of feeling such an impressively large penis inside her. I gently turned her around in the water so Stinger could step into the tub behind her even as he slipped on a condom. She kept saying she shouldn't do this even as she bent over and braced herself on the edge, and then it was too late as he penetrated her, gripping her hips and swiftly taking possession of her cunt with his rending hard-on, transforming her half-hearted murmurs of protest into helpless gasps of pleasure.

I couldn't believe I was watching the man I loved fuck another woman right in front of me and that I was feeling only an intense satisfaction untainted by jealousy (which is more than I can say about the people watching from the other side of the room). I circled behind my Master, observing his erection pumping into another pussy from every possible angle, while he kept his eyes on my face almost the whole time as we smiled at each other.

'Do you want to come inside her?' I asked him, thinking I might as well cross yet another terrifying threshold tonight since I was feeling so good and confident.

'Oh no, I'm not even close,' he replied a bit breathlessly but very firmly, and it thrilled me to know he was not having to make any effort at all to save his orgasm for me.

He fucked Linn hard and fast, keeping his erection deep inside her as she moaned beneath his uncompromising thrusts, and I wished I could get a better view of his big cock surging in and out of her little slot just above the surface of the water.

'Does that feel good,' I asked her, reaching down to caress her taut breasts and then slipping my hand down towards her clit. 'Would you like to come, sweetie?'

Her only response were soft cries as the forceful dimensions of my Master's erection relentlessly ramming into her pelvis overwhelmed her. I don't know how long he banged her before he suddenly pulled out, and we all stepped out of the hot tub together and onto the more comfortable cushions surrounding it. He sat down and leaned back against a wall with his legs stretched out in front of him, and I perched beside him as he made Linn face him and crouch down over his dick with her legs spread open on either side of her. She was doing all the work now as I lay back and enjoyed the show of Stinger's rigid shaft forcing her shaved little cleft open around it. Her delicate labia was flushed a pretty pink around the cool pale rubber sheathing him as she leaned back on her arms to keep moving her hips up and down, and it pleased me to know she was making a considerable effort to keep quickly stabbing herself with my Master's towering erection. I was lying back against some cushions a few feet away caressing myself in the hope that my own personal porno film would start turning me on more than it was actually doing physically. It didn't matter though, because it was all about how fulfilled I felt to be able to arrange this pleasure for my Master without experiencing any emotional pain; any physical pleasure I achieved would just be an added bonus.

'Missa, come here,' he said.

I quickly moved so I was sitting pressed up beside him, and watching his thumb working Linn's clit as she rode him seemed to have more of an affect on me than on her.

'So, are you two married?' she asked breathlessly.

'We're more than married,' my Master replied, and a few moments later added, 'It's your turn now, Missa.'

Before I knew it, I was face down on the cushions with his naked hard-on pulsing and swelling deep in my pussy as Linn watched, stroking herself and talking dirty, 'Oh yeah, I want to see you come inside her, come on...' I was touching myself too, and I came wonderfully close to climaxing with my Master. I loved the feel of his long hair mingling with mine as he buried my body beneath his, so I felt the explosion of ecstasy reaching as if to the core of both our bodies as he suffused my innermost self with the hot essence of being.

The Monday after our landmark Saturday night at Plato's, I sent my Master this e-mail at work:

I'm getting so hot , Master, I can't stop thinking about you... and about how next time my Master and I fuck another girl I would like to put your condom on and hold and caress your erection as I guide it slowly inside her... I would like to spread myself out beneath her and lick and suck your balls as you fuck her from behind... I would like to stand behind you and move my hips in time with your hips to feel how together we are deep inside... I would like her to spread herself on her back on top of me so I can play with her breasts and you can lean over and kiss them and then kiss me and then all three of our tongues can play together while you fuck her pussy with your cock and at the same time fuck my pussy with your hand... I would like to watch you come while she sucks you down and I lick your ass, then I would love to watch you pulling out of her mouth and feel you coming all over my face and breasts...

There's a lot more I would love, but I have to get back to work now,

Master. I hope you're feeling good.

Purrrrrrrrrrrrrrrrrrrrrrrrrrrrrrr,

Missa

And he replied:

Now I'm getting really hot dear. I love the images, I have had amazingly similar fantasies myself, lets makes them cum true. You're such a turn on and I love you.

S

When I asked him what his favorite part about Swinging with Linn had been, he said, 'The look in your eyes the whole time, Missa.'

We visited Plato's Repeat on two or three more occasions before we left Miami. One quiet Sunday evening we found ourselves playing a friendly game of pool with a young Latin couple. Only the girl spoke any English, but being fluent in Spanish myself, I was able to communicate with her appealingly shy and handsome partner. We all ended up in the hot tub together, of course, where I sat on the edge caressing by pretty new boy toy's shoulders before boldly moving my hand down to his handsome cock as his girlfriend energetically sucked my Master down just above the water. There was no danger of anything except hot water rushing into her mouth, because it is nearly impossible to make my Master climax orally, and I have yet to see him come inside another woman. She was a plump young lady who looked better naked than in the tight clothing she had been wearing, and I suggested we all adjourn to a private room. I personally don't like fucking in a Jacuzzi. I have a hard enough time coming as it is without water dulling my vaginal and clitoral sensations, and I found a mirror-framed bed much more to my liking. There was only one problem – the young man was so excited he couldn't stay erect. In contrast, my Master could not have been harder, and he fucked me passionately as the girl sucked her boyfriend into functional firmness again. Then she spread herself on her back with her face beneath me where I was crouched on my hands and knees taking it from behind, and I heard my Master groan appreciatively as she licked his penis and my pussy at the same time while her boyfriend fucked her desperately.

As we shifted positions, I gave my Master a conspiratorial smile and told the girl he wanted to fuck her now. She appeared willing, and I asked her boyfriend in Spanish if he wanted me to suck him down using a condom. He said, 'Si', but I never had a chance to slip the chocolate-flavored rubber on his penis because it wilted again, and Stinger wasted his own condom as the girl turned towards her struggling lover and considerately devoted herself to his needs. Then she suddenly got her period, and we crawled, perspiring profusely, out of the unventilated room and said a polite, if rather frustrated, good bye. Yet it was an important encounter for me. I had found myself Swinging with a light, carefree heart, untroubled by the thought of a full swap knowing it would turn my Master on to watch me being taken by another man while he penetrated another girl. It's very important to me what a man looks and feels like, and that Latin boy was so sweet and clean and beautiful, taking his young cock into my pussy would have been an effortless task for me. It may be all about pleasing my Master, but doing so should not be an unpleasant chore for me, either, which goes hand-in-hand with the fact that it is more enjoyably stimulating for him to watch my body being possessed by a man physically worthy of such a gift.

Our last Saturday night at Plato's I saw a young man who made me think of Jim Morrison in the company of an attractive blonde woman. The club was packed with bodies, but I caught a few glimpses of them as we walked around, after which I told my Master, 'They're interested in us.' Stinger can be quite humble at times, and he thought I was only imagining their attraction to us. We were standing at the bar wrapped in our white towels, and I was having another shot of tequila with salt and lime, when the blonde suddenly appeared beside me, right beside me, pressing her naked body against mine while her partner stepped up just behind me. I gave my Master an I told you so smile and we proceeded to get to know them. The woman was a stripper who could afford extremely expensive bottles of tequila, one of which she proceeded to share with us even as she literally forced me to take my towel off. I was still a bit shy and uncertain about my body at the time, but the way they both looked me up and down as I exposed myself went a long way to boosting my self-confidence.

'Beautiful,' he murmured. At this point he was standing on my left with his girl friend on my other side and Stinger just behind her, so that we were all as close to each other as possible. My admirer was so handsome I found myself shamelessly drawn to him, and just a bit dismayed by how much time I spent looking at his face instead of back at my Master. During one such glance I saw Stinger caress the blonde's lithe body, but I was distracted again when her partner cupped my soft pierced mounds in his hands and breathed, 'They're like brand new breasts!' squeezing and kissing them in awe of their firm round perfection. His girl friend also seemed more interested in my body than in Stinger's, but by then I was so deliciously wasted I didn't really care. I was having a great time, until we all inevitably ended up around the Jacuzzi, where I suffered the sight of my Master bending over to hungrily eat the stripper's shaved little pussy where she sat on the edge of the tub with her legs spread wide open. I didn't feel good about it at all, and my distress was compounded when she essentially commanded me to lick her. As my Master smilingly yielded his place to me, I was tempted to obey her despite myself, but I resisted.

'I can't,' I muttered.

'Why can't you?' she asked a bit peremptorily while her boyfriend urged me on more kindly but just as intently, standing beside me in the water fervently caressing me.

I looked desperately to my Master for help, but none was forthcoming. All he said was, 'Tell her, Missa.'

'Because I have a slight cut on the side of my lip,' I muttered.

'Oh really, and what's that from?' she asked suspiciously.

'From eating a Cuban sandwich,' I replied truthfully. 'The toasted bread was really sharp and hard and cut the side of my mouth a little.' I removed myself from between her slender thighs, buffeted more by my emotions than the water's hot jets. I didn't like the way this woman was taking control of everyone, and I relished the situation even less when I found myself submitting to her determined oral attentions as my Master honored her with his and her boyfriend hungrily kissed my mouth and breasts. Then, without warning, he lost control and tried to penetrate me without a condom. I shoved him away with a cry. My Master tells me he also pushed him away at the same time, assuring me that even though his tongue had been working on the stripper's cunt, he had had his eye on me, and was aware of what was going on, the whole time. Nevertheless, I was relieved when she decided we should all walk naked out onto the dance floor crowded with fully dressed people. I must have been seriously inebriated because I didn't feel in the least bit shy as I cavorted naked in public, alternately clinging to one of the three bodies attached to me, always glad when I ended up in my Master's arms again. Not only was I not embarrassed, I found myself making wanton eye contact with another woman's tall, handsome partner, and I was disappointed when she pulled him away to the other side of the room because he kept returning my smiling attention.

We lost track of our new friends, and the next thing I remember is sucking my Master's cock in the large playroom when I was startled to feel someone lovingly caressing my ass from behind. The stripper was back with her cute boyfriend, and I submissively asked my Master if he wanted to fuck her. He obviously did because he promptly reached for a condom, but she abruptly stood up and cried, 'Who needs another woman?!' She received several responses, and my Master and I found ourselves alone with her abandoned partner, who eyed me with hopeful despondency. Feeling sorry for him (and yes, I was also angry and upset with Stinger for immediately having had oral sex with her) I pulled a condom out of my purse and wordlessly offered him the pleasures of my pussy to make him feel better. But it was my Master who took it from me and led me out of the room.

We learned a few lessons that night, including the need to sense when couples aren't really together and avoid them. I also fervently expressed the main conclusion I had come away with, 'As far as oral sex is concerned, Master, I don't believe everyone deserves that honor from us!' and he agreed I perhaps had a point and he should be a bit more discriminating in the future. Nevertheless, I was punished for the angry, sullen way I expressed my opinion on the matter, which always happened when I failed to talk to him about something that was bothering me and let it fester inside me until circumstances made my feelings burst out of me. It's not easy being a hot-blooded Cuban slave.

14 Wrapping Up The Present

I am hauling in a very special kill on Tuesday night, a lovely young woman whose submissive compliance to our desires is a mystery to me that opens up a whole new dimension. All she gets out of it is sensual pleasure, and that seems to be enough for her. We're getting all to ourselves what most couples can only dream of – a pretty girl to play with. I am so proud I have been able to arrange this for my master's pleasure, and mine, because seeing him so empowered and fulfilled will make my soul purr, and this feeling will translate into pure sensuality in my flesh. It will be so nice to have two bodies to please him with, to extend my own sensuality through this other girl. It will be a landmark event, one of those gems of memory that make up the soul's mysterious trousseau. It will be a victory for me over lesser, weaker parts of me, and as a beloved slave whose wonderful Master deserves that she arrange such treats for him. And it comes only a day before we leave for Brazil, where we will be together almost every day for over two weeks. It is such an exciting time for us, and yet that has been the case ever since I met my Master. I am leaving behind the limited dimensions of my past and entering a whole new realm with my Master. He is always telling me how proud he is of me. The more time passes, the less wounded, frightened parts of me sabotage Missa's confidence and happiness. It seems the more people my Master and I interact with, the closer we become.

Why do I think that I'm afraid of everything when the truth is that I'm in love with everything?

Linn was late. The gourmet finger foods my Master and I had purchased together at Wild Oats were laid out on the coffee table along with three empty glasses of champagne waiting to be filled. I was wearing my white and clear extreme high-heels with my black starry minidress and a ritualistic abundance of silver jewellery crowned by my nipple rings. I was afraid she wouldn't show up after all and was relieved when she called from the highway. To say that she was a bit of a flake is an understatement, but that worked in our favour because she hadn't realized how far away we lived when she agreed to come over and play with us. Finally, she rang again from the parking lot and my Master went down to meet her. I was elated, even as part of me could still scarcely believe what was happening. I had willingly, of my own free will, arranged for another woman to enter our home so I could watch the man I loved fucking her!?! And yet, as Stinger kept stressing to me, it was all about us fucking her together, the way we had at the club, but better, in our own space where we could control everything that happened.

Linn had cut her long wavy hair to her shoulders and dyed it red. She looked very different, and in a black vinyl mini skirt and skimpy black lace shirt she looked cheaper than I remembered. Yet I sort of liked that; it was good that she looked like a skinny little tart, because all my Master and I wanted her for was her body. Nevertheless, we were the soul of politeness to her at first, seating her on the couch between us and offering her champagne and gourmet goodies and even allowing her to smoke cigarettes in our living room. It turns out she wasn't much of a drinker, and that she had not yet developed a taste for seafood, so all she did was smoke and chat, smoke and chat, as my Master and I sipped our drinks and pretended to listen attentively.

I was beginning to wonder how we were going to cross the threshold of politeness into a sexual dimension when I saw my Master's fingers gently insinuating themselves beneath her flaming hair and very gently, almost imperceptivity, caressing the back of her neck. She kept on talking nervously, and I watched his hand move to her delicate bare shoulder in fascinated excitement. I was sitting in my own living room watching the man I wanted to spend the rest of my life with seduce another woman, and I was loving it.

'Why don't we take this off?' he suggested, and Linn let him pull her shirt over her head.

I immediately reached over to fondle one of her breasts while my Master played with the other, and it was strangely thrilling to explore another girl's body with him. Then I sat back and suffered the exquisite torment of just watching him kissing and caressing her. He was so beautiful I couldn't get enough of looking at him; just the way his jaw moved as he worked his tongue into her mouth turned me on, as did how much of her slight body his large hand could cover at one time. Then he made her stand up between us so he could pull her skirt down her legs, giving her no choice but to step out of it. All he left her wearing were her come fuck me shoes as he spread her legs apart and looked intently up at her vulva. I waited breathlessly for him to lick her, but he only talked to her in a soothing voice as he fingered her labia, opening her up to his scrutiny, and I realized later he was inspecting her to make sure it was safe to have oral sex. Finally, he took half her little pussy in his mouth and sat sucking and tonguing her for a few moments I found agonizingly delicious as I reached up beneath my dress to stroke my clitoris.

'Now it's your turn,' he told me. 'Take off your dress, Missa.'

I obeyed him, and suffered a stab of jealousy when he stood up and I saw the impressive erection already tenting his black slacks. It seemed to me I had never gotten him that hard so fast. 'Hey, I wanted to do that,' I protested petulantly as he quickly pulled off his pants.

'Too late,' he replied shortly.

His dismissive attitude stoked the jealousy smouldering inside me, but I somehow managed to put it out. I'm very glad I did, and later he explained it was the prospect of fucking both of us that got him so hard so fast, which I had to admit made sense.

Once again, I recruited Linn to help me suck his dick, but she wasn't any better at it than before, and moments later my Master led us both by the hand into the bedroom. I had lit atmospheric oil lamps, placed condoms in strategic locations everywhere, and mood music flowed softly from the stereo. He instructed me to lie on my back across his king size water bed, then he made Linn spread herself on top of me as he knelt on the yielding mattress behind her. I knew when he entered her because she moaned in my ear in response to how swiftly he opened her cunt up around his hard-on. Her pelvis rubbed against mine in a subtly stimulating way as he thrust into her body while passionately kissing me, and I experienced the profound satisfaction of knowing I was doubling my Master's pleasure in everything tonight. He told me to come out from beneath her, and I glanced at our shadowy reflections in a mirror as I knelt on the bed behind him, pressing my body up against his, more than ever loving the warm, smooth texture of his skin against mine. Linn was up on her hands and knees now, and feeling his erection surge back into her pussy, I found myself fucking her with him; moving my hips back and forth in rhythm with his as I fervently stroked my clitoris. I didn't realize how intensely turned on I was until I started coming almost at once. I literally couldn't stop myself from climaxing as I moved back slightly, afraid I was putting too much pressure on him as an orgasm laid waste to my insides for a few glorious seconds. Later, my Master told me he was just as turned on as I was, and that he missed me when I pulled away from him.

After that, Linn requested we take a break so she could smoke another cigarette, and we filed out into the living room again. There was more chatter from her, then my Master was sitting on the couch and I had one high heel perched on the edge as he licked my pussy and Linn blew him. But I knew he couldn't be getting much out of it, so I tried to give her a lesson in fellatio. I'm afraid my efforts were wasted but for the fact that my Master enjoyed them, especially when I crouched on the floor before him and sucked his balls while she laboriously worked the ring of her lips up and down the top half of his erection, unable to get anymore of him into her small mouth.

We were soon back on the bed, where my Master lay on his back so I could sit on his cock as, facing me, Linn struggled to position her sex over his mouth. I helped steady her by cupping her breasts, and his hands rested on my hips as I began working my pussy up and down his shaft while caressing her. The pleasure I felt surprised me, but the longer my beautiful Master's face remained buried in another woman's vulva the less I was able to get into it. He didn't even seem aware of me he was so intent on fucking Linn with his tongue. I didn't realize at the time that he could see me and was loving the sight of my body riding his penis. I must have made my distress known because he told Linn to switch places with me, and soon it was my wet pussy smothering his features as her cleft slid up and down his erection. Everything was fine for a few seconds, then suddenly I panicked when I realized his lips and tongue were coated with her vaginal juices, which were now mingling with mine and making the condoms he wore when he penetrated her redundant. Without warning, I lifted my sex off his face and crawled off the bed.

'Missa?'

'I'll be right back,' I said tightly, and disappeared behind the wall of my dressing area to desperately wipe myself clean with a tissue.

'Oh come on!' I heard Linn say plaintively.

A wonderful feeling of triumph wiped away the fear and despair threatening to possess me. Stepping back into the room, I saw that the action had come to a complete stop in my absence even though I had just heard Linn doing everything in her power to keep it going.

'Is something wrong, Missa?' my Master asked me soberly.

'No, I just had to do something.'

'Are you okay?'

'I'm fine,' I assured him, and the expression in his eyes as he looked up at me with his erection embedded deep inside another woman's body confirms what he told me afterwards – that he felt lost when I abruptly left the room and all he could think until I returned was, What am I doing here?

The next thing I remember is Linn and I lying side by side on the bed, as close together as possible, while my Master fucked her. The pyramid of his arms supporting his weight as he pounded into her pussy encompassed both of us, and I stroked my clitoris gazing rapturously up at his face, which was even more beautifully defined by the overwhelming pleasure of possessing two women at once. We kissed each other passionately as Linn looked on placidly, and I don't think I ever loved and desired him more than I did as I caressed strands of his soft hair behind his shoulders so it didn't get in the way.

'Can you feel my pussy milking your cock?' Linn asked him, dirty talk being her forte; the rest of the time she was listless as a fuck puppet.

'Oh, yes!'

'Do you like fucking my pussy?'

'I love fucking both of you...'

'Oh yes, Master,' I gasped, 'yes... oh, yes...' I couldn't feel his penis inside me, but I could feel his pleasure as his hips pumped vigorously against her just beside me, and as it escalated, so did mine. I spread my legs wider almost literally feeling myself penetrated by the invisible force of his ecstasy as I stroked my clitoris to another blindingly powerful orgasm. It was as though I was mysteriously possessed by his pleasure. 'I don't know what's wrong with me,' I said afterwards, laughing breathlessly, 'I just can't seem to stop coming.'

My Master, however, was saving his climax for me, and it was a longed for moment when he penetrated my pussy at last. He fucked me just as hard as he had fucked Linn, yet I struggled with the terrible feeling that I was only second best; that it excited him more to be inside her because her cunt was relatively new and fresh and different from the one he had access to day in and day out. He has since made it clear to me it is ridiculous for me to feel this way because he loves me and he loves fucking me and I am never second best, on the contrary, and not only because mine is the only pussy he gets to feel without a condom. It goes much deeper than that, but at the time I was afraid my vagina was not as tight and enjoyable to him as Linn's had been, so I offered him my anus, secure in the knowledge that no pussy could ever grip him as tightly as my sphincter. And so my Master finally climaxed in my ass, his penis so unbelievably hard my moans of excruciating fulfillment filled Linn's mouth as she kissed me in sympathy.

Afterwards the three of us lay side by side on the bed watching Sensual Exposure (one of the most tasteful adult films ever made) without sound, and I wondered at the way the music emanating from the stereo synchronized with the action as Linn smoked and chatted, asking us questions about ourselves my Master provided monosyllabic, contentedly relaxed, answers to. Then at last she announced she had to get up early to go to work in the morning so she would be leaving shortly. I was pleased to hear it since she had more than served her purpose and I wanted my Master all to myself again now. She smoked another cigarette while putting her clothes back on, and then she was out the door and my Master and I were back in his bed, where he fucked my pussy again passionately, this time from behind, as I filled my eyes with images of beautiful naked women spraying themselves down with a powerful hose. My sensuality was in such full bloom I felt all the female flesh I was seeing as part of my own erotically charged skin the way Linn's body had been while she was with us. My Master came again, even more violently than before, as I blissfully suffered my third climax of the night. Sated at last, we adjourned to the living room to relax in front of the TV and eat the nearly untouched feast, sitting on our loveseat feeling happier and more together than ever.

My Master declared the evening could not have gone better. 'She came over, we fucked her and she left, it was perfect, and you did exceptionally well.'

My Master is always sure to swiftly replace the bottle of champagne he takes out of the refrigerator with a new one as though performing a heart transplant. It struck me as so amazingly wonderful and cute when in the midst of Swinging with Linn he suddenly remembered he might not have performed this vital operation when he went for a second bottle, and he immediately rushed into the kitchen to fill the void in our refrigerator. This seemingly insignificant event showed me how much our life together meant to him and reinforced how unimportant

Linn was – her blood cells might as well have been champagne bubbles contributing to our sexual intoxication with each other and then vanishing into thin air forever.

I have since learned that what the other girl looks like matters much more to me than it does to my Master. He takes a more abstract approach to Swinging as something made possible by our intense love for each other that enables us to fully experience our oneness with the world. With him it's not about a primitive male need for variety. When we dive into the sensual whole of humanity through Swinging, it mysteriously deepens our individual bond. His term for the girl we're with is 'Missa's other pussy' and she herself is nothing except the orifices she kindly lets my Master and I use together for our mysteriously combined pleasure.

Almost a year into our relationship, my Master was offered a prestigious position up north and so we began making preparations to leave Miami, at least for the time being. We were extremely busy, and one weeknight we decided it might be fun to go and relax at Velvet, which touted Thursday as Player's Night. The prospect of meeting couples who weren't only into Soft Swinging was intriguing, but mainly we were in the mood to play together in a luxurious venue we would have pretty much to ourselves. The food was free, we could bring our own drinks, and it was only a twenty minute drive. It was around Christmas time, and it pleased me to dress in the spirit of the season in a purple velvet corset with pearl buttons, a snow-white mini skirt, stay-up white lace stockings, and my white-and-clear extreme high heels. I felt lusciously sexy as my Master and I strolled in to the nearly empty club. They had made some pleasing changes in the décor since our last visit, and it was nice having so much space to play with. There were no hardcore Swingers to be found, however. I was slightly disappointed not to be afforded an opportunity to intensify the pleasure my Master took in being there with me, but I was happy to have him all to myself. We were entering a stage in our relationship (that would be reinforced by our new home in a different State) where it felt good to take a break from Swinging. I had proved to my Master that I could take a positive approach to us fucking other people together, so there was no longer a pressing need to go to sex clubs all the time so I could cross this milestone in my training as his slave. That quiet Thursday night at Velvet we only played with each other, and had a wonderful time. I had fun because I let go of the tense belief that I had to have an agenda – that I had to find a girl or a couple for my Master and me to play with – for the first time fully believing him when he said he was perfectly happy just to be there with me.

We had an audience for a while in the form of a single man who stood at a respectful distance from the couch where I was reclining with my Master kneeling before me as he fucked my pussy. I was touching myself, and when the voyeur pulled a huge cock out of his pants and began stroking it in rhythm with my Master's penetrations, a wicked excitement triggered my climax. Afterwards, my Master helped me up, retrieving my white lace panties from the carpet and handing them to me.

'Just a moment,' I said, and seating myself directly in front of the man still watching me, I raised both my legs high in the air as I slipped my panties back on, giving him a good view of my naked pussy in the process. Then my Master helped me up again, smiling in approval of my generously wanton gesture.

We concluded the evening upstairs on one of the plush black divans that had replaced the beds in the mirrored corridor, lying in each other's arms as though in our own palatial home.

We tried Velvet one last time on a Saturday, during which my pierced nipples were sucked and tweaked by countless people. By the time we left I was in serious pain. At one point my Master was fucking me from behind in one of the smaller playrooms, and a slender blonde woman crouched in front of me to suck down her partner who stood before her looking down at me. She had the cutest little ass I had ever seen, and I was more than happy to caress her for my Master's pleasure. I actually had to resist the temptation to bury my face in her sweet crack and hungrily fuck her asshole with my tongue. My Master sometimes has me lick his anus and I love doing it, but I didn't know this couple for anything and so hygienic reticence kept me from succumbing to the dirty desire.

My Master whispered in my ear, 'Would you like to feel his cock inside you while I fuck her?'

'No!' I responded beneath my breath, blinded by jealousy at the thought that he was so desperate to fuck this cute little blonde he was willing to trade me off to her less appealing spouse, as if I could possibly want to feel his cock inside me instead. Then I regretted my furious reaction. Separating myself from my Master to lie seductively on my side, I looked the man directly in the eye and smiled as I reached for my small black coin purse, from which I slowly and deliberately extracted a condom. He made a move to get on the bed, but his partner quickly rose and slipped on her robe saying something in a tone that made it clear she was not at all happy. Then they both left the room. I was upset on so many levels, it took my Master a long time to untangle my feelings when we got home.

'Missa, I asked you if you wanted to feel his cock inside you and you said no and that was the end of it. I wasn't going to make you do anything you didn't want to do. Have I ever made you do anything you didn't want to?'

'No,' I said, staring fixedly into space, 'but how could you even think I would want his cock inside me instead of yours? You were just dying to fuck her, weren't you?!'

'Missa, I was not dying to fuck her. He and I were communicating and it was obvious he was willing to go all the way so I asked you if you wanted to. You said no, and that was that. It wasn't about her at all.'

I looked up at him beseechingly. 'In those moments you didn't want her more than you wanted me?'

'No, I didn't. I never want another woman more than I want you, just like you never want another man more than you want me.'

'I'll say!'

'It's never about someone else, it's always about us, dear. When will you get it?'

'I never want to go back to Velvet!'

'I agree that's over for us. We've gotten as much out of that scene as we could and now it's time for us to move on. There are other ways for us to explore together. And there will be times when we'll want to just be quiet and safe together. There's no reason for you to be upset or afraid. I love you, Missa, more than anything. One day you'll realize just how much you mean to me.'

After our last visit to Velvet, just a few weeks before we left Miami, I sent my Master this e-mail at his office:

Dear Master,

I just had an epiphany in the shower. It may seem obvious, but I think it is a vital clue to help your slave Swing more smoothly in the future and make her Master happier.

If at Velvet Saturday night instead of asking me "Would you like to feel his cock inside you while I fuck her?" you had said, "I want to see his cock inside you while I fuck her" it might have turned me on enough to get past the fact that I was not attracted to him, and made me happy to think you wanted to watch ME as much as I feared you wanted to fuck that other girl. A command rather than a question would also have kicked in my submissiveness and aroused me by not making it my decision and responsibility.

I have never used my safe word, but in the future I think it will become more relevant in situations such as this. If in such moments in the future I truly feel I cannot possibly comply with your command because I am having a serious emotional crisis, then I will respond with my safe word "violet" which will have the same effect as my saying "No" had on Saturday night. I hope this makes sense, Master, because I think it is important. This way, you'll be able to look out for your slave's feelings without being put in the unmasterly position of asking your slave a question in crucial moments when you should be commanding her, and thus helping to turn her on by arousing her submissiveness and taking the decision out of her hands. Making anything my decision and responsibility when we're Swinging is NOT a good idea, and this way you can be totally in command and relaxed, free of the concern that you will make me do something I will resent later, because if I really feel that's the case I will use my safe word to prevent it and discuss it with you later in private.

Love, Missa

My Master responded:

Excellent work, my dearest. I agree fully. You've mentioned this before about commanding at Velvet, but I didn't have a way to check in, and the suggestion on how to do it is excellent.

My Master, Merlin and I left Miami for our new home in northern Virginia, and for a few months we were indeed just 'quiet and safe' together sipping Chardonnay by the fire. We celebrated our first anniversary, and shortly after he removed my slave rings. They had given me more pain and discomfort than pleasure; I had never really grown accustomed to them, or happy with their presence. I had found myself longing for the time when my Master as well as other people could lick and suck and fondle my nipples without me cringing in dread. My Master realized that the sexual pleasure I took in my breasts had been adversely affected, and so one night after we returned from dining out, he personally removed my slave rings. I prefer not to dwell on the event, which my abject terror made more painful than it should have been, but finally they were off and I was sobbing, mainly with relief, but also because I had treasured the symbolic meaning of these rings and their loss frightened me.

My Master took me in his arms and held me close as he told me he did not feel I needed these symbols of my slavery anymore, and that he really didn't care if I wore nipple rings or not because he had no desire to cause me pain. The only thing he needed to be happy was for me to be a good slave. 'You wore your rings for almost a full year, you tried, Missa, you didn't just give up, but for some reason you never got used to them, and that's all right. They were only a symbol of the fact that you belong to me, and their being gone doesn't change anything.' He held me at arm's length and looked down into my eyes. 'You're still mine, Missa.'

'Oh yes, Master.' I wrapped my arms around his neck and clung to him, sighing, 'I worship you!'

As I write this it has been over a year since I have felt another man inside me except my Master, and I am so happy. I didn't realize until I confessed it to him how afraid I was that he would be casually and constantly giving my body away to other men, making me endure the full swap scenario with other couples on a regular basis. For me that always meant settling for less and was a profound chore. So it was an infinite relief that lifted a crushing weight off my submissive psyche when my Master told me he was not interested in trading me for some other woman all the time. 'I love you, Missa, I'm not just going to casually give you away to other men. I also like it better when it's just you and me with another woman, and as far as other men are concerned, it's nothing you need to worry about. When was the last time you had another man inside you?'

'Almost a year,' I admitted.

'That's right, because it's not something we need in our life. I love you, Missa. Have I ever done anything to hurt you?'

'No,' I admitted again, 'but I was afraid once we got back in the Swing of things, I would have to suffer other men inside me all the time… every week!'

He took me in his arms and assured me that was definitely not the case; I wasn't going to suffer other men inside me all the time and Swinging wasn't something we needed to do every single weekend. 'Have I ever given you any reason to feel this way, Missa? Why are you so afraid?'

The fear that had been eating away at my heart was this – that a man who shares a woman with other men doesn't truly love her. I already knew for a fact this wasn't true, and yet it would have become true if my Master had desired to give me away constantly and enjoyed swapping me for other women on a regular basis, but that was never what he intended for us. It wasn't only that opportunities for a full swap didn't actually come up very often; even if they did, my Master wouldn't blithely take advantage of every one because I'm precious to him and that isn't all Swinging is about for us. Ideally, Swinging is an intense sensual communion with others through which a couple worships the mystery of their special love for each other, not a cold-hearted meat market where you simply go to trade one body for another. And as my Master keeps telling me, 'We're us and they're them, and why other people do something makes no difference, all that matters is why we do it, together.'

So ends this account of my first fifteen months of training as a slave, and although the pace is not as urgent and the lessons are increasingly subtle, my training continues... submission is a miracle of love that slowly becomes an enchanted state of mind. I love my Master, Stinger, more than there are days and ways to express, but I'll keep trying... And already new and exciting seeds have been sewn here in D.C. that make me realize I am still very much growing in my slavery as I glimpse even deeper and higher levels of submission latent within me where every fear and pain becomes love and ecstasy. For example, I just now sent this e-mail to my Master at work:

> *I always tell my Master what I'm thinking, which includes what I'm fantasizing about...*
> *I'm getting so hot thinking about that private dungeon... about being bound, and beaten, and fucked by you, and then by you and by other people at the same time, and then just by other people as you take pleasure in watching my body being used knowing I belong to you absolutely, and how many other rubber cocks and lifeless dildos I suffer inside me is directly proportional to how deeply and intensely I love you... I'm imagining being bound in a different position and beaten again, and then fucked even more by you and/or by those you give permission to use me, not for their pleasure because that's irrelevant, but for the pleasure you take in watching the beautiful body that really belongs only to you being played with; the pleasure you take in knowing I am helpless not only physically but in my whole being since how much I love you*

makes it impossible for me to resist whatever you desire. So even if what you desire is to have my orifices and flesh abused by others while you plunge your cock into another hole, the feel of your eyes on me and the sense of fulfilling all your desires will transform the torment of being physically separate from you into the subtly profound ecstasy of absolute submission to your will. The pain of being beaten and fucked by anyone besides my Master will make me mysteriously come and come inside with the knowledge that by being the perfect submissive slave I am doing everything in my power to show you how much I love you.

And this would all be possible because I would finally really trust my Master implicitly and surrender all my frightened need to maintain some control over the scene to his judgment. I would be secure in the knowledge that he would never let anything bad happen to me or let anyone really hurt me, i.e. I wouldn't need to keep an eye out to make sure condoms were always worn, etc. I would trust him to be aware of everything that was going on the whole time, because even in moments when we were separated physically in every conceivable way, we would always be completely together in our hearts and souls, and I would be able to relax secure in the knowledge that my Master was sensitive to everything happening to me at every moment.

Of course, I do not presume to know what would actually turn my Master on in different circumstances; I was merely fantasizing about the most terrifying, and ultimately submissive, scenario possible for me as his slave - what would be the hardest thing for me to endure while still managing to believe in, and truly feel, our connection to each other.

Meow,

Missa

Epilogue

MISSA'S LIST OF FIRSTS a section of my journal that grew exponentially during the first few months with my Master:

- Experienced an irresistible magnetic attraction to my Master, Stinger, the second I met him.
- Truly in real life, not just in fiction, desired to be a man's, Stinger's, slave and do whatever he says.
- Been collared by my Master, Stinger.
- Went out in public without any panties on.
- Sucked my Master's cock in public.
- Had my pussy licked by my Master in public.
- Watched other people fucking in real life and in public.
- Had sex with my Master in a public Jacuzzi full of other couples fucking.
- Been touched by another man while being fucked by my Master.
- Fondled a woman's breasts and kissed her nipples on a dance floor, in public.

- Was introduced as a slave by my Master, Stinger.
- Had group sex in public:
- Kissed a girl while fondling and kissing her breasts as we were both being fucked; played with her clitoris; spanked and licked her bottom; and was spanked and bitten and had my clitoris fondled by her.
- Kissed and fucked another man, a complete stranger, with my Master's permission.
- Licked a woman's pussy.
- Sucked my Master's cock while being penetrated from behind by another man.
- Watched my Master caressing and kissing another woman, and felt more excited than jealous (it was just a little upsetting, yes, but I guess I'll have to work on that).
- Had my breasts kissed and fondled by a man while another stranger, a black man, licked my pussy.
- Was fucked up the ass by my Master while four guys watched.
- Went to a nude beach, and walked around with my Master feeling perfectly happy and natural; bathed completely naked in the ocean and had my breasts and bottom, and everything else, exposed to the sun.
- Peed standing against my Master on his command.
- Walked around in "fuck me" shoes, and was fucked by my Master in a porno movie store booth.
- Been so happy and completely myself with someone, Stinger, my Master, every time and every second.
- Performed a Lap Dance for my Master in public; danced around a pole for my Master in public, exposing my pussy to passers by.
- Watched my Master fucking another woman right in front of me.

- Had sex in a public bar with my Master.
- Lifted my dress and exposed and touched myself in a public bar for my Master's pleasure.
- Went to a spa and was beaten by oak leaves by my Master.
- Was fucked in the dark laundry room a pub by my master while a live band played.
- Had sex in the Penthouse stairway of a hotel with my Master (after having my first dirty martini)
- Watched my Master kissing another woman, slipping his hand up another woman's dress, and licking another woman's pussy in front of me, the latter on my request.
- Flirted with and kissed and fondled another couple in public with my Master.
- Danced for my Master and another couple while they both touched my ass.
- Dressed in skimpy fetish wear in public for my Master, even exposing myself to Playboy cameras.
- Was led around in public on a leash by my Master in full slave attire.
- Had my pussy licked by a woman while my Master watched.
- Had a man and my Master sucking on my nipples while my pussy was licked (by a woman.)
- Had my nipples fondled by my Master to the point where I was almost hypnotised with pleasure.
- Been fucked in the pussy by my Master while bound hand-and-foot and half suspended.
- Had my breasts put in bondage by my Master.
- Been severely punished by my Master with a crop, a split bamboo cane and a thick leather belt while blindfolded and bound; had the soles of my feet beaten.

- Had an orgasm while being fucked in the ass by my Master without touching myself.
- Licked a woman's pussy at the same time as her lover while also kissing him as my Master fucked me from behind and watched.
- Had two orgasms in public while my Master fucked me, and affected another woman's orgasm with my own.
- Experienced a "violet wand" in public, and for my Master's pleasure, over my breasts, torso, navel, vulva and inside my vagina. Was burned by the wand's "red" attachment and had the marks photographed and posted on the web by my Master.
- Danced nearly naked on top of a chair in a club for my Master's pleasure.
- Had my nipples pierced while my Master held my hand.
- Exposed my pierced nipples to various people in a public place on my Master's command.
- Went to strip bars and tipped the strippers, once with the dollar held between my teeth as I bent over the bar and placed it between her breasts, another time walking up to the stage to place it in her garter.
- Actually watched real slaves, being flogged, spanked and paddled in public by their Masters, and was introduced as a slave to other slaves and their Masters by my Master.
- Was fucked and spanked by my Master while imprisoned in a stock in public, and then watched my Master offer my bound form to another man to fuck from behind while he fucked another woman right in front of me.
- Licked my Master's balls through his black vinyl pants while kneeling before him in public.

- Was flogged by my Master in public with several different floggers, and started going into a trance-like state that left me feeling deliciously weak and peaceful afterwards.
- Caressed a woman's strap-on, on my Master's command.
- Had a butt-plug used on me by my Master to prepare my ass for penetration by his much larger erection.
- Pulled my dress off and walked naked out of a strip bar, on my Master's command.
- Had sex in the woods during the day with my Master, and on two other occasions leaning against a tree in a public parking lot at night.
- Had sex in a lifeguard house at night.
- Swung with another couple in private, during which I was bound by my Master and fucked while bound; watched him kissing another woman, fondling her breasts; kissed my Master while he fucked another woman and another man fucked me from behind.
- Watched my Master going down on another woman from behind.
- Watched my Master putting his fingers into another woman from behind while he went down on me.
- Had my pussy licked by a woman at the same time that she licked my Master's cock as he fucked me from behind.
- Took off all my clothes except for my skirt and heels on top of a lifeguard stand on a public beach.
- Sucked my Master's cock with another woman.
- Kissed another woman while at the same time licking the heads of two cocks.
- Watched another woman kneeling in front of my Master sucking his cock while also looking into his eyes and kissing him as I felt him being pleasured.

- Watched another woman alternately sucking my Master's cock and her boyfriend's cock while having my pussy played with by, and kissing, my Master and the other man.
- Alternated between sucking and handling my Master's cock and another man's cock while kneeling between them.
- Watched my Master going down on another woman while another man went down on me and she and I fondled each other's breasts.
- Was part of a four-way kiss with my Master and another couple.
- Sucked a man's cock while a woman licked my pussy.
- Fondled another man's penis while alternately kissing my Master and a woman.
- Had my pussy licked by a man and a woman at the same time while my Master sucked my nipples and kissed me.
- Exposed my ass and my pussy from behind on a public sidewalk and was spanked.
- Had my pussy licked on a public sidewalk.
- Experienced a double penetration, with my Master in my pussy and another man in my ass.
- Helped my Master put his cock inside another woman.
- Licked my Master's cock while another man licked my pussy and my ass from behind.
- Watched my Master fucking another woman in a variety of positions while another man fucked me for a prolonged amount of time.
- Had an orgasm at the same time as my Master watching him fuck me from behind in the mirror.
- Fucked another girl with my Master, kissing and caressing him, and her, while he pounded her from behind, and touching myself while she rode him and he thumbed her clit. Then my Master said it was my turn and he came inside me while she watched.

- Had an orgasm in the ocean.
- Had the pleasure of feeling my Master's cock in my ass two times in the same half hour.

For more about Missa and her second year of training as a slave, visit her website at *www.TheStoryOfMAMemoir.com*